'This book is like real life; funny, sad and wise and true.'

Paul Burke, author.

for Rachel
with love
Joan x

Enjoy Ella.

I am Ella. Buy me.

Joan Ellis

For my darling Mum.

With thanks to:
Adland in the 80's: Maison Bertaux
and Patisserie Valerie for the best croissants in town;
advertising legends Trevor Beattie, Paul Burke
and Jeanne Willis for always being there;
Wight Writers for sorting the wrongs;
Doug for everything else.

CBA ADVERTISING
100 Dean Street, W.1. Telephone: 01 734 1000
20 November 1982

Dear reader,

My name is Peter Richards, Creative Director par
excellence of CBA Advertising. Thank you so much for
buying this book. With your help *I am Ella. Buy me*
will hopefully be a success and Joan Ellis will embark
on a career as an author instead of continuing to
masquerade as my copywriter in my advertising agency.
With her gone, I can hire a new little hottie.

Can you believe I caught Joan typing up this
manuscript on company time? I mean, why should I pay a
girl who won't sit on my lap and would rather write
books than ads?

I even discovered my secretary reading this book
when she should've been sorting my holiday in Bermuda.
She tells me it is a novel for anyone who has ever had
a bad day at the hands of a bad boss or a bad
boyfriend. I have no idea what she's talking about.
Rumour has it the Creative Director character is based
on me, but he's a sexist pig so obviously not yours
truly. Oink! Oink!!! Seriously, I've got my lawyers on
it and will sue Joan's arse to hell if needs be.
Clearly Joan is Ella with her 'small boobs and fat
thighs'. What a giveaway!!!! And I discovered the
complete manuscript on the company photocopier. No
wonder it's always out of toner.

Before joining me at CBA, Joan worked in some of
London's top advertising agencies as an award-winning
copywriter. She penned what she likes to refer to as a
'back-page funny' for a glossy magazine. She also ran
her own comedy club, writing and performing sketch
shows, even appearing on the same bill as Jo Brand.
Just the once, I imagine. Personally, I've yet to see
her smile. She doesn't get my jokes unlike my naughty
little secretary who finds me utterly hilarious. The
minx.

It might also be worth mentioning that my wife has
run off with her aerobic-instructor leaving me
blissfully free. Should any young lady reading this

want to help me clear my chakras I would love to meet
for a drink. What's the company plastic for if not to
spread a little joy?

In the meantime, I sincerely hope you enjoy the
book. Apparently, there's plenty more where this came
from. I feel a duvet day coming on!

    Yours truly,
    Peter Richards

Chapter one

Know your product

I am a ginger tom. I am a boy racer. I am a housewife. I am a success. I am a pain in the arse.

And that's just the day job. By night, I am a lush. I am single. I am a failure. I am still a pain in the arse.

I am a copywriter creating advertisements for everything from abandoned cats to luxury cars. To do this I get inside people's (or cats') heads and discover what makes them tick.

Welcome to my world. Welcome to Adland where creative odd-balls like me preen and party, snip and snipe. It's the only place to reward our egos, our hang-ups and our fornicating, setting us to work in ivory towers, encrusted with diamonds and surrounded by a moat of champagne.

Yeah, right.

My office is on the third floor of CBA, one of London's top advertising agencies in the heart of oh-so-sordid Soho where red telephone booths are awash with pee and calling cards promising French lessons from pneumatic blondes. But, when I glimpse these girls leaning in doorways, their skimpy tops reveal breasts as flat as fried eggs. They are paid to satisfy their clients' needs by fulfilling fantasies and pretending to be someone they're not, just like I do. Luckily, they don't have to pander to my boss, ageing lothario, Peter Richards. Or at least I hope they don't. No amount of money is worth that.

Today, I am Marmalade, a ginger tom abandoned outside Kitty Rescue, the home where he now lives with his moggie mates. He 'writes' letters to cat-lovers asking them to finance his board and lodging. By a cruel irony some of the money he raised paid for him to be neutered. I imagine him, lying on his side, one back leg pointing skywards, his head where his balls should be, trying to figure out where they went.

1

To ensure the letter hits the right emotional chord, I write the missive with my mum in mind. As she is not allowed pets in her rented accommodation, Marmalade and his crew fill the space in her heart, left by my dad after they divorced. She enjoys helping the cats and is always delighted to receive another letter from Marmalade, complete with the 'love and meows' sign-off, two kisses and a paw-print.

Now after three re-writes, I am ready to show his latest letter to Peter for approval. By a cruel twist of fate, he is both the Creative Director and my Art-Director, which means we are obliged to spend unnatural amounts of time together thinking up ideas. It's like a marriage without the sex, so just like a marriage. Peter's got it sussed. I do the work and he takes the credit. However, it is unlikely we'll be fighting on the winner's podium for the much-prized Golden Crayon Award with this one.

'Dear Mrs. Miggins,

Can you imagine how desperate I felt before Kitty Rescue found me? I was ...'

'Ella, let me just stop you there. It sounds rather lame to me. Would Marmalade really use a word like 'desperate'?' Peter asks, his voice buzzing around the room like a bluebottle trapped in a jar.

We've suspended disbelief this far, I think.

'Any thoughts?' he prompts waving his soft, expensively-manicured hand at me.

'How about 'hopeless'?' I suggest feeling the same emotion.

'Old women think of cats as toddlers in furry suits ergo Marmalade must talk like one,' he says slowly as if explaining to a toddler in a furry suit.

It's not easy working out what makes a feline eunuch tick. It's a bit like being an actress, which is what I wanted to be until my teacher told me I would never make it without family connections or family money to see me through the lean times. Not only was my dream of appearing on the silver-screen in tatters but the cloud's silver-lining hung in rags too. The following day, Mum left Dad and we went to live with Grand-dad in his Victorian hovel, taking with us just two suitcases and a birdcage. One case contained our clothes, including Mum's shift dresses, and my rather alarming, shocking-pink poncho that made me look like an anaemic bat. The other was crammed with Mum's beloved collection of Nat King Cole singles. In the large steel cage sat my irascible parrot, Beauty Column-Sixpence. ('Beauty' because she was, 'Column' because the most exciting part of my week was sitting, importantly on Dad's lap, deciding which columns to put the crosses in on his football pools coupon, and 'Sixpence' because that was my pocket-money.) Grand-dad's house was very different to ours. It was an old, cold three-storey terrace, heated, inadequately, by a single bar electric fire. To claim the house was ever 'heated' would be a lie. Even 'taking the chill off' would have been pushing it. The plumbing amounted to a temperamental cold tap in the kitchen, one minute gushing out rusty red water, the next not parting with a single drop. The outside lavatory provided shiny toilet paper stiff enough to double as tracing paper on geography homework nights. And my old plastic baby bath, which my beloved Mum had kept for sentimental reasons, was given a new lease of life as I washed in it as best I could every night. What had been the perfect fit when I was just eight pounds was somewhat wide of the mark when I weighed in at eight stone. Mum would set the bath on a towel covering the living room table and fill it with boiling water from the kettle and a pan of freezing water from the tap. Then she would leave the room as I washed with a flannel and a bar of Lifebuoy soap while watching Bruce Forsyth on our rented television set. None of my friends believed me when I grandly announced I had a TV in my bathroom.

After having my hopes of becoming an actress dashed, I marched into the careers section of my local library where I threw a fittingly dramatic tantrum, on the off-chance a casting agent or film producer was loitering. It must have been their day off because no-one offered me the lead role in their latest epic. Forced to flick, desultory, through the drawer of job index cards, I discarded the one titled 'Acting' and plucked out the one next to it marked, 'Advertising'. My future was decided on the turn of a card and I became the rarest of beasts in Adland in the early 1980's, a woman.

Cosmopolitan magazine rated being a copywriter amongst the top ten best careers for girls. If it meant I got to live the life portrayed within its pages that was good enough for me. The only thing I knew for sure about the industry was it paid well. Not only would I be able to afford super-soft loo roll, the sort Golden Labrador puppies favour but I would earn enough money to buy Mum a music centre so she could actually listen to Nat King Cole instead of just sliding the vinyl from its cover, examining the 'A' and 'B' sides and imagining him serenading her.

I made both our dreams come true with my first wage packet. Seeing her weary, worried face transform into a smile as Nat worked his magic was worth every penny I earned flogging floor cleaner.

'Ella?' Peter prompts.

I owe Mum everything. She cared for me when we had nothing. And she didn't just read to me. She taught me to write. Every Friday, we would be set a composition as our homework. Linking words together to form a story was an anathema to me. I couldn't even spell. Confronted with a sobbing eight-year-old, Mum would often write the essay for me and I would copy it out. One week, she finished her tale with the line, 'And all that was left was a burnt offering.'

'Burnt offering?' I asked, appalled. 'I can't say that.'

A vision of Joan of Arc being incinerated at the stake sprung to mind. As the only Church of England pupil in a Catholic school, I couldn't say a word out of place.

'It's a great ending, write it down,' Mum urged.

As I handed in Mum's story, I hoped to spontaneously combust and save the nuns the job. By a miracle, I got ten out of ten. Or rather Mum did. The bar having been raised, she had to beat her best efforts each time. After a few weeks of her writing it and me copying, I got the hang of it. In feeding me the words, she taught me to write.

I wish she was here now. She would know what Marmalade would say. I need to crack the cat's vocabulary in the next five minutes (and let's face it, the chances are slimmer than the Nimble girl's waist) or I won't make it to the wine bar to meet the gorgeous Alan Ferguson, and Marmalade won't be the only desperate one. Alan is one of London's most sought after Art-Directors. Having recently won his third Golden Crayon, he is now using it to write his own pay cheque and rewrite the terms of his contract with CBA. Officially allowed to use the pub as his office, he only pops by the agency to present Peter with yet another award-winning idea and challenge the boys in the studio to a game of table-football.

'Perhaps Marmalade feels 'sad,' I suggest encouraging Peter to channel an emotion other than self-love.

'Sad?' roars Peter. 'He's been kicked in the balls.'

'But he hasn't got any,' I say.

'The cat has been betrayed by the one person he thought loved him. All his home comforts have gone. He has lost everything. 'Sad' doesn't begin to cover it.'

Here we go again, Peter's recent marriage break-up. When his wife left him (and who could blame her) she purloined a couple of essentials, namely the penthouse and the pool-boy, to tide her over until a full and final settlement could be thrashed out between their respective lawyers. We all know the story. Peter never misses an opportunity to bore anyone sycophantic enough to listen. He blames his wife for the split, never mentioning his numerous dalliances with a succession of PAs - all of whom he recruited less on their shorthand skills and more on their resemblance to porn stars.

'How about 'alone'?' I ask picturing him rattling around his Highgate pad with just his executive ball-clicker for company.

'Ella, I don't think you're getting this. We need something more Marmalade, more honest,' he pontificates.

I just want to have a big glass of wine and forget all about the wretched cat.

'I've got it, 'sad',' he declares as if he has secured peace in the Middle East.

'But I suggested that and you...' I protest.

Then I remember Peter's ability to hire and fire in the same sentence and shut-up. I need the money to pay Mum's rent and keep her in freesias, her favourite flower, the one she chose for her wedding bouquet.

'We'll finish this later. Time for a drinkie-poo,' Peter says, pulling on his fashionably over-sized, over-priced overcoat.

The silk lining is hot pink to match his cashmere scarf. One of the art-directors tried to strangle him with it earlier this week. Now I know why. I can't think of anything I'd less like to do than have a drinkie-poo with this piece of doggie-do but we're in a recession, best not to argue.

'Okay, Peter, let's have a quick one,' I sigh.

I see his salacious expression, realise what I've said and want to fall on the nib of my Mont Blanc. But that would be a pointless waste of a very good pen.

We head for Kettner's Champagne Bar on the corner of Romilly Street. The cafes and bars on Old Compton Street are filling up with suits flexing the company plastic. Peter pauses to look in the window of one of the many sex shops. There's not much on display, just a few risqué videos. The hard-core stuff is inside, under-the-counter.

When we arrive at the bar, it's standing room only. I order a Kir Royale as compensation for having to spend a minute more than I am contractually obliged to with Peter Richards. The heady mix of champagne and Cassis, French blackcurrant liqueur, slips down easily and my glass soon empties. I watch Peter's reflection in the enormous gilt-framed mirror as he nods at the barman to pour me another. To my horror, he leans his head on my shoulder and whispers something urgently in my ear. Luckily, it's too noisy to hear what he's saying but the gist seems to be 'never go out to work while your wife works-out with a personal trainer, half her age.'

His hand rides up my thigh, slipping underneath my skirt.

'I've never had you, have I?' he asks with an unflattering level of uncertainty.

'No and you never will,' I say, draining my glass and leaving.

If my Mum knew what went on, she would be horrified. But Peter's pawing is a small price to pay to keep her in the house she loves.

I run back along Old Compton Street where I am shocked to spot a well-respected TV presenter exiting a sex shop, clutching a brown paper bag. I'm guessing it's filled with furtively selected guilty-pleasures. He voiced a television commercial for me last week. Had I known his penchant for porn, I'd have paid him in luncheon vouchers.

The Fox, where I've arranged to meet Alan, is Adland's most popular watering-hole, always packed with media types peering earnestly at each other through expensive designer glasses. Even people with twenty-twenty vision buy frames with clear lenses just so they can be seen sporting the latest, must-have accessories. Alan is already at the bar. I climb up onto the vertiginous stool next to him. This man is so laid-back he doesn't even speak; he just brushes my lips with his. Alan's mouth on mine, I shudder with pleasure. Can life get any better? Apparently, it can, as I now seem to be clutching a huge glass of oaked-Chardonnay. He whispers something in my ear. I don't catch it but that doesn't stop me laughing, in what I contrive to be an alluring manner, and falling off the stool. Alan pretends not to notice as I try and fail to clamber back on. I lean on the bar as casually as I can with what feels like a broken arm. We spend the next two hours drinking, staring into the middle distance and saying very little. This is as deep and meaningful as I've ever got.

I weave my way back to the agency. Having spent lunchtime in the company of a man I adore, I am confronted by a man I loathe, Josh Jenkins. Standing beside my desk, he is every inch the Senior Board Account Director in his pink and white candy-striped shirt and hand-made suit. His unenviable job is to liaise between the agency and the client. His enviable salary reflects the amount of flack he gets from both sides. He is the man for the job, his honeyed drawl exuding the brand of effortless charm only years at a fee-paying school can instil. Charming but unlikeable, I don't understand how that works.

'Ella, there you are. Sorry to hassle you, but I can't find Peter and we need to fax the copy over to Kitty Rescue before close of play. The client's chasing us - been on the phone all afternoon.'

All afternoon? Just how long have I been out to lunch? Judging from my response, I still am.

'Okelly-dokelly, Joshie.'

No, please tell me I didn't just say, 'Okelly-dokelly, Joshie' out loud to Josh Jenkins. I can hear Peter's secretary sniggering so obviously I did. Fortunately, Josh is far too well-mannered to react.

With 70% proof fuelling my cavalier attitude, I insert a fresh piece of paper into my typewriter and hit the keys. If Peter wants me to be more 'honest' about Marmalade's feelings, I will be. I lay bare his thoughts on the snip and include a few choice words regarding his feelings towards the vet who wielded the knife. When I've finished, I read it through. It has a rare integrity not often found in advertising copy. I glance at my watch. I must crack on with the real version for the client. The booze has gone straight through me. I run to the loo. When I get back Marmalade's letter has disappeared.

'Who's been in my office?' I ask Peter's secretary, desperately trying to sound sober.

'Josh took the Kitty Rescue copy and asked me to fax it to the client,' she replies in her bird-like voice.

'Can I have it back, please?' I say slowly as if trying to persuade a small child to part with a sweet.

'Sure, all done,' she says, picking up the paper as it snakes out of the fax machine and handing it to me.

Why did she have to choose today to be efficient? Usually, she's happy to be an air-head. I throw the copy, along with what's left of my career, into the bin.

I run back to the toilet. Very appropriate, given I'm in deep shit. I head for my cubicle – second from the end. It's the one no-one else seems to use so it's always well-stocked with paper to mop up my useless tears. I feel safe here, just like I did in the loos at infant school. I hated that place because it meant I couldn't be with Mum, eating currant buns and 'Listen With Mother' on the radio. Such safe, joy-filled days. All I had to worry about back then was how my two dolls, Susie and Carol, would cope without me to take them for walks and brush their hair? Every weekday morning, I would get into a state, sobbing and begging Mum to let me stay with her and not leave me at such a terrible place. A place where they ignored me as I sat with my hand up, begging for permission to go to the loo only to be told I should've gone at play-time. No five-year-old can plan that far ahead. A place where the nuns delighted in making me wear knickers from Lost Property after I had wet my own.

After a week of tears, Mum came up with a plan. If I went to school, she would wait outside all day, no matter what the weather, just below the toilet window. So when the teacher humiliated me for getting my spellings wrong - an every-day occurrence since I was under the mistaken impression I had only to glance at a list of words in order to commit them to memory, I could run to the loo and tell Mum all about it. Luckily, the window above my cubicle was too high for me to see out of so her cover was never blown. Little did I know then, as I was pouring my heart out, she was pouring herself a nice cup of tea, at home.

Now, here, in my addled state, I like to imagine she is outside, all ears, in her silk headscarf, shift dress and stilettos. I let rip.

'Kitty Rescue will go ballistic when they read Marmalade's letter. I could blame the cat; after all he wrote it.'

I'm not sensing any reassuring vibes coming my way. Mum's not there. She never was. I unlock the door and slope back along the corridor. I may as well clear my desk, but decide to clear off before someone spots me. How could I have been so stupid? I need time to decide what to do next. Like sign on the dole. I zip in the lift and push the button for the ground floor. The doors glide open.

'What's this, half day?' Peter slurs as he bowls in, barring my exit with his shoulder pads. 'You left me alone in the bar; naughty girl.'

He leers before stumbling forward.

'I'm just popping out, Peter.'

'So I see,' he mutters, his eyes level with my cleavage. 'Oh by the way, I dropped into The Fox and had a chat with Alan Ferguson. Had no idea you were a fully paid-up member of his fan club. I don't know what you girls see in him. He's ginger.'

'His hair is chestnut,' I correct, regarding Peter with disgust. 'And he is a very kind person.'

Then I remember some sobering facts, the country is in the grip of recession, unemployment is rife and I have undoubtedly just lost the agency a major client. I adjust my sneer into a smile.

'Fancy a ride home in my Porsche, young lady?' he asks taking a condom out of his pocket and waving it at me.

'I'm going by tube.'

'I'm going past your front door.'

Unfortunately, we live just three streets apart in Highgate. I'm in Crouch End. That's 'Highgate borders' in estate agent's speak. Peter loves the fact that his N6 post-code is worth more than my N8. Thankfully, our paths rarely cross at weekends but since his wife left, I live in fear of bumping into him in the Marks and Spencer Food Hall, cruising the meals-for-one section.

Peter had had enough to drink when I left him in Kettner's. He's well over the limit now.

'Why not stay in the company flat tonight?'

He may be a scumbag but I've met worse and he has had a tough ride recently. Besides, I don't want him ending up looking like one of the crash victims, with scars like tramlines, who stare out from the posters in the government's anti drink-drive campaign.

'Stay with me, Ella,' he whines.

'See you tomorrow, Peter.'

For once, I really hope I do, for his sake and mine.

When I get home, I am as close to sober as I'm going to get. A mortgage rate of 9% has that effect. I spend the evening alone fretting about the consequences of my stupidity. Kitty Rescue will have read Marmalade's letter by now. They will fire the agency and Peter will fire me. So not only am I a pain in the arse, I am also a fool. I must add it to my CV. I lurch around the kitchen in an attempt to make myself a drink but am incapable of boiling a kettle let alone opening a packet of tea-bags. I give up and go to bed early. I just want this day to be over. I lie awake, worrying about the consequences. If I lose my job, Mum loses her home. I can't let that happen. She's been through enough.

The next morning, I force myself to get up and go to work. As soon as I arrive. I am greeted by Peter's secretary, looking thinner than ever. It's a marvel the poor woman's still alive. She speaks slowly as if trying to conserve the few calories she has permitted to enter her body. Even her voice is weak.

'Peter wants you in his office.'

'If he wants me that bad he can pay for a room at The Ritz,' I retort.

She looks at me and I remind myself not to take my frustration with him out on her.

'What does he want?' I ask.

'Don't know but I shouldn't bother taking your coat off,' she replies before turning away to admire what little there is of her reflection in the mirror behind her desk.

Wally, the night-watchman ambles past and gives me a reassuring wink as he heads home after his shift. He used to work next door. Had his own little business. A café. I used to nip in there most mornings before work and we'd chat as he made my regular order, a lovely ham sandwich, on brown, no butter, salt and pepper. Then, one day, he wouldn't accept any money, said it was on him, a 'thank-you' for all my custom. He was shutting up shop for good. The landlord had increased the rent to an astronomical amount. He was being squeezed out, just like Mum's landlord had done to her.

'What will you do, Wal?' I asked.

As he turned away to clean the knife, I quickly took a twenty pound note from my purse and left it beside the till for him to find later.

He looked back at me and shrugged.

'Something will turn up. Always does. I've told the wife not to worry but she do. Born worrier, thinks the bailiffs are goin' come knockin'. D'you wanna cake with that, young 'un?'

A wasp flew through the open door and crawled slowly across the row of iced fingers, waving its antenna at me.

'No, thanks Wal,' I say. 'And I'm really sorry. I'm going to miss you.'

The following week, the caretaker at CBA retired. It seemed the obvious solution. I had a word with Wally and then put him forward for the position. Most people at CBA had been in his café at some point so he was well known and liked. He got the job. He even cannily upped his money by offering to double-up as a night watchman. As job descriptions go it was fundamentally floored but Wally could cope with most things. If a gang of thieves ever breaks while he's in the basement fixing a burst pipe say, he would probably make them all tea before asking to borrow their monkey wrench.

Now, he looks at me, his watery eyes, wrinkled with concern.

'Chin up, young 'un, it might never 'appen,' he whistles tunefully through his dentures.

'Peter's going to fire me, Wal.'

'Give him a smile and you'll be fine,' he grins. 'See you tomorrow, young 'un.'

He waves as he disappears slowly down the spiral staircase, torch in one hand, today's newspaper in the other. For someone who has been up all night, he's surprisingly upbeat. I never thought I'd envy him his late-shift but it must be better than doing battle with the Prince of Darkness in broad daylight. I breathe in and knock sharply on Peter's door. He is sitting smugly behind his vast desk with Josh at his elbow like an obedient sentinel. A wave of nausea overwhelms me and my stomach flips. Before I can recover Peter throws the opening punch.

'I suppose you think it's funny to compromise the agency's reputation with one of our most valued clients,' he says sending the Kitty Rescue copy skimming across his smoked glass table-top towards me.

This desk could tell some tales, like the one that ends with Peter naked on top of it. No. Not now. I'm in enough trouble thanks to a speaking cat; I don't need a talking table too. The offending piece of paper, still on its flight path, narrowly misses his cup of coffee made by his secretary with one brown French sugar cube, just how he likes it.

Josh clears his throat and fixes his owl-like eyes on me. He leans across the desk and I am treated to the full force of his halitosis.

'I was unaware Peter had not seen the copy. And I certainly had no idea you had made such sweeping changes, Ella,' he says, neatly side-stepping any share of the blame.

'But I thought ...' I falter.

Peter halts my words with a look, making me wait as he drains his cup before unleashing the full force of his fury.

'I am the Creative Director. You are just my writer. I say what happens here.'

'Sorry, the client was never meant to see it. I was being honest like you suggested and went a bit over the top.'

'A bit O.T.T.? Why not just post Marmalade's gonads to Mrs Miggins and have done with it?' blasts Peter.

'Wow! Peter! Great idea! That would certainly make the letter stand out!' exclaims Josh.

The sycophant.

'Josh took the wrong version,' I lamely tell Peter.

'You shouldn't have written such damaging rubbish. And you know I have to approve everything. Nothing leaves this agency without my signature.'

'But you weren't here.'

'All work must have my 'P' on it,' he snaps.

'Yes, Peter must do a 'P' on everything,' echoes Josh.

I snigger. Why? It's not funny. I'm not funny. I am a loser. Add it to the list.

'You seem to think everything is one big joke,' says Peter.

He's right. I make light of things; it's how I cope. My hand hovers over my mouth but I can't prevent a huge guffaw from escaping.

'You're fired,' says Peter.

Stop laughing you fool, he means it.

'No, please,' I say desperate to keep my job, my morning cappuccino and almond croissant, my champagne cocktails, my gym membership, my flat. Oh no, not my beautiful flat with its stripped pine floors and Victorian star-glass doors. And what about Mum's rent? I can't let her lose her home.

It's no use appealing to Peter's better nature. He doesn't have one.

He looks away. I turn to Josh but he's disappeared. Before I can stop myself, I'm running round the desk, tugging at Peter's tie. This may be Adland but we're still in England where unemployment is running at 124%. I visualise a dismal dole queue, snaking into oblivion, like the one depicted by Saatchi and Saatchi in their 'Labour Isn't Working' poster. And Mum, me and Beauty-Column-Sixpence holed up in a bedsit. And every time the landlord turned up to collect the rent, we had to hide the parrot and hold its beak shut so as not to breach the 'No pets' clause.

'I'll do anything, Peter,' I tell him.

'If I'd have known you were this easy, I'd have sacked you months ago,' he says lasciviously.

I look down. My hand is on his leg. How did it get there?

'Don't worry,' Peter says. 'I'll tell Josh to schmooze Kitty Rescue over lunch somewhere ridiculously expensive. We've done them a few favours; they owe us one. Now, stop snivelling; snot is not a turn-on.'

He reaches into his breast pocket and hands me his pristine white handkerchief. I blow my nose in it and give it back to him. He drops it in the bin.

'I'm glad we've come to a Little Arrangement. See you later,' he winks. 'And don't forget your toothbrush.'

My relief at this reprieve is immediately replaced by terror. Peter thinks I'm going to sleep with him to keep my job. He plans to hold me to something I said under duress. His ego is so out of control it should be kept under licence.

Chapter two

Know your competitors

I'm on the horns of a horny dilemma.

Do I sleep with Peter to keep my job or look for another position? (Anything but the missionary.) The first isn't an option, the second isn't viable; advertising is always the first thing hit in a recession.

In this business, it's not what you know, but who you know and I know Adam Hart's number off by heart. I'll give him a call. As my best mate and Deputy Creative Director of one of London's top agencies, Adam is well-placed to advise me. If he can't help, he'll know a man who can. We joined CBA within a week of each other and spent most of our time working our way through the free boxes of chocolates provided by our confectionery client. The trouble was, when the agency needed them to shoot the TV ad, we had eaten the star of the show. Nonetheless, he is a precociously talented writer, and it wasn't long before a zealous young recruitment consultant head-hunted him for his current role. Adam doubled his salary overnight. A stroke of luck given Peter was planning on firing him. Not because Adam was bad at his job but because he was too good; Peter couldn't handle the competition.

I dial, put the receiver to my ear and eventually hear the familiar purr of the dialling tone followed by the reassuring click as someone picks up the other end.

'Adam, it's me,' I whisper into the mouthpiece. 'Listen, I need a job. Anything going at your place?'

He recognises my voice instantly.

'Ella, what's up? Thought you were still at CBA. Richards hasn't fired you, has he?'

'Jumping before I'm pushed.'

'The man's insane, you're good,' he assures me.

'It's my own fault. I blew it. Drunk on the job,' I confess.

Then, I tell him about Marmalade's latest letter.

'Awesome. I've always wanted to do something like that,' he says once he's stopped laughing.

'Tell me what to do, Adam.'

'Go and see my mate, Steve Winter. Peter fired him just before you joined CBA. Best thing that ever happened to him. He's Creative Director at KO'd now. Give him a call. Tell him I sent you. Good luck. Let me know how you get on. By the way, there's a new restaurant opened in Frith Street, we ought to check it out next time we have lunch, heard they do a lovely chocolate mousse.'

Then he gives me Steve's direct line and hangs up. I replace my receiver. Adam is just like me, comes from nowhere but is determined to go places. Even if it is only the nearest cake shop - we share a passion for patisseries.

Using the arm of my typewriter as a mirror, I re-apply my lipstick before dialling Steve. Silly, but a quick slick of lippy makes me feel more confident. To my surprise, he answers straight away.

'Steve Winter,' he says confidently.

I introduce myself as quickly as possible; he's a busy man – pitches to win, secretaries to bed.

'Friend of Adam's? Wicked. And you work for Pete? Poor you. That sucks! Yeah, come over. Be great to meet you.'

He's enthusiastic, like he is asking me on a date but I need a job not a boyfriend.

'Are you looking for a copywriter?' I ask nervously suddenly sounding like I'm inhaling helium.

'No, we're cutting back. Just laid off one of our best creative teams. But it's always good to see good people. If we like you, you're first on the list when things pick-up. Can you get here tomorrow after work, with your portfolio? Say six-ish?'

'No problem,' I chirp before putting the phone down and bursting into tears.

No problem? Big problem. I don't have a portfolio, I have a cardboard box full of ads, the most recent written by a cat. It might work on dear old Mrs Miggins but it certainly isn't going to cut the mustard with Steve Winter, one of the hottest Creative Directors in town. My Kitty Rescue work isn't about to set the world on fire. Best thing I can do is take a match to the lot.

Where can I find creative briefs to work on at a moment's notice? Then I remember what we did at college and scoot downstairs to gather up armfuls of magazines. Back in my office, I leaf through them to find rubbish adverts. There are plenty of offenders. Someone, somewhere is getting paid big money to come up with this dross. But I can use them to glean the facts about the products and hopefully, come up with better versions of the ads. I examine an unforgivably poor Pro-High hair mousse ad; a mishmash of colours and a headline so lame it needs amputating.

'High-Pro. A hair-raising new idea!'

An exclamation mark has been added to ensure we get the joke. But no amount of punctuation can save this stinker. At least it shouldn't be difficult to improve it.

I'm moonlighting and it's not even dark. I work all afternoon, making notes, identifying what makes each product unique. Usually, everyone except Wally is out of here by six at the latest. But not tonight. No, this evening they are in it for the long haul, nicking and necking chilled beer from Peter's fridge. Alan Ferguson has turned up and is pouring whiskey chasers from the bottle he keeps in an empty filing cabinet. (The only filing Peter's secretary does is her nails.) My heart sinks when I hear

Darren, the studio manager suggest a game of table football. Trust him, the man with the knack of looking busy when he's doing nothing; unlike me who has the knack of looking like I'm doing nothing when I'm busy. I listen to the incessant thwack of the ball, followed by the shouts and jeers as goals are won and lost. I have to stop myself cheering out loud when the final triumphant cry goes up.

'Everyone down The Fox. Loser buys the first round,' Alan shouts.

What he says goes. I hear them all heading past my office towards the lift and sneak a look at Alan through the door. His face is partially obscured by his long auburn hair. There's no way that's ginger. Peter's just jealous. Alan exudes a gentle vulnerability and is the only man I know who can get away with wearing jumpers knitted by his mother from homespun wool. He looks like he got lost in 1950's Britain and has landed back here thirty years on, bemused and beautiful. I could dream about him all night but I must crack on. When the coast is clear, I raid the stationery cupboard for paper and pens. I pull the top off the thickest black marker and inhale. The acrid aroma reminds me of every campaign I've ever conceived, evoking hope and fear, success and failure. I rip the front cover off a pad and look down at the most terrifying sight a writer can face - a blank piece of paper. Unfortunately, it reflects my current state of mind.

Obviously, I'm going to have to work alone on this one without the benefit of an Art-Director's input. Then again, I work with Peter so I'm used to flying solo.

There's nothing like a deadline to focus my thinking. 'Deadline' is a horrifyingly appropriate word but right now, I need a lifeline. Sadly, the only person who can provide one is me. I set about filling the bin with discarded scribbles. Seeing the waste-paper basket overflow is part of the process, making it look like I'm getting closer to the Big Idea. When I start to wane, I visualise the alternative - Peter without pants, panting on the shag-pile. I don't want carpet burns. I mentally dress him in a sturdy pair of Y-fronts and some loose-fitting trousers. That's better.

I spend the next three hours coming up with new versions of the High-Pro ad, one of which could be a winner. As I reach out to receive the coveted Golden Crayon Award in front of an elite crowd of media greats at The Grosvenor Hotel on Mayfair's Park Lane, I feel the heat from the spotlight on my face.

'Thank-you,' I gush. 'Thank-you ...'

'No worries,' says Wally shining his torch in my face. 'I heard a noise, thought it was Pete up to his old tricks with one of his young ladies. Not hiding him under there, are you?' he chuckles flashing the beam under my desk.

I shake my head and laugh nervously. Wally never bothers to check the third floor. He usually gets as far as the second before nipping back down to the basement to enjoy a well-earned mug of tea and a packet of biscuits before giving his wife a ring on the company phone.

'Sorry, Wally I've got loads to do by the morning. Okay with you if I stay here the night?'

'Kip 'ere? You'll get me shot, young 'un. Go on then but only if you promise not to come downstairs and have your wicked way with me. I know all about you young career girls.'

If I was planning on sleeping my way to the top, I wouldn't start with Wally's bottom.

'I hope Pete's paying you double-time. Wouldn't catch me working all night,' he snorts at his own joke and taps his watch-face.

I am surprised he can even see it as it's virtually obscured by thick grey whorls of arm-hair. I can just make out the faded inky blue tattoos he acquired during the war.

'You women's libbers got more than you bargained for. You thought ...'

'Yeah, thanks, Wal, I owe you. One last favour, please can you ring me and make sure I'm awake by seven? Don't want Peter walking in and finding me asleep at my desk.'

'Yes, certainly, and what would madam like with her early morning call? Tea, toast and a bacon sarnie?'

He smiles, closing the door behind him as gently as a man with upturned hams for hands can. He reminds me of my Grand-dad, unimpressed by money and most of what it buys. Provided he can pay his bills and take his wife for the occasional meal at the Berni Inn, he's happy.

All Grand-dad asked for was a few quid to spend on the horses. Sometimes, he let me read through the runners and riders and would let me pick the ones to back. At ten I was too young to study form but was a sucker for names like 'Whooping Miss Molly' or 'Daisy Darts Off'.

'The odds are a hundred to one,' he would say. 'The bloody thing will never win.'

He was right. Daisy didn't so much dart off as die. During the steeplechase, she jumped and landed badly. The cameras moved away quickly and I knew it was the last race she would ever run. As a distraction, Grand-dad reached down the side of his arm-chair, produced a small, paper bag of toffees and handed it to me. Dad never shared his sweets, eating half pound bars of chocolate to himself in full view of me and Mum, feeling no compunction to offer us so much as a square. Probably why I like Adam so much; he's always the first to discover the latest confection and makes sure I'm the second.

'One day I'm going to buy you a new house with a bath and hot water,' I remember telling Grand-dad as I washed my sticky hands under the solitary cold tap.

'When you get to my age, little 'un, you'll know time is more valuable than money.'

Now the clock goads me, 'One hour gone. Tick. There goes another. Tock. Still haven't cracked it, have you? Tick Tock.'

Peter's secretary will be here in a couple of hours. Unlike most people who get ready for work before work, she gets ready for work, at work, arriving early to ensure no-one sees her without make-up. Wally spotted her one morning and escorted her off the premises thinking she was a bag lady. An easy mistake to make given she often turns up with a bundle of dirty laundry, her smalls which she puts through the company washing machine in the upstairs apartment. She leaves the same day with it all clean, dry and, by some miracle, ironed. No one minds. Except me. I get absurdly irritated by it. I'm working my arse off in the office while she's washing her pants in the agency penthouse. Can't be right.

I wake up with my head on my layout pad. I feel terrible. At least my new campaign for High-Pro hair mousse seems to have passed the overnight test. But is it strong enough to blow Steve Winter's designer socks off?

Now Peter's secretary waltzes in, a challenge given she is wearing a tight-fitting satin skirt which permits only the smallest of movements. She shuffles into my office like an Arian geisha and squints at me.

'You scared me,' she says sharply, her hands fluttering to her face to conceal her pallid complexion. 'What are you doing?'

'Work - you remember, it's what we get paid to do when we're here.'

I resent the fact that she seems to do very little but gets paid very well. She even has a company car. A Porsche. One model down from Peter's.

She tuts at me and makes her way, as best she can, over to her desk.

My phone rings. It's Wally.

'This is your early morning call, madam!'

'Thanks, Wal, I'm up,' I tell him quickly replacing the receiver before I alert Peter's secretary to my nocturnal activities.

I catch her smiling at herself in the mirror, checking her teeth for lipstick and spinach.

'Just nipping upstairs for a quick shower,' I say loudly startling her.

'You're not allowed up there. It's only for clients and the board.'

'That's me - I'm very bored. Won't be long,' I say as Peter appears.

What's he doing here? He's never in before ten.

'Didn't I fire you?' he says lighting up a long pink cigarette with a golden tip.

He draws on it hard and stares at me from under his hooded eyes. He slides closer and winks at me.

'No,' I tell him defiantly. 'No, you didn't. Why would you? I do all the work.'

'Oh that's right, I remember. We came to a Little Arrangement, didn't we? Let's just call it a change in the terms of your contract. I'll get my secretary to type up the new clause now. Let the bonking begin.'

'This rutting season is a long way off,' I tell him.

He laughs. He is so close I can smell the smoke on his breath and recoil. He widens his eyes at me, like a wolf spotting its prey. Suddenly, he morphs into a corporate animal. I'm not sure which version is more terrifying.

'We're pitching Friday morning,' he barks.

So that's why he's here. He flicks open his briefcase and takes out a wad of papers.

'Briefing, my office, nine a.m. It's worth a million so I want you firing on all cylinders.'

He must be joking. After last night, I'm burnt out.

'Oh and we're up against That-Little-Shit, Steve Winter at KO'd.'

I wonder if Peter's told the award-winning copywriter formally known as 'Steve Winter' that he has changed his name to 'That-Little-Shit'.

Now we're pitching against him, it certainly compromises my interview. Talk about bad timing.

'It's essential we get our ducks in a row on this one, Ella.'

Why can't Peter just say 'be organised'? No one would guess he works in the communications industry. I run up the stairs, two at a time and take a quick shower. When I come down, I help myself to a large mug of Peter's Blue Mountain coffee.

'Fresh coffee is only for the board,' Peter's secretary squeaks her mantra and waves her newly polished red nails at me in an attempt to dry the varnish.

'When I was upstairs, I noticed your washing had finished so I whacked it in the tumble-drier for you. Put it on the hottest setting so it would be ready sooner,' I tell her, nonchalantly.

'My silk knickers!' she exclaims leaping up. She's so small, shrunk pants should be the perfect fit.

I just hope the brief we're about to get is as tight.

Chapter three

Know your client

Meetings are dangerous places. Even before anyone has uttered a word, life-changing decisions must be made. Like what to say, too much and I risk saying something stupid, too little and I look like an air-head. It's a lose-lose situation. Choosing where to sit is another minefield. I can't be in Peter's eye-line. I'm not up to him picking on me. My mind wanders to thoughts of a freshly-baked, warm almond croissant. If we can wrap this meeting up before ten there's a chance the patisserie will have a couple left, one for me and one for Wally. Fingers crossed.

I find an empty seat at the end of the table and sit down. To my horror, Josh plonks his files next to me.

'Didn't Peter fire you?' he asks moving away as if getting the sack was contagious.

'Oh you know Peter, says stuff in the heat of the moment. We're fine now,' I say sounding ridiculously optimistic.

I eye up the freshly-made sandwiches and salads tantalisingly placed just out of my reach in the centre of the table. Getting a top-notch in-house caterer was all down to Adam. He told the board, if a client has two great agencies on their shortlist they'll always pick the one that provides the best tuck. He wasn't wrong, feed their egos with quail's eggs and smoked salmon and you've got a client, not just for Christmas but for life.

I haven't eaten since yesterday. My arm reaches across the table and my fingers inch towards a plate of thickly-coated chocolate biscuits. I pull it towards me.

'I'm guessing you've smoothed it over with Kitty Rescue and charmed them into staying with us, Josh?' I ask shamelessly buttering him up like a warm croissant.

But Josh isn't biting.

'If you mean did we do lunch, then yes, we did. We went to L'Etoile and pulled out all the stops, champagne, fillet steak, the works. But if you mean did I make it okay for you, then no, I didn't. That's not my job. Obviously, they are still very uptight about that stunt you pulled with the copy. Apparently, the client's wife saw it and told her husband to fire us. Luckily for you they are getting divorced so he ignored her.'

He glares at me as he arranges his papers in obsessively neat piles.

'That's good,' I murmur, trying to remember what it was I'd heard recently about the client's wife.

'Good? The man is losing his five-bedroom house in Primrose Hill not to mention his prize-winning pedigree pug. That dog's worth a fortune in pet food endorsements alone.'

'Who got custody of the kids?' I ask suddenly remembering the slim white envelope that arrived two days after my twelfth birthday.

At first, I thought it was a late card for me but it was addressed to Mum and typed in neat black print. I handed it to her and went off to set about my quest to teach Beauty-Column-Sixpence to talk. She was incapable of mustering more than an irritable squawk, eyeing me suspiciously before standing on one leg and simultaneously cleaning her claws and doing a dropping. Having been roundly dismissed by a parrot, I wandered back into the living room where Mum sat holding a sheet of stiff white paper, the empty envelope discarded on the floor.

I can still remember the look on her face, crumpled and confused. It was an expression I would become horribly familiar with. Without money as a shield, life deals some harsh blows. I went to her and put my arms around her neck.

'Why are you crying?' I asked her.

'He doesn't want to see you,' she told me.

'Who?'

'Your father.'

I glanced into the hall at the parrot. She yawned and showed me her thick, grey tongue.

'Oh.'

It didn't matter to me. I didn't want to see him either. We had our life and it didn't include him. True, it was nowhere near as comfortable but we were well rid of his ranting. Once, I remember him cornering Mum in the hall by the front door. She said something and he grabbed her around the throat making her face twist and eyes bulge. He tightened his grip before releasing her and running up the stairs. Then, he stopped half way, and doubled in size, taking hold of the wooden banister and wrenching it out of the wall, as effortlessly as pulling a weed. It lay there for weeks, like a dead animal, surrounded by little piles of cement rubble and masonry nails.

Mum had held the letter tightly. I tried to read it over her shoulder but she lay the piece of paper in her lap, face down.

'His solicitor has written to say he wants no further contact with you.'

Her eyes filled with tears and her mouth opened wide. So, it did matter, it mattered that he had said 'no' to me.

Now Josh, stands beside me. I seem to have upset him too.

'Who cares about the bloody kids?' he snaps. 'If I were you, I'd focus on sorting out your own mess. Obviously, you're off Kitty Rescue so you need to win this one.'

'Watch me,' I tell him defiantly.

Despite the bravado, I know he is right. As delighted as I am to stop being Marmalade, Kitty Rescue is, was, my main account. Luckily, I have got experience on other business. In the past, I've written ads for everything from lager to loo cleaner (some people might argue they're the same thing). I also helped win the Nighty-Night Beds account but the agency was forced to resign the business after Peter was caught doing a spot of product testing with one of our junior account executives. She was unfortunate enough to be laid, and laid off by Peter.

Yet, somehow he got to keep his annual bonus. He gains in stature from his antics yet I mess around with one piece of copy and I get screwed. Peter's a smooth operator. No qualifications apart from a Degree in Schmoozing, he has cunningly wormed his way in with both the board and the clients. The men want to be him and the women want him. He has an easy charm designed to disarm. If the boys fancy a long weekend in the south of France, Peter gives them Cannes, with can-can dancers. And if the women clients fancy a little extra for their fat fee, Mr Big will oblige. He lays claim to anything decent to come out of the creative department and expects me to take it lying down. But I will not sleep with him to keep my job. I have to convince Steve Winter to hire me this evening.

Easy peasy, lemon squeasy.

Oh no, I just said that out loud. I said 'Easy, peasy, lemon, squeasy' within earshot of Josh Jenkins. Add that to 'Okelly Dokelly' and he is forgiven for questioning my supposed winning way with words. For once, I am both delighted and relieved to see Peter. If anyone can create a diversion, he can. He doesn't disappoint. The poser swaggers in like advertising royalty flanked by his minions, Mr Media and Mr Planning. His homage to punk looks like several kilts in clashing tartans, fastened with giant safety pins and fashioned into something resembling a suit. Not his finest sartorial hour.

Peter stands and addresses the room, looking like he might undress any minute. He clips and unclips one of the larger safety pins holding the whole ensemble together. Like Nero fiddling while Rome burns. I have visions of the outfit coming asunder and Peter standing like a grotesque Venus, swathed in plaid. I don't know what men wear under their kilts and I don't want Peter to show me. Mr Media and Mr Planning take it in turns to say 'Yes, Peter', 'No, Peter'. 'Three bags full, Peter,' must be Josh's line.

'Essential we get our ducks in a row on this one because coming second is not an option.'

Having exhausted all the jargon he currently knows, Peter eases his left buttock onto the edge of his desk in an attempt to appear both laid-back and cutting-edge. He looks like he's got piles.

'Okay, we know why we're here, a million pound pitch on Friday morning. Our main competitor is That-Little-Shit-Steve-Winter over at KO'd so we must crack it. No excuses.'

He nods towards the back of the room where Mr Media and Mr Planning fight to turn off the light. Even Edison would have agreed it is an unedifying sight, grown men jostling for position in Peter's pecking order. No wonder, with a million quid up for grabs and heads on the block, even the most insignificant tasks become competitive. Do they believe that on the day of reckoning, when Peter draws up his list of names for the chop, he is going to think, 'Oh we can't lose Mr Planning, he's a whizz with a light switch. Same goes for Mr Media, if you've got a petty job needs doing, he's your man.'

As if to prove the point, Mr Media steps self-importantly into the limelight and presses the 'play' button on the video recorder with such aplomb I expect the room to explode. And it does, as we watch the big bang, Peter having sex with the client's wife, Mrs Kitty Rescue.

That's it, I remember now, last year's Christmas party. Peter gave Josh strict instructions to keep Mr Kitty Rescue out of the way, while he plied Mrs Kitty Rescue with vintage champagne. The last I saw of them they were slow dancing and snogging to 'Silent Night'. Very festive. Their affair lasted about six months. It was common knowledge; Peter made no attempt to hide it. She was an ex-model and certainly raised his kudos.

Apparently, the pair of them thought they had it sussed. On the pretext she was walking her poodle, she'd nip round to Peter's. The client never dreamt his wife was up to no good with Adland's bad boy. Then again, the fact her pedigree pooch was tied to the lamp-post outside his house when it got run over was a bit of a giveaway.

Now, none of us can take our eyes off the film. Judging by the tasteless decor, gold wallpaper and a gilt mirror on the ceiling, it was shot in Peter's bedroom. But how the tape came to be in the machine is anyone's guess.

Peter is admiring his technique, cocking his head from side to side, appreciating his performance from all angles. I'm laughing so much, I'm crying. This is the most fun I've had since Adam bought me a whole tin of Quality Street for Christmas. Josh, exasperated by my prurience, quickly ejects the tape before handing it to Peter as if it were nuclear waste. Peter looks all set to take a bow but Josh shoots him a look of such disgust it even permeates Peter's hide. He settles for putting the tape in his briefcase, doubtless to enjoy later in the privacy of his own bedroom, his finger firmly on the 'pause' button.

Josh demands Peter's secretary tracks down the correct tape. I take advantage of the ensuing mayhem to have a sandwich. Thanks, Peter. This is the closest we will ever come to doing lunch but that's fine by me. Poached salmon or brie and grape? I can't decide. Before I make my move, Peter's secretary sashays in with another cassette. She bends down to put it in the machine and all the men in the room lean to the side at a ninety degree angle to watch her. They quickly sit up straight just before she gets up and four pairs of eyes follow her out of the room.

Peter's impromptu performance is engrained on my brain. Whenever I try and think of something lovely, Alan Ferguson or eating cake with Adam, there's Peter's peccadillo. I'm scarred for life. That could constitute an industrial injury - perhaps I can get counselling on expenses.

'Okay. Let's try again,' says Josh attempting to restore order as he switches on the video player.

It's a commercial for High-Pro hair mousse. I'm ahead of the game. We're pitching for High-Pro. I just might win this one. I feign interest in the ad but it's so bad I'd almost prefer to watch Peter perform again. The ad opens with a disturbingly energetic girl gyrating about the screen shaking her big moussed-up hair to the sounds of a sanitised punk rock track. She ends by thrusting a giant phallus at the camera. On closer inspection I realise it is a can of High-Pro. The words 'A Hair-Raising New Idea!!' appear along the bottom of the screen in big type. And, in case you nip out to make a cup of tea and miss it, the voice-over helpfully shouts the line so loudly you're bound to hear it, even over the noise of the kettle.

'Total crap so it won't be difficult to beat,' smirks Peter, still thrilled by his moment in the spotlight.

Pompously, Josh reads us the brief. Out loud, word for word. This isn't a briefing; this is story-time. For a moment I'm back in the fuggy atmosphere of my classroom, the one that smelt of wee and furniture polish, listening to my teacher, Sister Mary Francis.

'Sorry, Ella, did we wake you up?' asks Josh, his educated drawl clotted with sarcasm.

I sit bolt upright and pray he doesn't ask me anything. The last thing I remember seeing was a close-up of Peter's rear view. Now, it sounds like he's talking out of it.

'I think we're all singing off the same hymn sheet so we just need some awesome ideas to run up the flag-pole and see who salutes.'

That's a full house in Bullshit Bingo. Now I know how Peter Richards justifies his mega-buck salary.

I wait for everyone to leave and then help myself to the sandwiches curling unappetisingly at the edges. Pudding consists of two biscuits, like bars of chocolate with a thin layer of shortbread underneath, Adam's favourites. Heaven.

I'm reluctant to present my High-Pro ideas to Peter. After all, I'm only here because he thinks I'll have sex with him. Perhaps I should show my work to Steve in the hope he likes it enough to hire me. Then again my salary pays my mortgage. And Mum's rent. More importantly, there's no guarantee Steve will want me. I stick with the devil I know.

Peter leans across his desk and views me suspiciously.

'High-Pro ideas? Already? You can't have anything worth looking at. I've only just briefed you. I want stuff that's right, not rushed. Oh yes, grab your Filofax and let's put a date in for our Little Arrangement.'

He leans back in his chair, legs apart, hands resting on his thighs. I stare at the chair, willing it to topple over. Please, oh, please.

'I had a thought in the meeting, just wondered if you think it's worth developing?' I say, approaching his desk.

'Show me,' he demands.

I quickly fan out the sheets across the smoked glass.

'Think it's on the right lines?' I ask.

I shift from foot to foot, hoping he'll like it.

'You're a girl and this is hair gunk so you've got a head-start,' he says, the corners of his mouth twitching like they do when he thinks he's struck advertising gold. 'Hey, 'Head-Start' is a great slogan. It could work for High-Pro. See what you can do with it.'

I can bin it, that's what I can do with it.

Peter clicks his fingers at me.

'We might have a brief coming in for cough syrup, another one right up your street.'

'Why?'

'Because you're a woman.'

'So?'

'It's for kids.'

'I don't have any.'

'You must want them, you're a girl.'

'Do you like this?' I ask forcing him to focus on the work.

He stares into the distance, his eyes wide and his pupils dilated.

'Every woman I know wants babies. My babies. They'd have looks and talent, a rare and winning combination. But I'm not getting tied down. No way. That's why I'm splitting with my wife.'

No, I want to tell him, your wife is divorcing you because she got tired of you playing the field and decided to have some fun herself. She had such a blast; she left you.

Reluctantly, he stops talking about himself for long enough to review the work. He flicks through the ideas, giving each one no more than a second of his time. He screws up his face like he's in pain. Oh no, he's not having a heart attack. Not now, we've got too much to do. It could be a delayed reaction to his sex-tape coming to light. I thought he was playing it cool earlier, obviously suppressing his anxiety. Don't collapse on me, Peter, please. I can't give you mouth to mouth or you'll get the wrong idea and I'll be starring in your next porn flick.

'Is this another one of your jokes?' he asks tossing aside the layouts.

'No. I want to win this.'

'We're pitching for a million pound account on Friday against That-Little-Shit Steve Winter and you show me this? Go home and do the washing-up or whatever it is you women do all day,' he rails.

'I don't understand. What's wrong with it?' I ask warily, never having seen him quite so angry before.

'What's right with it?' he rages sweeping the work onto the floor.

I see ornaments, porcelain figurines of little girls in headscarves wearing simple skirts and blouses lying on the floor, hands severed from arms and heads broken off necks. And I hear Mum screaming and crying in disbelief that her husband could, with one swift action, destroy her beloved collection.

'The work's good, Peter.' I tell him as I snatch up my work and leave the room. 'You should be pleased we've got something to present at such short notice.'

He can't treat me like his whipping boy. He needs me. I work. He shirks. But, he has the power to keep me on or erase me from the payroll. He can do whatever he wants. Just like Dad. Mum stayed with him, clinging on for crumbs, hoping he would change back into the man she fell in love with.

If I walk now, I'll go back to where I came from. Nowhere. And it's easier to find a job when you've already got one, another of life's little ironies. I'll work for CBA for as long as it works for me. After all, I am Ella. I am not my mother. I don't have to put up with Peter. No amount of money is worth that. But before I walk, I need to know where I'm going.

Chapter four

The idea is king

'Hello Steve, it's Ella, Adam's friend. Just confirming our meeting tonight?' I whisper anxiously into the receiver, trying not to be overheard.

'Just about to call you; I'm going to have to cancel.'

His voice is aloof. He has better things to do than look at my work. But this is my opportunity to get out from under Peter.

'Shame, I've got some interesting stuff I'd like to show you.'

'If it's good, it'll keep,' he says.

He is flip, dismissive. I imagine him leaning against a huge black lacquered desk, flicking through this week's copy of *Campaign* checking out the shots of himself, posed on the iconic spiral staircase in his agency's atrium alongside yet another report detailing yet another million pound win. He has had plenty of lucky breaks. I just need this one.

'Limited offer – today only,' I tell him.

I can't let him turn me down. Not now. I coil the flex through my fingers as I wait for his response.

'Okay. I'm hooked. Drink in The Fox in five?'

'See you there,' I say putting the phone down.

I grab my best High-Pro ad and put it in my handbag before re-applying my lippy and galloping downstairs.

When I arrive at the pub, I spot a tall, thin expensively-dressed man waving at me from the bar. He is wearing round, yellow-rimmed glasses, the designer logo etched on the sides.

'Hello, Ella. I'm Steve.'

'Hi, how did you know it was me?'

'You're the only girl in here. Drink?'

He laughs and catches the barman's eye.

'White wine, please,' I tell him.

Steve orders two large glasses and hands over a fiver, telling the barman to keep the change. When the drinks arrive we look each other in the eye and say 'cheers'. We laugh. We talk. We laugh some more. It feels like a date. I feel on top of the world. I've only known him two minutes and already I'm planning what to buy him for Christmas, silver cufflinks in the shape of aeroplanes. 'High-flier'. Oh no, I've been working with Peter for too long. I hope mind-reading isn't one of Steve's many talents.

Steve's teeth are big and white, his skin golden brown. Is that a smear of foundation on his shirt collar? Surely not?

'You come highly recommended, young lady. Adam really rates you,' he says smiling. 'He's a good bloke.'

'Yes, yes he is,' I say remembering the time he did my shopping for me for four weeks after I'd broken my arm and refused to let me pay for any of it.

'How's the wine?' he asks.

'Nice,' I hear myself say. 'Really nice.'

'Nice'? I'm trying to convince one of the greatest Creative Directors in the business to hire me as a writer and the best I can come up with is 'nice'? And I said it twice. Not nice.

'Come on then, let's see these awesome ideas.'

He looks expectant, like I'm about to show him the meaning of life. I'm pretty sure it's chocolate but judging by the way he has drained his glass, it's white wine all the way for him. I thrust my hand into my bag and take out the crumpled piece of paper. Embarrassed, I smooth it out with the flat of my hand on the bar.

'Steve, I probably shouldn't be showing you this; it's for High-Pro.'

His eyes widen.

'My first thought, probably not great, but...'

That's right, Ella, you sell it to him. Who in their right mind can say 'no' to that pitch?

'Mega!' he exclaims. 'Love it.'

'Really?' I squeal trying to swallow the incredulity in my voice.

Steve Winter likes my work. This is it. There is life after CBA.

'Peter thinks it sucks,' I tell him.

'If he hates it, I love it. The guy's a dinosaur. None of the kids in my creative department have even heard of him.'

'He has refused to show it in the pitch.'

He looks at the work, then back at me for a moment longer than is comfortable.

'I'll present it,' he says decisively, taking another mouthful of wine.

'What?'

'I'll pitch this to High-Pro.'

Peter may not like my idea but I like Steve's. Shame it's not moral or ethical. It's probably not even legal. And when Peter finds out, I'll lose my job. I can't risk it.

'Thanks, Steve but I don't think so.'

I fold up the layout and slide it back into my bag.

'If we win the business, I'll hire you. How much do you want?'

We all have our price. I wonder what mine is? I am tempted by his offer but the stakes are too high. I shake my head.

'No, thanks, Steve.'

'Why are you so loyal to that bastard? He'll stab you in the back first chance he gets. Did Adam tell you what he did to me?'

I nod.

'And you know Peter was gunning for Adam too? Peter's a leach. He did one half-decent ad back in the 70's and he probably ripped that off from some junior art-director. He has been living off it ever since.'

'Yes, the trouble is the board love him. As long as he keeps the clients happy, they're happy.'

He turns away and orders two more white wines. The barman sets them down on the polished wooden counter. Steve looks uneasy about his outburst. He plays with the knot in his tie and begins to calm down as he talks about what's going on in the industry. We have a lively exchange about new campaigns. Suddenly, he stops and looks intently at me. I don't like the silence and start to gabble, trying to appear bright and witty when inside I'm still the kid wearing someone else's knickers. Mum couldn't afford to buy new clothes and took to shopping in Oxfam. She picked me out a crocheted bolero. A bolero? I didn't even know where Spain was, let alone want to dress in their national costume.

I should try to impress Steve, not blame my shortcomings on the Balearic islands. Before I can convince him he needs me, he leaps up.

'Gotta go. Let's hope one of my lot has come up with something on High-Pro or I'm looking at an all-nighter. I'll give you a bell and we'll sort a date.'

'A what?' I ask my voice high-pitched with excitement.

'A date for you to show me your portfolio, yeah?'

'Oh yes, of course.'

What am I playing at? This is Steven Winter, Creative Director of KO'd. He might, if I stop behaving like a complete fool, offer me a job but he certainly doesn't want to ask me out. I might turn up in a bolero.

'Think about what I said, Ella. You've got my number. Call me.'

He puts his hand on my hip and goes to kiss my cheek just as I turn my head. His lips meet mine, fleetingly. I laugh, embarrassed but oddly delighted. He smiles and briefly touches my forearm. Charming, but I can't help thinking a handshake would be more appropriate.

When I get back to the agency, Peter is reclining on the leather sofa, in his lair. I can see cigarette smoke snaking through his open door. He spots me. Damn.

'Ella?'

Tentatively, I go in. Fortunately, his mood seems to have lifted. I note the empty crystal tumbler at his feet and the half-drunk bottle of whiskey on his desk.

'Sit down,' he says patting the space next to him.

I perch tentatively on the edge. For some inexplicable reason, I find myself sympathising with him – after all it's his neck on the line if we lose this pitch. It has to be right. I should cut him some slack. Then, I catch sight of the large silver-framed photo on his desk, a picture of his loved ones. It's Peter in his Porsche. I stop feeling sorry for him.

'Peter, I don't think you should have spoken to me the way you did. My ideas are on brief and …'

'Forget about all that. I've cracked it,' he declares.

He spreads his work out between his well-shod feet, planted a yard apart. Smug is Peter's default setting. He seems to have added deluded to the mix. The work is all style and no substance, just pretty girls with big hair. I'm not known for my diplomacy.

'Where are you going with this, Peter?' I ask.

I've heard Josh use this one, many times. When he says it, it sounds neutral and honeyed like he's reserving judgment and is genuinely interested as to how the idea might pan out. When I say it, it sounds like, 'I can't believe you're actually getting paid for this crap.'

'Where am I going? I've arrived,' he says repeatedly stabbing at each advertisement with his forefinger. 'Look!'

I look but can't see much.

'Sex sells. Even if you are too uptight to admit it, Ella.'

Peter would use sex to flog lettuces to tortoises if they could afford them.

'Darren's drawing up my layouts as we speak,' he declares defiantly. 'Obviously, we're keeping the strap-line, 'High-Pro – A Hair-Raising New Idea' because the client loves it.'

Does he? Are you sure? If he loves a bad pun so much and is delighted to be the laughing stock of the hair and beauty industry, why would he put his business up for pitch? Why doesn't he just stay with the agency that produced the dross? I imagine he wants some fresh thinking for his million, a flash of brilliance that makes everyone with hair want his products. Peter glares at me, waiting for me to heap praise on his big head.

'We know that for a fact, do we Peter?' I ask sounding all sarcastic.

Peter sounds all bombastic.

'Yes, we do, as a matter of fact. The Planning Director did some research among the target audience.'

What? Mr Planning asked Mrs Planning? Great, we're basing a million pound hair-mousse pitch on a sample of one. A woman with no hair. Poor Mrs Planning is completely bald, her alopecia no doubt brought on by the stress of being married to Mr Planning. A man so anal, he insists on sitting in the same seat at every board meeting, next to Mr Media.

'I do not have to justify my decision to you,' Peter booms. 'I am the Creative Director. You are just my copywriter.'

'I thought we were supposed to be a team,' I say incredulously.

'Can you manage to write the copy or shall I brief someone else while you pop home and run the vacuum round?'

I stare at him in disbelief. What was it Steve called him? 'A dinosaur'.

'And this time, no funny business,' he says fixing me with a look. 'Don't want you arranging the first letter of the first word on every line to spell out some obscenity.'

As if. I've got a much better idea. I go back to my office and dial Steve's number.

'You can present my High-Pro stuff,' I tell him defiantly.

Actions speak louder than words and this is me telling Peter enough is enough.

'You sure?' he asks unable to conceal his glee.

'Yeah, go for it.'

With any luck, it'll win the pitch and I'll land a job at KO'd. Knock-out.

'Shall I fax it over?' I ask him.

'No need, I can remember it.'

I pause then say quickly, 'If it wins, you said there's a chance of a job at your place, didn't you?'

41

He takes so long to respond I think we've been cut off.

'Whoa, easy tiger! Let's get the pitch under our belts first.'

I bridle at the condescending comment. I'm not sure I like where this is going.

'We need to be clear,' I tell him coldly.

'Your call, either I present it. Or Peter doesn't.'

Now I see how Steven Winter got to where he's got. In less than ten words, Mr Adland has persuaded me to do what he wants.

'Fine, present it. But remember it's my idea,' I say. 'At least you won't have any competition from Peter. His stuff sucks and he expects me to write the copy for it.'

He's not listening.

'Awesome. Thanks, Ella. Gotta go. Gotta pitch to win,' he says and hangs up.

I put the phone down and stare at it. What the hell have I done? I've just handed Steve Winter my best work, an idea he believes will win the pitch. Let's hope he has a shred of integrity woven into his bespoke suit and honours his agreement to hire me if it's successful. This is my golden opportunity. I should be presenting the concept myself, not giving it away to the first bloke that asks. Ouch! That sounds familiar. Don't go there, Ella. Focus on work. Reluctantly, I churn out the copy for Peter's ad.

'I'm off now,' he says, putting his head round the door. 'Leave the work on my secretary's desk; I'll check it in the morning. Oh and I've unplugged the fax machine and locked it in my office, just in case you think it's hilarious to give the client a sneak preview. I know your tricks – still haven't forgotten Kitty Rescue. You're a very naughty girl. I like that.'

He approaches my desk and stands behind me. My body tenses. I feel him put his hands on my shoulders, very gently. He is so close I can smell his breath. Whiskey mixed with nicotine. His lips brush my ear.

'I was going to wait for you tonight,' he whispers urgently. 'Thought we could have some fun. Enjoy our Little Arrangement. But I got a better offer. Night-night.'

He spins my chair round to face him, laughs and walks off. The pungent stench of his oh-so-expensive aftershave lingers in the air long after I hear his Porsche roar off. It smells like he's still in the room, watching my every move, waiting to ponce, I mean pounce.

My fingers shake on the keys. Somehow I manage to finish the copy. I read it through. It's not good enough. I rip it out and put a fresh piece of paper in the roller and rewrite it. I check it again and spot a couple of spelling errors. I paint correcting fluid over the mistakes and blow on it to encourage it to dry quickly before retyping the words. Now it's as good as I can make it. I remove it from the typewriter and leave it on his secretary's desk.

I give Adam a quick call before I leave. It's later than I thought; he's already left the office. I feel a pang of disappointment when his answerphone machine clicks in and I have to settle for leaving a message.

'Thanks for the tip-off. Steve was really nice. Ringing him was a good move. If you fancy breakfast at Pat Vals this week, let me know, my treat. Bye and thanks again.'

Chapter five

Be careful who you cross on the way up; you might meet them on the way down

Swinging by KO'd to see how Steve is getting on with High-Pro could be fun but I must go over to Mum's. She sees my signature on cheques more often than she sees me. When I'm not too busy I go as often as I can but Peter isn't keen on his staff having a life.

I hurry towards Oxford Circus tube, step in a puddle and curse; my new black leather boots will be ruined. They are sky-high, with a price-tag to match but worth it as they make me feel a million dollars. It's raining hard now. Luckily, I can run in heels and just make the station entrance before another deluge. A crowd has gathered at the top of the stairs. Everyone wants to get down into the station but London Transport staff are anxious to avoid overcrowding on the platforms and are only letting a few people through at a time. A woman shakes her umbrella, I turn my head to avoid the spray and lose my balance.

Falling forward, I drop over the edge of the top stair. Sliding down headfirst, I grate the side of my face like a lump of Parmesan cheese against the serrated metal edges of the steps. A thick fog descends and envelops my head. I lie on the floor, my grazed cheek grateful for the cold comfort of the concrete. If my friends could see me now. What friends? I spend more time with Peter than anyone else. I must get a life. No, I must. I am about to die. Blood pools like gravy in front of my eyes. I'm no doctor (much to Mum's disappointment) but even I know this is not good. Oxford Circus can't be the end of the line for me. Then again, I'm already six foot under; it will save on the burial costs. But I can't die - I've got a pitch to do.

'Help me,' I murmur.

No-one comes. I am alone. My mouth fills with a metallic-tasting liquid. Then nothing.

When I open my eyes I am in a wheelchair being carried up the stairs by two men. I'll die of embarrassment if the brain haemorrhage doesn't kill me first. My eyelids fall like shutters, blotting out reality. If I can't see it, it's not happening.

Now, I am in bed with a stranger looking deep into my eyes. He's a fast-worker, obviously not a London Underground employee. He snaps on a pair of rubber gloves, the sort doctors wear when they examine you in places you don't want to be examined. And I thought the evening couldn't get any worse.

'What is your name?' he asks gently.

'Ella.'

He's already got me into bed; it's a bit late for pleasantries.

Plastic tubes, red blankets, a man in green. Why am I in an ambulance? I struggle to remember.

'Is Peter okay?' I ask anxiously as I picture him drunk with his Porsche keys in his hand.

My head feels heavy, full of pain.

'Peter? Who's Peter?' the man in green asks.

'Peter Richards.'

'You were alone in the station when we got to you. Now, Ella, are you going to be a good girl and come to the hospital with me?'

He talks slowly like he's considering having me sectioned. I can save him the paperwork. I work in advertising. It's like an asylum but with more stylish jackets.

'I must go and see Mum. And I've got a presentation in the morning,' I say struggling to sit up.

'Don't move, please. What is the Queen's name?' he asks.

The man's a fool. He should apply for a job at CBA. He'd walk it.

'Ella, look at me. Can you tell me the Queen's name?'

If this is his idea of a chat-up line, he's got a lot to learn. Oh I get it; it's a trick question.

'Elizabeth, Elizabeth the second!' I tell him triumphantly.

You don't catch me out that easily. I'm not some lunatic imagining I live in the sixteenth century with the Virgin Queen still on the throne. He observes me closely but says nothing. Perhaps he wants to know her surname. Does she even have one? I don't know. Did we do this at school? No, but we did study the war poets and our English teacher insisted, '*The Naming of Parts*' by Wilfred Owen was about sex when it was clearly about a rifle. That's the sort of teacher we had back in the '70's.

'Slough,' I shout triumphantly. 'No, Windsor. Her surname is Windsor.'

Not satisfied with that, he's got another brain-teaser for me.

'Who is the Prime Minister?'

'Maggie Thatcher milk-snatcher,' I chant.

He looks at me, notes down what I've said and adds a few comments of his own in the margin. No doubt, 'Delusional drunk.'

I try to twist my head to read what he has written. He angles his pad away from me.

'Margaret Thatcher, that's right. You caused quite a commotion earlier, the station had to be closed because of you, young lady.'

Patronizing and delusional, he could give Peter a run for his money.

'I'm going now. I'm fine.'

He shows me my reflection in a hand-mirror.

'You'll have a real shiner there tomorrow,' he says.

'Is there anyone you'd like me to contact for you?' he asks.

Adam's the only person I can think of. At least, he'll bring cake. But, it's too late to bother him.

Much to my disappointment, the ambulance-driver doesn't deem my case serious enough to sound the siren. We arrive at A&E, unannounced; he checks me in and leaves.

Cries, like wailing bird song fill the air and people who look like they might expire at any moment, fill the seats. Others, who have just popped in to shelter from the rain buy tea and Mars Bars from the vending machines. A middle-aged man is sitting on the floor shouting randomly at anyone who will listen.

'Four bleedin' hours I've been here. I'm dying.'

'Ella David. Room two.'

I stand up quickly. Too quickly. My head feels like it is filled with slow-setting cement. I shuffle along the corridor, shielding my eyes from the fluorescent lights. A short, sweaty man who looks like he would be happier flipping burgers for a living, leaps out of a side room.

'I've got a junior doctor here, observing. Don't mind, do you?' Burger Man asks, indicating a young woman in a stiff white coat fiddling self-consciously with her stethoscope.

No point objecting, I just want to get this over with.

'You sustained quite a blow,' Burger Man tells me. 'It's possible you have a head injury.'

He looks up and I half expect him to ask if I'd like onions and fries.

I feel a bit sick and sit down. Burger Man holds up my left eye-lid with his fat thumb, and shines a deceptively powerful light in my face before

47

attacking my wounds with a ball of damp cotton wool. I flinch. It stings like hell.

'Been drinking?' he asks.

I shake my head and the room spins.

'Grab her, Jan! We've got a fainter.'

The doctor steps forward, grips both my arms and sits me back on the chair, like a naughty child. She makes no attempt to conceal her contempt for me, a lush who fell down the stairs and is now squandering valuable NHS resources. I don't blame her. She didn't spend seven years at medical school for this.

'Anyone we can contact for you?' she asks abruptly.

I feel worse than ever. I need a friend.

'Adam,' I say automatically.

She blinks. Twice.

'Give me his number and I'll get someone to call him,' she says.

I lift my head slowly and look at the clock. He would come, I know he would but he's got work in the morning. And there's nothing he can do. This is one time when the restorative properties of chocolate cake aren't going to cut it.

'Don't worry. I'll get a cab.'

Burger Man takes a closer look at my wound and screws up his eyes.

'You'll probably need a scan but you're going to have to wait; we're very busy as you can see.'

Thanks to him, scorching the back of my retina, I can't see a thing.

'I'll get you into see the consultant as soon as possible,' he tells me scribbling down some more notes.

I thought he was the doctor. If he's not, is he the Burger Man, a ketchup-wielding weirdo who lied about having a PhD and got to play God for the night? He tells me to sit in the waiting room. I don't have time for this. Using the pay-phone, I call a taxi and leave.

When I get home, I avoid the bathroom mirror and head for bed. Right now, I would love someone to take care of me, give me a cuddle and make me a cup of sweet, strong tea to drink through a straw. I've never felt more alone. Work has enveloped my life. Adland never sleeps. It learned that from Maggie Thatcher. Apparently, she survives on just four hours a night. I read somewhere lack of sleep drives you crazy. Who in their right mind would want to spend time with me? A girl obsessed with advertising. It's less about what I am selling and more about what it lets me buy. Peace of mind for Mum. While I'm paying her rent, she's free from money worries for the first time in her life. I owe her this. She gave me so much. And gave up even more. Having lost my home and my Dad, I clung to her, stifling any other relationship in her life. Now I know how she must have felt; the closest thing I have to a boyfriend is Marmalade.

I wake with a start, to the familiar buzz of my alarm, having dribbled on the pillow. And I wonder why I'm still single. I go to the bathroom, wash my face and rub it vigorously with a towel. I almost pass out. The mirror shows the left-hand side of my face is a muddle of purple and blue. It looks like someone's been at it with a potato-peeler. No amount of make-up is going to mask this mess. But staying at home is not an option. My body is stiff. With difficulty, I put on my black suit, the one with the huge shoulder pads, and set off. I pass a couple of schoolboys. One points at me and gurns. The other laughs. Undeterred, I slowly make my way up the hill through Queen's Wood to Highgate tube station. At the entrance, I see the deep stairwell and shudder. Gripping the handrail tightly, I walk gingerly down. People tut and push past, anxious to get to work, eager to make money. I stand on the escalator letting others run down the left hand-side. Reaching the bowels of the station, I take up pole position on the platform, where I know the double doors of the train will slide open onto the first carriage and I will be perfectly placed to get on and grab a seat. I don't want to be jostled and hang back, letting the first two trains, packed with upright, uptight bodies go. Eventually, I arrive at the agency later than usual but still in time for the presentation.

Peter's secretary looks at my face, puts her hand over her mouth and runs off. Peter strides out of his office, wearing a hand-made suit and a made-to-measure smile.

'Good night, was it Ella?'

'The stairs at the tube were wet and I slipped.'

'Always knew you were a lush. Well, we can't have you in the pitch looking like an inebriated tramp so just write me a creative rationale, keep it loose, nothing too detailed - make me sound good. Should be easy enough. Then you can go home. Don't want you putting everyone off their croissants,' he says.

'I'm here to present.'

He laughs, long and throaty. I can see his fillings, mercury like bullets between his back teeth.

'Listen, sweetheart, if you didn't want to sleep with me, you only had to say. Obviously you're out of the running with me until that face has healed. It would be like bonking Quasimodo.'

He makes a gagging motion. He is the least funny man I know. But I might have the last laugh. If he finds me having a face like a pizza a turn-off, I hope it takes forever to heal.

'Peter, I am going to the presentation. I'm part of the team.'

I step forwards. He bars my way, wagging his nicotine-stained forefinger in my face and scrutinizing my bruises.

'Did you throw yourself downstairs deliberately? Try and top yourself because I rejected you the other night?'

50

He laughs.

The bastard. How dare he? I would give anything not to be beholden to him. But he has the money and the power. If I tell him where to stick his job, I'll be the one stuck where the sun don't shine.

'Ella, I pay you to do what I tell you to do. Creative rationale as quick as you like.'

He calls the shots and I can't afford to be fired but something snaps inside me.

'I don't feel well. I'm going home.'

I push past him and go to the kitchen for some water. I hold the cold glass against my forehead. It eases the pain momentarily. When I come back Peter's secretary is watching me closely.

'Ella, your driver is here, white Mercedes at the back of the building,' she tells me looking at my face. 'Are you okay? That looks painful.'

'Few bruises, nose bleed, nothing serious,' I reassure her.

'Good,' she says.

She turns away and starts typing, her slender fingers flying over the keys. She must be doing a hundred words per minute. I've never seen her move so fast. I'm impressed.

Laughter is coming from the boardroom. I can't resist putting my ear to the door.

'Sorry, you're not allowed in there. Peter says you'll frighten the client,' she tells me, clearly embarrassed to be the messenger.

'Fine by me. It's a lousy campaign anyway,' I shoot back.

Just then Darren appears, carrying a pile of slickly drawn layouts.

'Here's the High-Pro stuff. I've made the logo bigger and changed the typeface, like Peter asked.'

Curious to see just how bad the finished ads really are, I take a quick look.

No, it can't be. It is. It's my idea. The one Peter said was rubbish. Now, he's about to take the credit for it. No wonder he didn't want me in the presentation. The scumbag.

'Please don't touch Peter's work,' says his secretary snatching the boards up.

'Peter's work?' I ask incredulously. 'The only thing he's any good at his stealing other people's ideas.'

She wiggles past me into the boardroom. I want to run in after her and, like in the movies, leap on the table and unmask Peter as a fraud but I am not convinced the glass top would take my weight. Then I remember the Christmas party when it supported two people, one of whom was Peter. Perhaps I could burst into song, a real show-stopper about how a no-good, down and dirty guy did me wrong and strut about pointing at my esteemed Creative Director. Josh would try and have me thrown out but the client would prevent him, seeing me for a gutsy-girl-made-good and sweep me into his arms. Everyone would applaud. And Peter would be forced to flee the agency in disgrace, never to darken its doors again.

'Bet you're not getting much action with that,' says Darren eyeing my black eye.

'My face will heal but you'll always be a creep.'

It hurts to talk but that was worth the pain.

Now I must phone Steve before it's too late.

'Sorry, Steve, you can't present my idea. Peter is pitching it to the client as we speak.'

'You're kidding! It's all I've got. They'll be here in an hour.'

'How do you think I feel? It's my idea and ...'

'Gotta go,' he says, hanging-up.

'Ella, your cab's waiting. Hurry up,' calls Peter's secretary.

'I'm not going anywhere. I want to be here when the presentation ends. I want to see Peter's face when he sees mine.'

Peter may have stolen my work but I am going to make him pay. Just because he's a lying bastard doesn't mean I have to take it lying down.

Chapter six

Know your strategy

At ten past twelve the board room door swings opens and six men, two High-Pro clients, Peter, Josh, Mr Planning and Mr Media, gush out on a tidal wave of testosterone. They talk too much, laugh too loudly and shake hands too firmly. Peter loosens his tie with one hand and slaps the senior client on the back with the other. I've never seen him look so thrilled with himself. Then he sees me.

'Go home,' he hisses out of the side of his mouth.

'Did the client like your work, Peter?' I ask sarcastically.

Mr Media and Mr Planning walk slowly down the spiral staircase, pausing to listen in. Josh pushes past them.

'Peter, if your secretary can get our coats, we'll be on our way,' says the client, pointing at me.

'No problem, Mike,' he tells him before turning to me. 'Ella, fetch the coats.'

Everyone gets one moment, a point in time when they can do or say exactly what they like. One moment to savour before their world comes crashing down. This is Peter's. He just doesn't know it yet.

'Enjoy the presentation, Mike?' I ask ignoring his side-kick who is hovering nervously at his elbow.

'Yes, very good but we do have another agency to see before lunch so if we can have our coats...'

Peter steals my idea and the client robs me of my dignity.

'I am not Peter's secretary,' I assert. 'I am Ella. I am his writer. I worked on this campaign.'

'Really?' Mike asks as if I've just told him I've seen the Tooth Fairy.

He turns away to face Peter, 'So you think you can bring the commercial in under budget?'

'Leave it with me,' says Peter.

With nothing to present, Steve Winter is out of the running. That means High-Pro is as good as ours. I cannot stand back and let Peter take all the glory. No way. That one idea has not only won us the business, it could win me an award, promoting me to the same league as Alan Ferguson. Time to take control.

'Mike, let's do dinner. Peter, ask your secretary to book a table for three at Le Caprice tonight.'

The client's eyes widen with greed as he anticipates antipasto and aperitifs. Peter looks like he's going to vomit.

'Le Caprice! Fantastic! I've always wanted to eat there. Can we say about seven thirty?'

Love at first bite. One mouthful of nouvelle cuisine from one of London's hippest restaurants and he'll be eating out of my hand.

Not wanting to disappoint the client, Peter reluctantly nods at his secretary to make the call. He walks Mike and his shadow to the lift. The doors close on the two men and Peter and I watch the display as it counts down the floors – three, two, one, fire!

'How dare you? Who the hell do you think you are? I won the pitch and you turn up and jeopardise everything,' screams Peter his shoulder pads heaving.

'But it's my idea. You told me it was crap then present it as your own. You're amoral. At least offer me a pay rise, don't just steal it.'

'Listen, Ella. I worked my arse off in there. I don't know what Josh was playing at but I was the one who turned the whole thing round. I persuaded the client to buy the idea.'

'The point is you rubbished my work and then took all the glory, like you always do.'

'Really? As I remember it, I briefed you, you couldn't crack it and I saved the day. And if you try and challenge me, believe me, I will wheel out the CBA legal guns and point them at you. Comprendez?'

'I no speakie bullshit.'

But behind my bravado, I know Peter and his cronies could see to it that I never work in advertising again.

'And, if you don't like the way I do things...'

'What, Peter? You'll fire me?' I ask, my tone reaching a dangerous level of defiance. 'You need me to progress the idea and come up with next award-winner.'

A flicker of realisation crosses his face.

'Look, Ella,' he says, backtracking, beads of sweat forming on his upper lip. 'This is all very simple; we came up with the same idea, at the same time.'

'That's not what happened and you know it. You haven't had an idea in years.'

He takes a step towards me, his voice low and menacing.

'I don't need you. Copywriters are queuing up to work for me.'

'Not good ones,' I mutter.

I want to tell him where to shove his job but as he has already 'worked his arse off' that's not an option. The days of walking out of one agency and straight into another are long gone. Everyone, no matter how unhappy, is clinging on to their jobs right now. If I leave CBA I may as well hand the keys to my flat back to the building society and tell Mum I won't be able to help her anymore. No matter how much I despise Peter, I have to put up and shut-up until something better comes along. The problem is I can't include the High-Pro campaign, my best work to date, in my portfolio now Peter has officially bagged it.

There's no copyright on an idea in this industry and there's no union so there's no hope of me getting justice. Besides, Adland is a small world and Peter is big mates with some big names; I can't afford to upset anyone.

Now, to add insult to injury, my face looks like a rotten cabbage; Alan Ferguson won't give me a second glance.

I call Adam but get his answer machine. So I do the next best thing and take up my favourite seat in the patisserie on Old Compton Street, the one with the best view of the cakes in the window. I am so uneasy on the eye, I put tourists off their choux buns which means I have no trouble keeping the table to myself. Greedily, I tuck into my croissant. As if it's not baked with enough butter, I lavish more on top. A pot of shiny strawberry jam also demands I open it; I squish a generous spoonful inside. My mouth is still sore. I lean awkwardly to one side, open my lips wide and, like a snake consuming an egg, insert the pastry and bite down. Jam oozes and drops onto my plate, flakes of croissant attach themselves like fly-paper, to my face.

'Hello, Ella.'

Alan Ferguson is watching me as he waits to be served. I am horrified he even recognises me looking the way I do. Of all the patisseries, in all the towns, he walks into mine. He looks divine, smiling while trying to catch the eye of the dark-haired Italian waitress arranging her rum-babas into neat rows with a pair of silver tongs. When she sees him, she beams. Silly girl, he wants a coffee, not your hand in marriage, I think watching her fiddling with the fronds of hair at her temple. She turns away to prepare his cappuccino and to show off her pert bottom. How can anyone work in a cake shop and not have a bum the consistency of clotted cream? Making a tremendous show of twisting silver knobs and handles, she stands back as steam bursts from the machine's every orifice. Using a thin silver tube, she magically turns cold milk into steaming white foam. You're making coffee not art, I think, watching him watch her. She pours fresh coffee into the Styrofoam cup and carefully spoons frothed milk on top before pressing the lid down. Taking a biro from her apron pocket, she scrawls a phone number, which I jealously assume is hers, on the side. As he takes the drink, he whispers something in her ear. Then, he walks over, sits down and points sympathetically at my face.

There are times when I long to talk to him. This isn't one of them. My face needs to heal. My hair needs styling. My legs need waxing. My body needs exercising. I need to look good enough for Alan Ferguson.

Just then, the waitress sashays over, deliberately brushing a perfectly taut thigh against his arm. He grins as she wafts past him into the kitchen before saying,

'Hear High-Pro went well. Wish I'd been there.'

'So do I.'

The story has already acquired all the hallmarks of an advertising legend. Agency in danger of dying on its arse in urgent need of resuscitation and ageing Creative Director desperate to prove himself one last time presents someone else's idea as his own at the eleventh hour to win a million pound account.

'Did you see the concept?' asks Alan.

'See it? It's my idea,' I tell him.

I feel the heat in my cheeks.

'At least, the agency won't go under now,' he says softly.

'What?'

'The board was about to call the receivers in.'

'Peter never said. Then again, he's not going to admit bringing the agency to its knees. The place has been bankrolling him for months. If he could have got away with charging his jacuzzi to the company, he would.'

But Alan is not listening. He is mesmerised by the waitress as she passes, holding a tray of perfectly domed coffee eclairs under her perfectly domed breasts.

I didn't think this day could get much worse. But the script that is my life, says it always will.

On the pretext of giving my table a quick wipe-over, the waitress leans across Alan allowing her bust to lightly brush the Formica surface. I keep forgetting only one side of my mouth works and when I speak, I snarl. My lips twitch. Alan must be having a job resisting me. Then the waitress whips off her pinny, the man of my dreams has is now centre stage in my worst nightmare. I can only watch, as he heads for the door, hand in hand with another woman. It's game over. I am no match for her with her honey, honed limbs and Mardi Gras smile but it still hurts. Like hell.

Think of the devil and he shall appear.

'Ella!' Peter yells across the tables. 'High-Pro. You. Me.'

Clearly, he is now so busy he can only speak in monosyllables. As usual he's making no sense.

'Taxi. Reception. Seven thirty.'

Obviously, he doesn't want to waste his breath on me.

I wander along the length of Shaftesbury Avenue, thinking about Alan, mulling over what might have been and trying to shut down the images of his paramour having her wily way with him. To be honest, we were never really together but there was an attraction, admittedly more on my part than his. I try to distract myself, looking at what's on at the theatres and reading the reviews posted outside. But my mind returns time and time again to mull over what Alan said about the agency being on Skid Row.

Peter owes me. Big time. But try as I might, I can't dispel the gnawing doubt that although my idea won the day, Peter will ensure I lose out.

Chapter seven

Keep the client happy

Peter sits in silence as the cab sweeps along Shaftesbury Avenue towards the restaurant in Mayfair, fluffing up his hair in the driver's rear view mirror. I am too angry to speak. Even the cabbie knows better than to talk.

When we arrive, Mike appears to have started without us. He raises his glass in his podgy hand, the skin stretched uncomfortably over his fat fingers. He stands up, swaying unsteadily, like a puppet on a string but the effort proves too great and he collapses back down onto his seat.

'Hi guys, what are you drinking?' he asks expansively which strikes me as odd given we are the ones footing the bill. No wonder the agency is on the brink of bankruptcy.

'G and T for me and whatever the little lady wants,' Peter tells him through a plastic smile.

'Kir Royale,' I say automatically.

If the geese are on the sauce, so is this gander. With the evening shaping up to be a disaster, I'll take my pleasures where I can.

Mike clicks his fingers at the waiter. In contrast, the young man is polite and attentive, pulling out my chair and placing a starched white napkin the size of a tablecloth on my lap. I smile at him, trying to convey, 'Sorry about the jerk.'

Much gets lost in translation because he asks, 'Yes, madam, I will bring you some water.'

'Water? This is a celebration. Shampoo all round,' declares Mike expansively, waving his hands across the table and knocking over his glass.

Clearly, we have some catching up to do. Not least to learn a whole new vocabulary.

'Good to see you again, Mike' says Peter.

He sounds so sincere. It's a gift, I'll give him that.

'You were awesome this afternoon, Peter. KO'd had nothing on you. Zero. Zilch. You are my man.'

There are few things more toe-curling than a rotund, middle-aged man from suburbia trying to sound cool. Thankfully, the waiter arrives with our drinks and saves Mike's life. I was about to stab him with my butter knife.

'Cheers, Mike. Here's to you,' says Peter as if they are life-long friends.

'You are not going to believe this, Pete,' says Mike falling under his spell. 'Steven Winter had no presentation. No work to show me, not even the tiniest 'ickle ad.'

Did Mike really just say 'ickle'?

I down my Kir Royale to drown them out.

'To be honest, it doesn't surprise me,' says Peter swirling the round the ice in his glass before taking a mouthful. 'Steven Winter worked for me for a while but I had to let him go, just not up to the job. I'd heard he'd started to turn things around but I guess he couldn't hack it.'

'Forget him. This is your night, Pete. Congratulations! You've just won High-Pro! Here's to you, champ!'

Mike gets up and lunges across the table, locking his arms around Peter in a clumsy bear hug. It lasts for longer than is strictly necessary. Thankfully, the waiter leaps forward with three fresh glasses and pours the champagne.

'Here's to you, Mike,' says Peter raising his glass and intimating to me to do the same.

I don't need any encouragement.

'Just doing my job,' says Peter like some sort of hero.

I catch his eye. Not a flicker of remorse, the thief is happy to steal my thunder. Suddenly, I am eight-years-old again and back at school. Never one to do things by halves, I had been off for months with measles and whooping cough. When I eventually returned, pale and wan, I had to take part in the annual prize-giving rehearsal where the teachers were using the previous year's winners as a guide. My name was called three times: Best composition. Best poem. Best writer.

After it was all over, I asked if I could please have my prizes.

'No, Ella. You may not,' the head-mistress told me.' You weren't here. We gave your book tokens to someone else.'

'But that's not fair. I was ill and couldn't come.'

She turned away to talk to another pupil as tears pricked the back of my eyes. I wanted to cry but I had to be brave. I ran home and told Mum but she couldn't fight her own battles, let alone mine. I would have to learn to stand up for myself.

Now, Peter orders a bottle of Sancerre and two bottles of Chateauneuf-du-Pape as I study the menu. Monkfish in a saffron reduction sounds interesting. How different from the frozen, boil-in-the-bag cod Mum and I lived off. Peter wants the sea-bass. It's his favourite. But not to be out-done by macho Mike's rare fillet of beef, he orders steak tartare - raw minced beefsteak, topped with an egg yolk which is about as alpha-male as you can get in Mayfair.

'CBA is very excited about working with you,' says Peter, snapping the menu shut with one hand and smoothing back his hair with the other.

'Likewise! Here's to a long and happy marriage!' says Mike.

I'll give it six months and hope Peter has a good divorce lawyer.

This place is a renowned celebrity haunt. Bored and frustrated, I look around hoping to see someone famous, an actress or a model dining on a designer lettuce leaf. I don't recognise anyone. Peter and Mike talk at length about their respective cars and houses. It seems the client's Morgan trumps Peter's Porsche. But Peter's Highgate postcode beats Mike's Morden. Peter knows it's smarter to let the client win and omits to mention his heated indoor pool.

Mercifully, our waiter reappears with our meals, three large white plates of beautifully presented food. But the portions are so small they look more like appetisers than main courses. Mine consists of small but perfectly cooked cubes of monkfish arranged not on a skewer but on a toothpick. Half a baby tomato is concealed underneath a bonsai basil leaf. It takes me mere moments to finish. If Adam was here we would have polished this lot off, then have nipped to the nearest fish and chip shop for some real food. I am tempted by the home-baked bread. Most people ignore it as if it's a sin to even glance in its carbohydrate-laden direction. Not me, I select a chunk of dark brown wholemeal studded with walnuts and sultanas and smother it in unsalted butter. Folded over several times it's small enough to squash into my mouth as fast as I can. Just as I am about to start chewing, Peter notices my empty plate.

'How was your fish, Ella?' he asks pretending to care to impress Mike.

My mouth is too full to speak. I could spit the lot into my napkin but Mike is watching me. I swallow hard but the lump catches in my throat. I take a mouthful of wine to try and force it down. My eyes are watering. I am sweating. Breathe. Must get out. Can't open door. Push? Pull? Choking. Door opens. Squat on the pavement and wretch it up like an alley cat having a fur ball. Marmalade would be proud of me. Immediately, I feel fine but the effort makes my nose run and eyes stream.

I go back in and take a serviette from an unoccupied table and wipe my mouth. I drop it into an ice bucket as I pass. When I arrive back at the table, Peter and Mike are lolling in their chairs, clutching half-drunk glasses of wine, barely aware I'm alive let alone that I almost died. Peter has hardly touched his meal and has pushed his plate to one side. Mike is still greedily forking in mouthfuls of raw beef.

'Fancy a sticky?' Peter asks me, pointing to the long list of liqueurs on the menu.

I was hoping for a panna cotta accompanied by fresh raspberry puree or a dark chocolate mousse laced with rum but sadly, we seem to have skipped pudding and three large glasses of Armagnac appear instead.

'Here's to CBA and High-Pro, the winning team!' says Peter warming the brandy balloon in his hands.

'And it's handy to have a girl on board. They know all about this stuff, don't they, Pete?' says Mike.

Enough. Not only has Peter stolen my work but he has deprived me of the opportunity to capitalise on it. This could have been the making of me. I could have used it to launch a brilliant career and taken centre stage as Creative Director of my own agency. As it stands, I've been reduced to a walk-on part.

'I don't use High-Pro. Then again I didn't drive when I won awards on a car account either. It's about being creative. Men already work on perfume accounts. They'll be advertising tampons next.'

The drinks, by-passing my virtually empty stomach, have shot to my head and are now doing all the talking. The client looks uneasy. Peter looks unhinged.

'Woh! I hear you,' says Mike throwing his napkin onto the table.

A corner of the serviette pierces the uneaten dome of Peter's egg. I watch as the once-pristine white linen turns a fatty yellow.

'Reel her in, Peter.'

'Apologise to Mike,' orders Peter. 'You're supposed to be a writer; you know the difference between 'assertive' and 'aggressive', don't you?'

Why is it that guys who stand up for themselves are deemed 'assertive' but when girls do the same they are 'aggressive'? I remember Mum trying to stick up for herself but was easily cowed by Dad. She would attempt to say her piece but he would tell her if she didn't shut up he would buy her a plaster for her mouth. I remember laughing when he said it. Then I saw Mum's face and stopped. She was crushed. Hurt to the core. Sadly, by the time she found the strength to walk away, she had no voice. I had to speak up for both of us, battling with the landlord to install an inside toilet, taking on shop assistants who tried to short-change her and fighting anyone who said a word against her. I was ten-years-old.

Now the word 'sorry' sticks in my throat every bit as stubbornly as the lump of bread. But again, it all comes back to one thing, money. It's always the money.

'I'm sorry you feel that way, Mike,' I say.

It's another one of Josh's favourites. Contrived and convoluted, he uses it to absolve himself of any wrong-doing and to put the blame squarely on the other person. The difference is when Josh says it, it works.

'Ella,' fumes Peter.

'It's okay, Peter, at least I know I'm in safe hands with you,' says Mike pointedly.

The vein in Peter's neck is throbbing. I am transfixed by it. Suddenly, he clicks his fingers. When the waiter brings the bill, Peter throws down the company plastic. When we get outside, the weather seems to have been pre-ordered to match the mood. It's raining. Pouring. A black cab pulls up with its light on. Mike gets in and leans out of the window.

'Next time, Pete. Leave the little woman at home, eh?'

'No problem, Mike. Next time I'll bring the girls.'

They both laugh. Peter and I stand on the kerbside and wave him off, like a married couple saying goodbye to a long lost friend. Once he is out of sight, we start arguing, like a married couple.

'Happy now? You could've cost us the account,' shouts Peter jabbing his finger in my face, rain running in rivulets off his lapels.

Another taxi arrives. For the second time this evening, opening the door defeats me. Peter takes charge and I clamber in. To my horror, he gets in beside me. I like to forget he only lives down the road from me. I squash myself into the corner of the seat, rest my head on the cool window and close my eyes. When I open them, Peter watching me. He slides closer. The driver makes a sharp turn enabling Peter to put his hand on my thigh as an excuse to steady himself. He gives my leg a squeeze. The driver pulls up outside the agency.

'What are we doing here, Peter?'

'Tweaking my script. Mike wants it first thing,' he replies smoothly, paying the driver.

'My script,' I protest stumbling onto the pavement. 'My script, not your script.'

Confused, I watch as the taxi's tail lights disappear onto Old Compton Street. After several attempts to fit the key into the lock, Peter manages to open the door. The reception is dark and quiet, I feel like we're about to rob a bank. A pair of tights over my face would do wonders for my appearance right now. Like a trusting puppy about to be flung into a sack and drowned, I trot behind Peter, following him across reception, up the stairs and into his office. He flicks on the light and opens the fridge. He brings out a bottle of Chablis before disappearing out of the door, presumably to locate some glasses.

I lie back on his leather sofa and close my eyes. Ah, that feels good. Now, not so good.

'Peter! Peter! I'm going to be ...'

Just as he appears, I vomit in his waste paper basket. Fashioned from a lattice of wicker-work it is not up to the job.

'You want me. You want... my carpet! Oh my God!' exclaims Peter retreating down the corridor.

'Peter,' I wail.

For once, I need Peter. I really do. Desperate for something to wipe my mouth, I stagger across to his desk and open his drawer. I thrust my hand inside and feel about. I find something soft and silky. A pair of knickers. Very small, very expensive silk knickers. I hear footsteps.

'Hello, Ella,' says Darren watching me from the doorway.

Navigating around the mess on the carpet and covering his nose with his arm, he helps me up.

'Sorry,' I blub.

I never play the 'helpless-little-me' card. It works for some girls in this business but I'm not pretty enough to get away with it.

'I'll call you a taxi. Let's get you downstairs,' he says picking up the receiver and dialling. 'You live near Highgate, yeah?'

He gives the person on the other end of the phone, the agency's address.

'They'll be here in five minutes,' he tells me. 'Were you with Peter?'

I nod vigorously.

'Lucky I was working late and turned up when I did. You're not going to be sick again, are you?'

Darren's not as bad as I thought. When the cab pulls up, I fall onto the seat where I slump against his shoulder.

'Don't throw up on me,' he says.

Chapter eight

Say something effective

I am awake. Alive. In my own bed. With someone next to me. No! We are lying back to back. The slightest movement and I can touch them if I want to. Which I don't. Who is it? Who did I sleep with? Because that's all I would've done. Is it Mike? No, I remember waving him off outside the restaurant. Thank goodness. Please don't let it be Peter. Even Mike would be preferable, at a push. Well, it would have to be more of a shove.

I struggle to piece together what happened after the meal. Peter and I went back to the agency. Big mistake. Should never have done that. I threw up. And he left me. Nice. How did I get back here? I have a vague memory of lolling in the back of a cab as it took the Archway roundabout at full tilt. The taxi driver? Perhaps, I didn't have the fare and I really am no better than the girls in Soho who wear too much make-up and too few clothes, smiling hollowly at men for money. I want to crawl away, not just from the person lying next to me but from the person I have become.

This is my bedroom. I recognise the Designer Guild wallpaper even if I don't recognise the feel of the man next to me. The embarrassment is paralysing. Unwanted images flicker across my brain. Gagging on the pavement, bringing up a pellet of bread. Shouting at the client. Throwing up in Peter's bin.

I turn over slowly so as not to disturb my sleeping partner. I have to see them before they see me. But, I am naked so they have already had an eyeful. Peeping beneath the covers, I am greeted by a long, muscular back. Now my eyes shoot down his spine, looking for boxer shorts or Y-fronts; I'm not fussy just so long as they're doing their job.

Naked buttocks, like two hard boiled eggs, side by side. I hold the covers down so I can't see the body, just the back of a head on my pillow. My Egyptian cotton pillow. My bed that up until last night, only I have slept in.

'Don't be sick on me,' Darren says, turning over and edging away.

'Darren, you...'

He shifts his weight momentarily and the soles of his feet rub against my legs. My unshaven legs. The shame. I have standards. No, apparently I don't, I am in bed with Darren.

'You undressed me?' I ask.

'You undressed me,' he says cockily.

'No, I didn't.'

'Not what you said last night,' he leers. 'I rescued you from Peter Pervert. You were very grateful.'

'We didn't...?'

He replies by lifting the duvet and inviting me to look inside the tent of shame. I pull the sheet around me. Too late for modesty, I have slept with Darren, the man who rejoices in putting his hands in his trouser pockets, lifting them up and thrusting himself at me, asking,

'What d'you reckon to that then, Ella?'

Now his bare, over-pumped, over-excited body is soiling my beautiful bed-linen, new white pillow-cases with pink rose buds hand-embroidered on each corner.

'No matter how drunk I was, I would never sleep with you,' I tell him. If I say it out loud, it must be true. 'Get out, Darren.'

He swings his legs over the side of the bed and stands up, facing me, challenging me to look at him. I turn away as he bends down, pick his boxer shorts off the floor and puts them on. Thank heavens for small mercies. Very small. I hear him pull on his jeans and zip up his flies.

'You were in a right state last night,' he says.

He is balancing on one leg, putting on a sock.

'What do you use for contraception, personality?' I quip quoting a put-down I had once heard a comedian use to great effect on a rowdy heckler.

'You weren't worth the cab fare,' he sneers buttoning up his shirt. 'And look at the size of those thighs.'

Darren has found my Achilles Heel. Well, my fat thighs. He sits on the bed and puts on his shoes. I kick him hard. He gets up and brushes his hair, using the brush on my dressing table.

'Thanks for having me,' he says, smirking at me in the mirror.

That old joke. It's not even funny let alone true.

'See you at work. Better not arrive together or people will get the wrong idea. Or the right one,' he winks.

I hear him go to the toilet. He leaves the door open so am forced to listen to him having a wee. As soon as I hear the front door close behind him, I get up. The bed stinks of his musky after-shave. I start to rip off the sheets. Last night's clothes are scattered like breadcrumbs around the place. I follow the trail into the bathroom and I slip on my bra. Grabbing hold of the sink, I just manage to save myself.

Standing in the shower, I rejoice as the spiky jets of water hit my flesh, washing Darren away. There he goes, scum spiralling down the plughole.

When I arrive at work, Wally's waiting for me.

'Morning, young 'un. You alright?'

'Been better. Fancy a cuppa?'

He nods and we walk towards the kitchen where I busy myself with the reassuringly mundane routine of making tea. I manage to put the bags in the mugs and boil the kettle but my hand begins to shake as I attempt to pour the water, it goes over the side, narrowly missing Wally's arm.

'Here, let me,' he says, gently taking the kettle with one hand and wiping up the pool of water with the other.

He hands me my drink.

'Careful, it's hot.'

He watches me as I take a sip and replace it on the counter.

'Here, Wally, I've got something for you,' I open the cupboard and bring out a tin of assorted chocolate biscuits, his favourite.

'Thanks very much,' he says, opening the lid.

His eyes light up when he sees the glossy selection of milk, plain and white chocolate cookies.

'Want one?' he says thrusting the tin at me.

'No, they're yours.'

He looks as happy as if I'd given him a gold watch. 'Tell you what, I'll leave 'em 'ere and we can share 'em with our tea of a morning.'

'Yeah, I'd like that.'

He chats away, munching through an entire stack of chocolate chip cookies. He dips a Bourbon in his tea and tells me how his wife is always on a diet and only buys rabbit food. With expert-timing, he lifts out the biscuit and puts the soggy mess in his mouth.

'Lovely,' he says smiling and licking his fingers. 'Right, gotta love you and leave you. The wife and me are going to the park to feed the ducks.'

Again, I see the joy in his face, like he's about to swim with dolphins.

He replaces the lid and hides the tin in one of the cupboards, behind a pile of crockery.

'Have a good day, Wally. See you tomorrow.'

He pops the biscuit he had secreted in the palm of his hand into his mouth and scampers off.

There's no-one in the creative department when I arrive, just a huge white, pink and mauve floral arrangement where Peter's secretary should be. Seems like a fair swop, a bunch of flowers could easily do her job. With her gone, we would save a fortune on washing powder.

'You look awful,' she tells me as she darts out from behind an orchid.

Stating the obvious is her one talent, apart from knowing how to programme the company washing machine.

'Thanks. Who are the flowers from?' I ask.

She blushes and looks away.

'Peter gave them to me,' she says rearranging them.

I raise an eyebrow.

'Oh, they're a 'thank-you' for all my hard work on the High-Pro presentation,' she tells me by way of explanation.

'Your hard work?' I ask incredulously. 'You mean making the coffee?'

Twisting the vase from side to side, she tries to align the blossoms next to her face as she pouts at her reflection in the mirror. I check my office to see what token of appreciation Peter has given me. Not so much as a dandelion.

'He wants to see you,' she tells me. 'He'll be back soon; just popped down to the studio to see Darren.'

No doubt Darren is enjoying telling Peter about last night in lurid detail. If the news has reached the creative floor, Peter's secretary will be the first to know. I search her face. She looks clueless. No change there.

We both turn when the lift doors open. Peter emerges like a beast exiting the gateway to hell. I fantasise about him being sucked back in to face the roaring flames of the underworld.

'You're fired,' he mouths at me as he draws his index finger across his throat. 'It's never okay to talk to a client the way you did and certainly not a million pound client. I've been on the phone to him all morning trying to persuade him not to resign the account. Alienating clients is the only thing you're good at.'

He strides into his office and I scuttle behind him like a beetle. Unwise, given he wants to crush me under his Gucci loafers. He sits down and toys with a long white envelope, flipping it adeptly through his fingers.

'Here's your P45 and a cheque. I've paid you 'til the end of the month - very generous under the circumstances.'

It's the 29th today so hardly magnanimous.

He drops the envelope onto his desk, swivels 180 degrees in his chair and stares out of the window.

'Please, Peter...' I implore, my voice shaking. 'This isn't fair. You wouldn't even have the client if it wasn't for me.'

He spins around to face me.

'Close the door on your way out,' he says trying to hand me the envelope.

'I'm not taking it. You can't do this, Peter.'

'I think you'll find I can. You were abusive to a client.'

'This is because I ran out on you last night, isn't it? You can't fire me for that.'

'You still here?' he asks yawning like a dog in my face.

I pick up the envelope and run downstairs to the studio. Darren is sitting with his feet on the desk, flicking through a body-building magazine,

74

looking at a picture of a triangular-shaped man flexing his huge biceps and showing off his tiny tackle. He must be Darren's role model. His team of drawing-board monkeys are drinking coffee, sketching and wielding scalpels like butter-knives as they slice through paper with surgeon-like precision. Given they are permanently befuddled on a heady mix of spray glue and marker pens, it's a wonder the place doesn't look like the cutting room floor of Sweeny Todd's.

'Get much sleep after I left?' asks Darren, licking his finger and turning the page.

'What have you been telling Peter?'

'For once, little Miss Know-It-All is the last to know,' he says closing the magazine and laying it down on his desk. 'Peter was just briefing us on a job. How's it coming along, boys?'

'Can't fit her legs on the page,' guffaws one of the lads holding up a grotesque caricature of me: big head, small boobs and fat thighs.

'Like your leaving card?' he asks.

Everyone laughs. I want to run to the loo to tell mum. But she is at home, too old to be hanging around outside advertising agency toilets listening to my sob stories. I slowly go back upstairs to my office.

'Peter's says you can't go in there ...' says his secretary without looking up.

I run in, slam the door behind me and pick up the phone. It's a long shot but perhaps there's a chance we can salvage something.

'Steve, hi, it's Ella. Fancy drowning your sorrows at The Fox this lunch-time?'

I do my best not to let him catch the worry in my voice.

'Oh it's you,' he slurs.

It sounds like he's already had a skinful.

'You told me Richards hated your idea and wasn't going to present it. You said he had come up with some crap of his own. Then, you call me, with only an hour to go before my meeting with the client, to say Peter is presenting your idea after all, leaving me with nothing to show the client. You stitched me up so CBA would definitely win. I could probably sue you for this.'

'No,' I protest. 'Peter stabbed me in the back. He's taken the credit for my idea.'

'Whoosh! Did you hear that, Ella? That flushing noise was my job disappearing down the pan.'

He slams the phone down before I can explain. I didn't plan any of this. I'm not that smart. I've been shafted. Not that he cares. Too busy clinging on to the rim of the toilet bowl of life.

Thankfully, I can't imagine his case would stand up in court but I don't know. I don't know anything anymore, except I have screwed up big time. My only consolation is never having been screwed by Peter. Or Darren.

I haul the cardboard box of work out from under my desk, toss in a couple of marker pens, three unused A4 pads, a stapler and a hole-punch. Not because I need them but because they are some compensation for Peter's skulduggery. Four pounds fifty worth. That'll teach them. I take my certificates off the wall, Golden Arrows, Euro Best, Campaign Press and Design and Art Direction, the Oscars of the advertising world. Pretentious, but true. Usually, they boost my confidence but today they mock me from inside their silver frames. Hopefully, they still mean something and will continue to open doors. This is it, my career in a cardboard box. But as long as Mum and I aren't living in one, I am still winning.

I can't tell her. She would only worry. With any luck I can get another job quickly and we'll be fine. Pigs might fly. This pig will soar. Well, once I've shifted a few pounds.

I walk past Peter's office. He's not there. Then I hear the familiar roar of his Porsche pulling away. When he took delivery of his new company car he insisted it was parked right outside the front door where everyone could admire it. Big, bold and black, it screamed success. He was mid-way through firing Steve Winter and had just delivered the well-worn line, 'This isn't me. It's you. I'm going to have to let you go,' when he spotted a young traffic warden slapping a ticket under the windscreen wipers. He opened the window and hurled an eye-watering volley of abuse at her.

'Get that f****** thing off my car, you bitch.'

Picking up his new electric typewriter, he hurled it through the window. Fortunately for her, he had forgotten it was plugged in so the wretched thing just dangled by its flex. Had it been a manual the traffic warden would be dead and Peter would be serving time for manslaughter. Progress can be a mixed blessing.

Not surprisingly, this tale has become an advertising legend. One version has Peter perched on the window ledge threatening to jump on her if she doesn't throw down her pen. As usual the board tolerated his outburst, reluctant to upset their golden boy, but they did refuse to replace his typewriter. So he just hired another secretary. One to make coffee and one to sit on his knee and take things down.

I carry the box awkwardly along the corridor and set it down outside the toilet where I disappear into my cubicle and bolt the door.

'Mum, I'm sorry,' I whisper up at the window. 'Don't know what I'm going to do now. Find work where there isn't any, I suppose.'

Someone has scrawled the words 'Peter is a perv' on the wall behind the cistern. Lest we are in any doubt, the word 'True' is etched into the paintwork next to it. I come out and catch sight of my face, still purple and puffy, in the mirror. My water-proof mascara has run, even that disappoints. I pick up my box and am half way down the stairs when I bump into Darren.

'Alright?' he asks stupidly.

I may have changed my sheets but no amount of water can wash away the memory that silts up my brain.

'You shouldn't have got into my bed,' I tell him, my face hot with embarrassment.

'Someone had to stop you choking on your own vomit.'

'You should've slept on the sofa.'

'Forget it, I have,' he laughs again and runs upstairs.

I sink down on a step where I curl up like a frozen prawn, pausing for a moment before going into reception. The only person I want to say 'good-bye' to is Wally but he'll be at home now, sleeping.

I spot the telephone on reception and call Adam.

'Adam? It's me. I've been fired.'

He recognises my voice instantly.

'No way? Don't worry, Ella. Looking for a job is like looking for a parking space in London, if you go round long enough, you'll find one,' he tells me confidently.

His optimism is contagious. He's right, I just need to get out there and start knocking on doors.

'Can't Steve help?' he asks. 'Want me to give him a ring?'

'No, thanks. Not exactly flavour of the month with him.'

'Really? That reminds me. There's a new ice-cream parlour in Leicester Square. Flavour of the month is double-chocolate-choc-chip. Meet you there in ten, my treat. I'll be the one with the triple scoop cone.'

For once, the last thing I want to do is eat but it'll be good to see Adam.

I rashly decide to leave CBA through the revolving door. It is going at quite a lick having just disgorged a thrusting young account executive, compelled to do everything at breakneck speed in case someone he wants to impress might be watching. I complete two and a half rotations before Mr Media joins me. What with me and my cardboard box and him and his briefcase, it's a snug fit. He manages to escape but when I try to follow, the aperture closes and a young couple get in. They become so passionately entwined I imagine she must be pregnant by the time they spill out into the reception.

Seeing blue sky on a weekday is not something I'm familiar with. The heat is enticing people to drink lattes in pavement cafes and expose their white, pallid limbs. I don't feel sunny. I turn right onto Old Compton Street, passing the studio where I edit, edited my commercials. The cool receptionist in her air-conditioned office, spots me through the window and waves. I smile back at her, unsure whether to go in or not. I stand on the pavement, without purpose, no longer one of the busy people who dart in and out of their shiny Soho offices.

When I was a client no request was too much trouble, be it a cappuccino from Bar Italia at ten o'clock at night or a plate of noodles from the Chinese restaurant on Brewer Street. Having cast the best actors and voice-over artists in my commercials, I would then have the privilege of directing them. They didn't need my help to turn in award-winning performances, transforming thirty-second commercials into works of art. A wealth of talent just to sell loo cleaner, no wonder people tell me it's a crap way to earn a living.

Unfortunately, not all the luvvies were lovely. One actress was particularly difficult. The radio commercial was for a body wash and the script required her to sing supposedly in the shower. The song was nothing more than a ditty, short and simple. But, she was having none of it, arriving at the recording with her long-suffering agent in tow.

'Tell her I don't sing,' she told him to tell me.

'She doesn't sing,' her agent said apologetically.

'You can hum if you like,' I suggested bursting into my own pathetic rendition and then laughing too loudly.

'Tell her I don't sing,' she snapped.

Time was ticking by. Studios don't come cheap and neither did she. With one eye on the clock, I had five minutes to re-write the commercial minus the song. Neither of us left the studio covered in glory that day. I hadn't bargained on a comedienne taking herself so seriously.

Now, someone pushes past me, nudging the box and almost knocking it to the ground. I reposition it, wedging it firmly on my hip.

I watch the receptionist as she answers the phone, no doubt making another lucrative booking. She nods at me, as if to say, 'Excuse me, this client is about to pay lots of money to rent our services by the hour.'

A young girl stands in a doorway, waiting for her client who pays very little to rent her services by the hour. She is about the same age as me but looks much older. She appears lifeless, mannequin-like, as if she has seen too much life and prefers to occupy the safe space behind her eyes. A man walks purposefully towards her. The poor girl must be wondering what he wants for his filthy lucre. If he's anything like Peter, he'll want her naked on a smoked glass table taking down minutes of their meeting.

I pass my favourite shop, the one selling cutting-edge, hand-tailored clothes. The trousers I am wearing cost a week's wages but are worth it because they make my thighs look like pencils. I covet everything on display. Why bother looking? I can't even afford to window shop. I weave through the tourists clogging China Town, past the cramped, huddled shops and restaurants smelling of pak choi and steamed duck and emerge into Leicester Square. A man takes a mouthful of a hotdog just bought from a nearby stand and immediately spits it onto the pavement. This is London where you are never more than a few feet from a rat.

Peter must be very close.

Luckily, Adam is closer, holding two tubs each stacked with three scoops of double-chocolate-choc-chip ice-cream. I could kiss him

Chapter nine

Discover your unique selling proposition

'That was good,' says Adam finishing his ice-cream before I've even started.

I watch him eyeing up the multi-coloured tubs in the window.

'What one next?' he asks.

He wants to help. He can't get me a job but he can get me a triple-nut-mocha with extra toffee sauce. I shake my head. For once, chocolate has failed to work its magic.

'So, Steve was no help? Thought you two would hit it off.'

I know he wants another tub but because I'm not having one, he declines when the assistant hovers over the display with her scoop.

'We did but it got messy. I wanted to play with the big boys but didn't know the rules.'

'There aren't any, Ella. You were just unlucky. Next time, it'll be your turn.'

When Adam says something, I believe it. If he told me I could drop a dress size overnight, I'd be down Oxford Street snapping up the size tens. A wave of reassurance washes over me, soothing the sickening panic.

'I know it will but I still need to find something else fast. I can't afford to do nothing.'

'You're good; you'll be fine. I promise. If anything comes up at my place, I'll let you know. And I'll ask around. There are jobs out there and there's one with your name on it.'

I smile at him. He's the kindest person I know in the industry. He's the kindest person I know. Full stop.

'Meet me in town for lunch every Friday. Then, you can arrange all interviews for that day.'

'Well, that'll certainly make the fare worthwhile.'

'My treat. They're paying me silly money. The way they carry on, you'd never guess we were in a recession.'

'Thanks, Adam.'

I know he means it. Unlike most people in this industry, who promise the earth but wouldn't give you the dirt off their shoes.

He asks for two sample spoonful's of vanilla bean and cherry pie and gives me the biggest one.

'That's nice. Like it?'

I shake my head.

'I'm going to have to take whatever's going, Adam. I need the money. Trouble is I'm not qualified for anything else. Without shelf-stacking experience, I probably can't even get a job in the local supermarket.'

'You won't have to. I'll make a few calls this afternoon. Stop worrying, it won't help.'

He's right but I'm a wrong place, wrong time kind of girl. I'm not sure even the winning combination of Adam and double-chocolate-choc-chip ice-cream can change that.

Chapter ten

Keep your communication single-minded

The next day, there's no time to waste. I get up early and drive to the Unemployment Office in my BMW. It's a company car and I won't have it for much longer so I might as well make the most of it. A slew of parking tickets for leaving it outside the agency on double yellow lines had deterred me from driving to work. Darren claimed the system was so inefficient, only one in ten outstanding parking fines was ever followed up. I was always that one.

The dole office is nearby but is a million miles away from the world I inhabit, inhabited. No complimentary coffee, newspapers or glossy magazines in this reception, only uninviting grey pamphlets about state benefits and intimidating posters warning me about the dire consequences of making fraudulent claims.

People stand in line, waiting. Waiting to be called by faceless clerks. Waiting to be processed. Waiting to be told their lives are on hold until they get on their bikes and get a job. I wouldn't dare ride a bike, not in London.

When I reach the front of the New Claims queue, I am rewarded with a bunch of forms. I sit down and leaning awkwardly on my lap, attempt to fill them in. I struggle with some of the questions but my National Insurance Number is one of the few useful pieces of information I know. The forms are incomprehensible. Perhaps I could offer to rewrite them so people like me can understand them. I fill them in as best I can and hand them in.

The recently unemployed are easy to spot. Full of hope, keenly studying the cards pinned to the notice board detailing vacancies and diligently noting down employers' names and phone numbers. I look to see what's on offer. These are the only ads I'll be looking at for a while, a far cry from what I'm used to, scripting a prime-time television commercial.

'Admin. Assistant. 20 hours a week. Experience essential.'

'Store-hand required. Nights. 40 hours a week.'

'Cleaner. Mornings only. Good references.'

My heart sinks. Being a copywriter doesn't qualify me for anything other than being a copywriter. Even my typing skills aren't great, always having had the luxury of relying on Peter's secretary to produce the final pristine draft. I clutch the white envelope Peter gave me. It is still sealed because I can't bear to open it, can't bear to see my P45 or my last pay cheque. It's too final and I am not ready to admit this is really happening.

One man clearly knows how to work the system. I recognise him. As I drew up, he was parking his top-of-the-range Jaguar in the loading bay outside the unemployment office to ensure he was first in line when the doors opened. Now I watch him take his battered dole card from his back pocket and sign on the dotted line when his name is called. He makes no attempt to disguise his trade, his brown hair white with plaster dust, his hands calloused and hard, even his boots are spattered with blobs of cement. Having secured his benefits for another week, he runs out, leaps into his car and takes off, no doubt heading for the nearest building site to work as a labourer and get paid cash in hand, no questions asked.

A lady with a long, grey plait stands next to me. She clenches and unclenches her fists and rises up and down on the balls of her feet. A piece of hair, like steel wool, falls across her mouth as she speaks.

'I try to live everyday in the light, do you?'

Well, I'd love to but Peter is the Prince of Darkness.

She moves closer and observes me, taking in my dyed hair, painted nails and make-up. Muttering obscenities, she sucks her teeth in disgust.

'David!' shouts a clerk.

Someone has the same Christian name as my surname. It happens all the time. No-one moves. Lethargy rules. It seems contagious. The sooner

I get home, the sooner I can phone round for work. The longer I'm here, the more chance failure will cling to me like mould, its spores destroying the last threads of my self-confidence.

'David!'

I check my watch. I've been here over an hour, long enough to have written an entire radio campaign. The hard-faced woman behind the New Claims Desk continues to leaf through a pile of piles as I approach her, smiling politely.

'Hello, my name is Ella, Ella David. I've been waiting a while and ...'

'Why didn't you come when I called, David?' she asks aggressively without looking up.

'Sorry, David is my surname, my name is Ella.'

'That's what I said, David.'

'But surely, I'm either 'Ella', 'Ella David' or 'Miss. David'.'

'Sit,' she growls.

'I'm not a dog.'

This is role-reversal at its worse.

'I'm not an inmate. I've done nothing wrong, just lost my job.'

'P45?'

She is a dangerous woman with power over the powerless. Fortunately, she is too stupid to realise. In another life she could be Peter's secretary. I hand her my white envelope and she recites her mantra, breathing garlic in my face.

'You must be available for work to qualify for Unemployment Benefit. Any jobs on the vacancies board you can apply for?'

'No,' I tell her truthfully.

'No? What was your last job?' she asks in disbelief as she scans my forms.

'Copywriter.'

'What, like legal stuff?' she asks.

Before I can explain, she jots the word 'copyright' onto her pad.

'No, not 'copyright'. I am an advertising copywriter,' I tell her helpfully pointing to the word on the page. 'I write TV and radio commercials.'

I do a helpful little mime of writing something in mid-air.

'So, you see it's 'copywriter', spelt c-o-p-y-w-r-i-t-e-r not 'copyright', spelt...'

When I look up, she is glaring at me as if to say, 'I hated you on sight. Now you've corrected me in front of a roomful of people, including my boss, I loathe you even more.'

'Surely you can type?' she sneers.

'No, I had a secretary.'

She sneers.

'What about cleaning? You can mop a floor?'

Sarcasm. I'm sure that's not in her job description.

'You have to be actively looking for work at all times to be eligible for benefit. Keep a record of all the jobs you apply for and the interviews you attend. Bring this information with you when you next sign on. You need to...'

She is talking but I am not listening. I do it all the time, just glean the bits I need to know as my mind wanders to a more interesting place, usually a café, eating cake with Adam.

'Sign here, David,' she demands, pushing yet another official form across the desk at me.

A cheap ballpoint pen is secured to the table by a length of string. Why? No one wants to steal it. It doesn't even work. The clerk turns her back to me. I unzip my bag and take out my Mont Blanc pen. The last time I used it was to sign my name was on my CBA contract. Same signature, different meaning. What was the difference? About five hundred pounds a week.

The clerk peers inside the envelope I gave her and turns it upside down before handing it back to me.

'Where's your P45?'

I start to panic, shake the envelope and feel inside. It's empty. The clerk takes great joy in telling me she can't progress my claim and orders me to return with the correct documentation. She warns me again that any work I do must be declared or I risk a fine or imprisonment. Although I'm sure she will make an exception and ensure I get both. But I can't see it being an issue. Given the recession, me finding work is as likely as Peter finding God.

The devil has surpassed himself. This is the most creative thing he has ever done. Either that or his secretary simply forgot to include my P45 and pay cheque. Yes, that's probably it. Uncertain as to whether I still have a job at CBA, I consider explaining this to the clerk but think better of it. Given she couldn't understand what work I do, there's no way she could conceive the workings of Peter Richard's mangled mind. My P45 will probably be on the doormat waiting for me when I get home. My world starts to shrink back to what it was when I was a kid with no money, no power and no choices.

I sit in my car, the only place where I am still in the driving seat. The soft, cream leather seat moulds itself comfortingly around me. I glance up at the dole office and feel a failure. I can't get away fast enough. I turn the key in the ignition, ram my foot down on the accelerator, shoot out into the flow of traffic and slam into the first car I meet. The driver leaps out of what's left of his vehicle and yells at me. Waving his arms like a spider directing traffic, his words hit me like flint.

'What the f***? 'You f******you just f****** pulled out! You f******! You didn't even f****** look! 'You f****** silly cow! 'Look what you've f******done to my f****** car!'

'I'm sorry,' I say, lowering the window a fraction.

Evidently, an apology from inside my car is not enough. He wants me to get out. He's not doing much to entice me. His moves his mouth like a monkey, his lips curling back over clenched teeth. I hastily retrieve my Filofax and rip out a page. My hand shaking, I write down my name and number. I get out of the car, waving the piece of paper at him like a white flag. But he's not ready to surrender. He means war. He fires off another round of expletives.

'F****** Filofax, *******yuppie! Think you f****** own the f****** roads!'

'Calm down, mate,' says a young guy. 'It was an accident. Leave her alone. Don't speak to her like that.'

'What about my car?' he shouts.

'The insurance will pay,' the young bloke tells him.

'Silly f******!' the driver tells him.

'Enough!'

Definitely the last word on the subject, delivered with the gravitas of a General handing down an order. Mr F-ing, his tiny tail between his tiny legs, gets back in his car, the two-seater now just a one-seater. Miraculously, it starts first time only to be halted almost immediately by an elderly woman crossing the road in front of him. I force a smile. He sticks two fingers in my face. I turn to my knight in shining armour. Well T-shirt and tight-fitting jeans.

'Thanks.'

'No worries. Can I call anyone for you?'

He points to the phone box on the corner of the street.

'No, it's fine.'

'Sure? Boyfriend? Husband? Anyone?'

I shake my head. We turn to look at my car slumped uselessly across the tarmac. A line of traffic curls round it like a giant metallic centipede.

'Are you in the AA?' he asks. 'I'll ring them.'

I hand him my membership card.

'I can't read your signature. What's your name; they'll need to know.'

'Ella, Ella David.'

'Nice to meet you, Ella,' he smiles as he heads up the road towards the telephone box.

Everyone wants to know who I am today but not in a good way. A stray dog cocks its leg against my car and then dives off to do the same to nearby lamp-posts as he marks his territory. That's quite a property portfolio he's got himself, no wonder the little cur doesn't have a care in the world.

My new friend jogs back.

'They'll be here in about forty minutes,' he says breathlessly.

He takes a packet of cigarettes from his pocket and offers me one. I shake my head. He lights up as he talks to me through a haze of smoke, his eyes creasing attractively at the edges.

'I'm trying to give up. I've gone from ten to twenty a day.'

He laughs and encourages me to join in. My face, still bruised from the fall, doesn't want to move.

'Another smash up?' he asks awkwardly looking at my cheek.

'I fell down the stairs at Oxford Circus tube.'

Then I tell him about the ambulance-man, the Queen and the Prime-Minister.

'Sounds like the start of a bad joke. But it's not funny. You should be more careful.'

I've been looking after myself since I was ten-years-old. Mum was so heart-broken when her Decree Absolute was granted, she spent her life mourning the loss of her husband. Although she left him for the way he treated us, she always hoped he would have a change of heart and come after her. He never did. Just set up home with another woman and her daughter.

'I noticed you earlier in the dole office. You're not the sort they usually get in there,' says the young guy.

I didn't notice him. How did he slip under my radar? Handsome and charming, not a combination often found at the Hornsey Unemployment Office. He smiles. I smile back, get all embarrassed and pretend to look for the AA man. Remembering my face, I turn away so he can't see the battered side.

'It's just a bit bruised,' he says moving closer to examine it. 'The other side is very pretty.'

'Pretty'? It's not how people usually refer to me. Someone used the word 'attractive' once but I think they were referring to my wallpaper.

'By the way, I'm not actually signing-on. Well, I don't think I am, not yet,' I tell him changing the subject.

'Well, I am. No shame in it. We've paid our dues; we're entitled to that money,' he tell me forcibly.

'Oh, I know. But, I think my boss may have just pretended to fire me.'

He laughs so hard he starts coughing.

'That's genius. Why would he do that?'

'Teach me a lesson? Who knows?'

'What a weirdo.'

'Yerp. He is.'

There is a silence.

'I'm Tom, Tom Gould. But I changed my name to Tom Tyler.'

'Are you famous?' I ask sounding like a star-struck teenager.

'I will be. I'm a singer. Just started getting gigs. Unpaid, of course,' he says with an exaggerated wink.

If he sounds half as good as he looks, he'll go far.

The AA man arrives and after some rudimentary tinkering announces the car is beyond a roadside repair. We wait another half hour for a tow truck. The time passes surprisingly quickly with Tom telling me about his dream of becoming a pop star. Just as the story gets interesting, the recovery van pulls up. From Hollywood to Hornsey in the turn of a wheel. Sadly, the driver is no movie idol, more of an idle mover, taking forever to attach my car to his truck. Eventually, he secures it and offers to drive me home before dropping my car at the garage. As tempted as I am by the opportunity to ride upfront in his jalopy, I hand him the keys and sign my car over. Right now, I am more interested in going places with Tom.

'Drink?' he asks.

'How did you guess?'

'I can read minds.'

He had better be kidding because right now mine is in the gutter.

'Cheeky!' he says with a smile.

'I didn't say anything.'

'You didn't have to,' he smiles.

This is the most fun I've had since the patisserie brought out a new hazelnut and chocolate éclair. We walk to the nearest pub, a Victorian monstrosity with a smoky atmosphere, music blaring from the juke-box and a flashing fruit machine.

'What do you fancy?' he shouts over the noise.

'You,' I want to say but I've only known him two hours.

'A Kir ...' I say then remember I'm not in Soho now.

'Brandy, for the shock?' he suggests.

Smart boy. Clearly, a trained first-aider.

I nod and walk over to an empty table, the soles of my shoes sticking to the carpet. I sit facing the bar where I have a great view of Tom's rear as he leans across the bar. The barmaid recognises him and whispers something in his ear. He laughs. She says something else and he laughs again this time much louder. He reaches into her breast pocket and takes out a packet of cigarettes. She takes one and lights it before putting it in his mouth.

'Cheers, love, keep the change,' he says, the cigarette stuck to his lip.

Slowly, he unfurls a tenner from a thick roll of notes. Even by Adland's standards, that's an eye-watering tip.

He carries the drinks over and hands me my glass. The single shot of brandy barely covers the bottom of the tumbler.

'Nice car, shame about the prang,' he says draining his glass.

'It's a company car. They'll sort it.'

'Company car, eh? I had you down as a secretary or a teacher.'

'I'm a copywriter. I write ads.'

'Advertising? Good money, eh?'

I look away, resenting the question. People like to judge me on what I do for a living, rating me alongside estate agents. They don't understand, we are all selling something provided the price is right.

'Think of a number and double it, eh?' he asks, his smile widening.

The only number I am interested in right now is his.

'Yeah, the money's great but the industry is very cut throat.'

'Yeah, I guess. But you won't be out of work for long. Something will come up; it always does.'

'Yes,' I murmur. 'Something will definitely come up.'

He grins and blows a smoke ring. Then another. I've never seen anyone do that before. I'm impressed. What's wrong with me? I must be mad. Mad about the boy.

Chapter eleven

Sell yourself

'How are the interviews going?' Adam asks, perusing the pudding menu at Soho's latest faux French brasserie.

'I had one this morning. Turned out he was great mates with Peter.'

'You didn't want to work for him then.'

'No,' I say looking at the other diners, well-paid and well-fed, their only worry what wine to drink. 'But I can't bear the thought of having to sign-on every week. That dole office is such a hell-hole I half expected Peter to be in charge. I crashed my car on the way out.'

'What?' asks Adam genuinely alarmed. 'You okay?'

'Fine. A really lovely guy came to my rescue.'

Adam looks at me. Usually I can tell what he's thinking but not this time. He catches the eye of a passing waiter and orders two desserts, 'Chocolate mousse and white chocolate gateau, please. What are you having, Ella?'

'Tarte tatin.'

'Apples? You can't just eat apples for lunch. Make that two mousses and two gateaux please. Thanks.'

The waiter makes a polite little bow as if everyone dining here has two puddings apiece for lunch.

'That's not your portfolio, is it?' he asks looking at my small, plastic folder.

'The only thing creative directors want to see are my ideas,' I say concealing it under my napkin.

'Not true. This business is ninety-nine percent presentation, one percent desperation,' he tells me.

The waiter sets down four plates of exquisite-looking confections. I carefully lift off the spun sugar Eiffel Tower standing astride my gateau and put it on Adam's plate.

'Thanks,' he says opening his mouth and devouring it. I watch as a triumph of engineering disappears in seconds.

'Have my raspberry,' he says spearing it on his fork and feeding it to me. 'When we've finished I'm buying you a new portfolio. And don't say 'no'.'

He pays the bill, batting away my offer of half, and we head for Cowling and Wilcox. The shop is full of artist's supplies and smells of paper and ink.

'Most people I interview, have something like this,' he tells me, holding up a large A2 black leather case.

I'm surprised he can lift it; the price tag is so hefty.

'No, this will be fine,' I say grabbing a small, plastic version.

'If that landed on my desk, I wouldn't even open it, let alone hire the owner,' he tells me. 'Just take this one and give yourself the best chance.'

He quickly unzips the portfolio and proudly presents the acetate sleeves, steel ring-binder and inside pockets. It's so impressive it could get a job all on its own.

'Okay, but only if I can pay you back.'

'You can get the croissants next time we go to Pat Vals,' he tells me handing the cash to the assistant and kissing my cheek. 'Gotta go. Good luck but you won't need it.'

I stride into my next interview, bursting with confidence and chocolate cake.

Chapter twelve

It's not who you know, it's who they know

It's been a while since Peter fired me. I don't like to count the days. That would mean this is actually happening and it can't be. Too much relies on me bringing home the bacon. But thanks to Peter telling porkies, life is looking dicey.

There's still no sign of my P45 or final pay cheque. I should call CBA and ask what's happening but I can't bear to hear the smug woman in personnel telling me that yes, of course, Peter fired me, the paperwork is in the post and no please don't ask for a reference as a refusal often offends. I've had a couple of interviews but no-one seems to be hiring. But with this month's mortgage due and mum's rent to pay, I can't afford to give up.

I ring round more top advertising agencies asking for work. As always, I am headed off at the pass by the Creative Directors' PAs all of whom are far more efficient than Peter's secretary. This doesn't work in my favour.

'Good morning, please may I speak to your Creative Director?'

'Who's speaking?' asks the snippy PA.

'Ella David.'

'Who?'

'Ella David.'

'Ella David?'

She stops short of asking 'Who the hell are you?' and settles for, 'Will he know what it's regarding?'

Not unless he has a sixth sense, I think.

'Sorry, he's in a meeting,' she replies without missing a beat.

Shame she didn't tell me that in the first place and we could've saved all this palaver. But we both know he's not in a meeting. He's probably in his office and she's in there with him, perched on his lap popping peeled grapes into his mouth.

'When is a good time to call back and speak to him?'

'Give me your number and I'll make sure he gets it.'

Don't call us; we won't call you.

By contrast my head-hunter is always delighted to speak to me. It's her job to find me a job for a cool twenty percent of whatever salary she negotiates for me. Our relationship is symbiotic; we keep one another in the style to which we have become accustomed. Her name is Charlotte and she's older than me but she's so hip and happening, she answers to Charlie. She greets me like a long lost niece.

'Ella, darling! How are you? Haven't spoken in ages. How lovely to hear from you! Still over at CBA? With the fabulous Peter Richards? Do give him my love. How is he - still adorable? Such a lovely man!   And so talented! I got him that job, you know. You're very lucky to be under him.'

I will never be under Peter. But I know plenty of girls who are.

'What's happening, Charlie? Much work about?' I ask as if it doesn't really concern me, as if I'm just making polite conversation. My insides are yelling, 'Get me a goddam job! Now!'

'Darling, you're not unhappy at CBA, are you?' she asks trying to sound concerned, her voice plumy and rich. 'I hear Peter's just won the High-Pro business. Clever boy! Great news! Worth zillions, isn't it? Wowza!'

I can hardly bear to listen to her ill-informed twaddle but I do because I need her. Even if I told her it was my work, not Peter's she would never believe the truth. Peter has built a career on lies. The clients neither know nor care. They just love him and life his agency cheque-book buys them.

'Why on earth would you want to move? CBA must be buzzing, right?'

Buzzing? Only with the sound of flies feasting off all the rot.

I can practically hear her flicking through her Rollerdex already looking for my replacement. Her loyalties don't lie with me but with the advertising agencies. They pay her fees. True, she got me the job at CBA but I never know whether to love or loathe her for it. For once, I think carefully before replying.

'Just curious Charlie, putting out a few feelers.'

'Well, this wretched recession is really biting now. I've had to cancel Bermuda this year and do Jamaica instead. Needs must and all that. We both know advertising is always the first thing to suffer. But don't you worry. Leave it with me darling. Your work is so gorgeous I want to eat it! I'll make a few calls and see what I can do for you. In the meantime, sit tight and don't do anything rash, there's a good girl. Speak soon. Bye, darling. Oh and give Peter a big kiss from me. Tell him Charlie sends her love.'

That's going to be harder than she thinks. Right now, I wouldn't give him the kiss of life.

Charlie likes to come across as everyone's favourite aunt. The act is lost on me particularly as my aunt, Dad's sister, was a witch of a woman who thought a naked doll smoking a cigarette was an appropriate gift for my sixth birthday. When Mum wrestled it off her, Auntie tried to strangle her. The doll went in the bin and I was sent to bed. So if Charlie thinks pretending to be a close relative is going to win my trust, she's mistaken.

I replace the receiver and immediately the phone rings again. It must be Charlie calling back to suggest I consider a cushy little number in Saudi Arabia. Middle Eastern salaries are tax-free and Charlie would earn a healthy commission. But if I took a job out there, I may as well bury myself up to my neck in sand for all the chance I would have of landing a London gig again. This city spawns some of the best advertising in the world and doesn't take kindly to people selling out.

'Charlie, I really don't think...' I begin before being interrupted by a man's voice.

'Hello, is that you Ella?'

I think I recognise the voice but why would Josh be calling me?

'Who is this please?' I ask.

'Josh, Josh from CBA.'

Yes, it had to be. I don't know anyone else who talks like he's related to Princess Margaret.

'Ella, are you still there?' he prompts nervously.

'Yes,' I reply twirling the coiled phone flex nervously around my hand.

What does he want? To amuse himself with tales of my demise? Or to discover how the other half live? Perhaps he wants to explain where my P45 and pay cheque have got to.

'Sorry, thought we'd been cut off,' he laughs but I'm not sure why, he hasn't said anything amusing.

'How are you, Ella?'

I don't like it when he uses my name. It's another of his tricks to win friends and influence people.

'How am I? I've no work, no car and no money so I'll have no flat soon. Oh and my mum will face eviction as I've just used the last of my savings to pay her rent. So, Josh, what do you think, am I 'A', 'delighted' or 'B', 'suicidal'? Peter had no right to fire me, we both know that.'

I have been polite to him for too long. I've nothing to lose. The pleasure of speaking my mind is fleeting. I remind myself Adland is a small place and Josh knows lots of people. I'm not doing myself any favours. This is getting to be a dangerous habit of mine. But I refuse to let myself be cowed. Mum showed me the way by eventually having the guts to walk

99

out on Dad. All I have to do is follow in her footsteps. Just in more stylish footwear.

Josh cuts across my thoughts.

'Sounds like I've called at the right time. I hope you will be 'A' 'delighted' because I am ringing to say your job is here, if you want it. We'd love you back.'

'What? You can just rehire me? Can't imagine the board would be too thrilled. Or the client, come to that.'

'Peter never fired you, Ella. You know what he's like. I told him it was a bad idea but...'

'The bastard! So, it was all just a joke?'

'Yes, but he took it too far.'

'Have you any idea what I've been through?'

'No, I've got a trust fund so probably not something I can relate to. But that's all in the past now. Can we move on?' he says glibly.

'Move on? Are you mad? You can't just expect me to come back like nothing ever happened. I got so upset at the dole office, I crashed the car.'

'Not the BMW? Is it a write-off?' he asks with the level of concern normal people reserve for close relatives in Intensive Care.

Josh had ill-concealed car-envy. My model was top of the range and came with all the bells and whistles. Josh had to settle for playing with his horn.

'Have you had any other offers?' he asks tentatively.

'A few,' I tell him.

It's true. I am considering my options, namely a series of indecent proposals from a young entertainer who performs best lying down.

'I am in talks with several agencies.'

Recruitment agencies but he doesn't need to know that.

'Yes, yes, of course. I understand. Look, Ella why don't you think about what I've said and get back to me tomorrow?'

I don't need to think. I'm done with being treated like a dog by a bitch at the dole office.

'Josh, is Peter okay with this? He seemed pretty angry with me the last time I saw him.'

'Absolutely, he asked me to call you.'

'Really? Then why didn't he ring me himself?'

'Too busy. To be honest Ella, I'm worried about him. We all are. He's not coping. The pressure of his divorce is getting to him. He spent all week in talks with his lawyer and all day in court, getting taken to the cleaners by his ex-wife. The you-know-what is really hitting the fan and the agency could go down the pan. Sorry, I think I may have mixed my metaphors there but you see where I'm coming from.'

Peter stressed, skint and covered in crap? Things are looking up.

'Let me think about it, Josh. Who else knows about all this?'

'Just Peter, Darren and the boys in the studio. No-one important,' he reassures me. 'The board just assumed you were on holiday.'

'Holiday? I need one to get over this nightmare.'

'We can compensate you, Ella. And it goes without saying we are more than willing to match any offer you may be considering.'

Bingo!

'Match it or better it, Josh?'

'I hear what you're saying but clients are slashing their budgets. We're all tightening our belts.'

'Josh, don't insult me.'

'Okay, Ella, let's stop horse-trading and cut to the chase. We want you back. We can't progress High-Pro without you. To be honest, Peter tried some stuff. It was pretty awful and the client blew it out. Name your price and let's get you back on board.'

He has shown his hand. How careless.

'Peter was out of order. He should be begging my forgiveness.'

'Peter is on his knees. Trust me. But let's not forget you were very rude to our biggest client. That cost the agency a long weekend in St Tropez for him and his mistress. We've done our bit, Ella. I'm sure we can come to some arrangement.'

Just like Peter's 'Little Arrangement'? I hope not.

'Get back to you soon,' I say replacing the receiver.

'Get back to me now,' Tom calls from the bedroom.

Chapter thirteen

Tell your audience something they don't know

'Take the money. Think of it as compensation for how that pervert Peter Richards treated you. He thinks he can do what he likes because you don't have a union,' advises Tom as he grates mounds of Cheddar directly onto the work-surface in my kitchen.

I resist the urge to grab the dustpan and brush and start sweeping up the strands of cheese as they fall on the floor.

'I don't know. That might be pushing it, Tom.'

My gaze is fixed on his shoes, willing him not to step in the mess and tread it into my new cream woollen fitted carpet in the bedroom.

Since we met, we've enjoyed spending time together. It's a commodity we've both got plenty of. We enjoy doing the simple things, walks up Ally Pally, swimming in the ponds for free on Hampstead Heath and window shopping, planning what we'll buy when he makes it big.

It's the small things that mean the most. Like this morning, I got up to find last night's washing- up all done and put away. Most importantly, we laugh about stuff no-one else would get. That's the real joy. Nothing matters quite so much when we're happy and together.

With Tom, I can be Ella. Not just Peter's copywriter, wary and forever on my guard. With Tom by my side, I can conquer Adland. Watch me.

That day outside the dole office, he rescued me. Now I want to rescue him right back. Since arriving in London, he has spent months crashing on mates' sofas. Not any more, he can sleep in my bed whenever he likes. Occasionally, when he's got a gig out of town, he'll stay at a bed and breakfast or if funds are really tight, sleep on someone's floor. When he's selling out Wembley, this will have been a small price to pay.

'You're good. CBA need you, they've said as much. Take what you can from the bastards. Got any white sliced, love?'

I shake my head and shudder slightly at the thought of plastic bread as I hand him a small loaf of fresh wholemeal.

'Sorry, just brown, unsliced. The knife's in the block, by the kettle,' I say watching him wield the blade like a saw. 'I can't afford to price myself out of a job.'

I watch in horror as he slices directly onto the work-top. 'Tom, do you mind not...'

I check myself. No-one likes a nag. Dad couldn't stand Mum's persistent fault-finding and used it as an excuse to punish her.

'Don't undersell yourself and don't let them take advantage of you. They're in the wrong, remember that. They owe you big-time. Ask for a five grand pay rise.'

I like that idea. Nice one, Tom. It's feels good to have someone batting in my corner. I hand him some fresh mayonnaise. He sniffs it suspiciously.

'No salad cream? Ah well, this'll have to do.'

I must quell my obnoxious tendency towards food snobbery. Too many expense accounts lunches have given me expensive tastes. Tom's brow furrows in marked concentration as he presses yellow worms of cheese onto the bread with the back of a tablespoon which he then uses to dig straight into the jar of mayonnaise and lift out a dangerously wobbly mound.

'Five grand?' I repeat. 'You think I'm worth that?'

'Of course. Go for it, love. The guy's offered you an open cheque.'

Please put the spoon down, I think as I wait anxiously for the oil-based sauce to spray up my newly-decorated walls, freshly papered with Designer's Guild finest.

I mentally calculate how much extra five grand would give me a month after tax and national insurance. He turns to sneeze into his free hand. I reach out and rescue the spoon from him.

'Bless you! Here, let me,' I say quickly smoothing the mayonnaise on top of the cheese. 'I was thinking more in the region of two thousand.'

'After what they put you through? No way,' he says wiping his hands down his jeans and slapping the second piece of bread on top. 'They haven't even apologised. They treated you like shit, Ella. Don't let them get away with it. Screw them for every penny you can. You're an asset or they wouldn't have asked you back. Times are hard. They can take their pick of talent. And they've picked you. Be happy.'

Using the heel of his hand, he squashes it all together causing cheese mulch to squelch out at the sides.

'For you,' he says, holding it out to me with both hands like a small boy having proudly made his mum a treat.

I don't want it but he is bursting for me to try it. I can't say 'no' to that smile. I take a small neat bite, remembering the unopened packet of smoked salmon in the fridge.

'You finish it. I'll make myself a salad later. Lost my appetite with all this stress.'

'You didn't fancy this, did you love?' he asks emitting a throaty laugh and pointing to his plate. 'I could tell by your face.'

'No, it looks lovely, I just wasn't hungry.'

'That's not true,' he laughs giving me a hug. 'You're right. It does look crap. But it was made with love and it tastes good.'

He takes another bite and chews it theatrically before swallowing it in one gulp.

'Play on that bastard's guilty conscience,' he advises. 'Peter Richards? Who the hell does he think he is, God?'

'Lucifer is more his style.'

Tom picks up the bread knife and says, 'I'll have a word with them, the bunch of ...'

'There's no need, thanks,' I say smiling at him hoping he'll smile back.

It works, which is a relief as he doesn't look nearly so attractive when he's annoyed. His face becomes all red and round. He sets about making another sandwich, thinly slicing wholemeal bread, layering on pieces of smoked salmon, squeezing over some lemon juice and adding a couple of twists of black pepper. He carves off the crusts before cutting it into quarters and arranges the pieces neatly on a plate.

'There you go - all yours.'

I take a bite.

'It's delicious, thanks' I say, trying to quell the shock in my voice.

'My pleasure, anytime. You eat the best bits and I'll have all the crap,' he says chewing happily on the discarded crusts.

That's the best offer I've had in a long while. I just hope it's not too good to be true.

Chapter fourteen

When you have nothing to say, use showmanship

I've always hated supermarkets. Too many products, too many irritating tannoy announcements and too many people getting in my way. I would like to go back to a butcher, a baker and a couture dress-maker all in the same street. But today, with Tom, this shop is a different place. He leaps on the back of the trolley and whizzes past the frozen foods into chilled meats where he grabs two packets of square ham and some orange coleslaw that looks like something Marmalade threw up.

'Fancy Spaghetti Bolognese tonight?' he asks lobbing in a pack of minced beef.

'Lovely,' I reply, remembering the cheese sandwich fiasco and inwardly fretting about the mess he'll make. 'Remind me to call Josh when we get home, before he changes his mind.'

I take my turn to push the trolley but it develops a wayward wheel. Just my luck.

'Make him wait,' says Tom. Treat 'em mean, keep 'em keen.'

'I'd love to but the longer I don't work, the less money I have,' I remind him picking up a packet of smoked salmon, check the price and replacing it in the cabinet.

'Have it if you want it,' he says reaching across me and selecting the largest size. 'I'm paying. Here, try this,' he says popping a sample slice of salami into my mouth from a plate on top of the delicatessen counter.

I chew on the salty, greasy meat and gag.

'Oh love, here,' he says looking around and grabbing a packet of kitchen roll off the shelf. He rips it open and tears off a square, holding it open for me to spit into lobbing the offending tissue into the air towards the bin behind the deli. It lands in a woman's trolley. Luckily, she is too busy examining the merits of fabric softeners to notice.

Tom laughs. The lady looks up and stares at us. I turn away. If I can't see Tom, I'll be okay. But I keep picturing his face when he threw it and imagining hers when she discovers it. Tom is clinging to the edge of the shelf, trying to remain upright but he creases over and slides onto the floor. My stomach hurts from suppressing laughter. It is the most intoxicating pain I know.

'Tom, get up!' I shriek.

Suddenly I'm crying. I haven't been this happy in ages.

Eventually, we get to our feet, embrace and kiss. When we eventually part the store detective is watching us. I know she is the store detective because she is always in there, traipsing up and down the aisles with the same three items in her basket.

'Fancy a film this afternoon? Matinees are half-price if you're signing on,' Tom asks.

'Really? We get something for doing nothing? Can't be right,' I reply feeling guilty about the idea of lounging around in the cinema all afternoon.

I'm programmed to work, not play. Going to the Odeon during the day would feel like bunking off school and I never dared do that either. Never bright enough to be able afford to miss lessons, I gleaned every ounce of knowledge, holding it in my head until I could regurgitate it on my exam paper. When the test was over, other kids handed in two sheets, three at the most. I always wrote six and somewhere in the overwhelming number of words was a text-book answer. All the examiner had to do was find it. Clearly they enjoyed the challenge as I managed to get nine 'O' levels, my passport out of poverty. Back then I naively believed, qualifications were a one-way ticket to success. But, if I'm not careful, I could find myself back in the gutter faster than I can say 'Sign on'.

I see Tom whizz past the top of the aisle. I run to catch him up as he takes the corner into the household aisle.

'Madness,' he says indicating the baffling selection of cleaning fluids and aerosols. 'My old flat-mate used his flannel to clean the bath and wash-up. Never did him any harm.'

I can practically smell that cloth and throw a pack of disposable sponges into the trolley.

'Why work with people you hate?' he asks loading up with lager, taking full advantage of the special offers on six packs.

He selects a bottle of whiskey and wedges it safely alongside the opened packet of kitchen roll in the trolley.

'There's no work around. I did look for other jobs. I'm not going back there out of choice.'

Tom aims for the shortest check-out queue.

'Screw the bastards for every penny then,' he says unwrapping a piece of gum and concealing the wrapper in his palm.

I look at him, disapprovingly and glance around hoping the store detective hasn't followed us. A woman reading her way through every glossy magazine has the nerve to eye him disapprovingly.

'Don't forget to pay for that, Tom,' I tell him loud enough for her to hear.

We inch forward in the queue.

'My work's picking up,' says Tom. 'People can still afford a cheap night out. Listening to some live music with a drink lets them forget their troubles for a few hours. The pubs and clubs are packed with punters. This recession is great for me.'

He reaches into his back pocket and brings out a roll of notes.

'Half,' I tell him. 'You can pay half.'

My independence is important to me. I have worked for everything I've got. I place each item on the conveyor belt. I didn't know they made so many types of crisps or beer.

'Everyone's waiting, love' he says reaching across me and dumping armfuls of shopping on the conveyor belt. 'Listen, *'Time Out'* is doing a piece on me next week. I've got a big gig coming up. I just need a manager and a record deal. I'll give Shaking Stevens something to shake about.'

'Excuse me, can you get that chocolate for me. The one with the nuts?' asks a short, elderly woman standing behind Tom, her plump hand outstretched in anticipation.

'There you go, darling,' he says handing her the bar. 'Anything else I can do for you?'

She looks him up and down approvingly, her rheumy eyes twinkling with mischief.

'Plenty if I was ten years younger,' she says.

Tom laps up the attention even if it is from an octogenarian.

'Is he yours?' she asks me.

Can one person own another? I don't think so. Tom is his own man. Nonetheless, I'm proud to be seen with him. She stiffens and lifts the tip of her walking stick to point at him, accusingly.

'Handsome is as handsome does,' she remarks with a dismissive sniff.

I have no idea what she means. Before I can ask her, she looks away.

To my horror, our bill comes to the same amount as I usually spend on a Christmas shop. They say two can live as cheaply as one. Clearly, 'they' have never met Tom. I open my cheque-book. Since I met Tom, it's rarely closed. Tom pays half the bill and I pay the rest. My bank balance is shedding pounds even if I'm not.

'I'll have my own TV show in six months, you watch,' he says as he helps me pack the bags. 'Now we're together I can start paying half of all the bills.'

I drop the box of eggs and look down at the bright yellow yolks intermingled with the clear albumen and shards of shell. I like him. He makes me laugh. He makes me happy. He makes love like a god. But making like we're a couple? It's too soon to be a twosome.

And paying half of all the bills? Surely he can't mean my mortgage? Because I don't care how exciting he is, I would rather be on my own than give someone I hardly know a stake in my flat. My place is my place – no landlord threatening me with eviction like poor mum has to put up with. No second-hand, chipped crockery in the cupboards – just beautiful china from Liberty's bought in the sale just after I joined CBA. My home is my security. I can't put that at risk for anyone, no matter how blue their eyes.

The cashier glares disapprovingly at me before enjoying her fifteen seconds of fame on the tannoy.

'Spillage at check-out number nine, please.   Spillage at check-out number nine. That's check-out nine, spillage.'

She leans forward, brandishing her 'Till Closed' sign at the elderly lady behind me.

'But, I need to pay now. I'm going to miss my bus,' the elderly woman protests, pointing at the contents of her basket.

'I'm closed. Sorry, madam.'

The cashier doesn't look sorry. She looks delighted.

Tom darts forward.

'What? You're refusing to serve an old lady? That's your job. It says so on your badge, '*I'm Sharon. How can I help?*' You can 'help' by doing what you're paid to do.'

I half expect him to follow it up with the classic gangster line, 'You heard the little lady, now do what she says and take the money, that way nobody gets hurt.'

But he just pulls a note off his wad and drops it by the cash register.

'There you go, love,' he tells the elderly woman. 'I've paid for your shopping. You shoot off and catch your bus.'

'Thanks, very much,' she says, packing her bag with the sort of alacrity reserved for elite athletes. 'Sorry, I don't know your name.'

'Tom, Tom Tyler. When I'm famous, you can tell everyone Tom Tyler picked up the tab.'

She tugged his sleeve and he bent down. After kissing his cheek, she hurried towards the exit.

'Manager to check out nine, that's the manager to check-out nine,' the cashier. Fifteen minutes of fame? The woman is now a celebrity.

'Come on, Tom. Let's go or we'll miss the film,' I say taking him by the arm and steering him towards the door as I see the manager approaching.

'You should treat your customers with more respect,' Tom tells him. 'You're quick enough to take their money, aren't you?'

Tom is shouting now. Everyone is looking. I hurriedly pick up our bags just as he kicks over the pile of hand baskets, they clatter across the floor preventing the manager from following us.

'What a wanker,' Tom shouts over his shoulder.

As we walk past the delicatessen, I can't help wishing we'd gone there. Supermarkets are like motorways; they're faster but bring out the worst in people.

'What was all that about?' I ask.

'The guy needed telling. That poor old lady. Anyway, let's forget it now. I'm not in the mood to see a film. Why don't I buy you lunch instead?' he suggests. 'Florian's do great Italian food. I've popped in there for a drink a couple of times before work.'

He kisses me gently and slowly.

I've lived in Crouch End for some time but I've never been in the wine bar. I've always wanted to try it but it's easier to socialise in Soho after work.

When we arrive, the waiter greets him like an old friend.

'Tom! Good to see you.'

'Eh, Franco! Hello!' exclaims Tom.

The only other person here is a grey-haired, olive-skinned man sitting alone in the window sipping a large glass of red wine. He looks like an older version of Franco. He must be his father. With some difficulty, he gets to his feet, pulls out a chair and motions us to join him. He speaks Italian to Tom who replies in English but with an Italian accent. They laugh and joke, appearing to understand each other perfectly.

'This is Ella,' says Tom pushing me forward and kicking the shopping bags underneath one of the other tables with his foot.

The old man looks confused.

'Remember, I told you about her?' says Tom smiling.

The man shrugs and turns to Franco who raises his eyebrows and laughs.

'She is Tom's girlfriend, Bella Ella, Papa,' Franco says pointing at me and grinning.

'Bella Ella?' says the old man incredulously, looking me over.

He laughs. My butt seems to be the butt of the joke. Embarrassed, I look away. The old man nods and we all sit down. He talks mainly in Italian, peppering his sentences with the occasional Anglo-Saxon word we can all understand.

A young woman wearing a tight white blouse and black skirt, emerges from the kitchen carrying a tray of antipasto – Italian cheeses, bread and a bowl of green olives marinated in garlic and herbs. She sets down the plates of food before expertly uncorking a bottle of Rosé wine. She looks at her watch and nods at Franco who gets up, locks the door and turns the sign to 'Closed'.

After a glass or two of wine, I relax into the afternoon and time passes in a delicious haze. So this is what people who don't go to work do all day. I can see the appeal but all the same I can't wait to get back to work. It's my life, what I am trained to do. For all its flaws, it defines me.

Tom entertains the two men who are mesmerised by his easy charm. I love that about him, the way he makes people feel special and makes them laugh.

At five-thirty Franco clears the plates and tops up our glasses again before opening the door. Gradually the place fills up with the evening crowd, mainly local business owners, jostling for attention at the bar, waving their cash demandingly at the staff. I mistake one of them for an actor off the television, before remembering he works in the fishmongers and I last saw him gutting cod. The old man gets up, hugs Tom and blows me a kiss before disappearing into the kitchen as Franco takes an order.

Alone with Tom, I am content in the warm fug of alcohol and cigarette smoke, in no hurry to leave. We watch people. A couple sharing stolen moments, rub each other's ankles under the table like a pair of lusty grasshoppers. Women stand in groups quaffing fizzy white wine and showing-off their designer hand-bags and heels. Others sit alone, nursing their drinks, talking to no-one. I am glad I am not one of them. I am glad I am with Tom, the most gorgeous man in the room. He makes up silly little songs about the other customers, mimicking their accents. I add in the chorus lines and we spark off each other, enjoying the riff. He tops up our glasses and turns my face towards his, kissing me gently on the lips.

'Happy?' he asks but he doesn't need me to tell him.

He can see me smiling from the inside out. I am so happy it feels like a new emotion. A shiny pair of shoes straight out of the box. A rainbow on a rainy day. A size ten dress that fits. The elation I feel when I do a good piece of work doesn't come close.

He kisses me again, softly and slowly. I look at him. He is smiling his beautiful smile. He is handsome. He has the sort of face girls pin on their bedroom walls and pine for. But the best thing about him is he is with me. Well, I never. Don't miss this one up, Ella, I tell myself.

We chink glasses. Is this my third or fourth? Who cares?

'Come on, let me take the pressure off you. You could even leave CBA and take time to find a job you really like,' he says drawing his fingers across the line on my forehead.

'No, thanks, I'm fine,' I murmur, sipping my wine.

'Please, I want to help,' he says his hand on mine.

I can't just hand over my life to him. It's too soon. Too fast.

'More wine?' he asks.

I nod and he orders another bottle.

'Good girl,' he says as I drain my glass. 'Work to live.'

I like the sound of that. I have been letting things get to me, downing a painkiller with virtually every cup of coffee. I would love to find another job somewhere I am appreciated and not have to put up with Peter making me feel like I don't measure up. I've had enough of that. I wasn't the daughter my father wanted, falling short on some hidden graph of life. Why else would he have behaved the way he did? Why else would he have told his solicitor he didn't want to see me? I don't know the answer, but I do I know Tom likes me. Tom Tyler could be the answer to my prayers, a rock God who, judging by the frequency he tops up my glass, turns water into wine.

Chapter fifteen

Invent a place or a character

On Tom's advice, I negotiated a four thousand pound pay rise with Josh. I have a few more days to enjoy before I go back to work. This is precious time with Tom and I am determined to make the most of every second. I may not be ready to share the bills but I'd love to go halves on a chateaubriand in Paris.

A weekend there would be wonderful. The last time I went was with my friend, Vera. Far more worldly-wise than me, she organised the whole thing, including our itinerary – a heart-stopping trip up the Eiffel Tower, huge cups of cafe au lait at Les Deux Maggots on St Germaine and the most unforgettable dessert at Le Bistro du la Garde. A bowl of chocolate mousse so huge, it was supposed to be passed from table to table with diners helping themselves to a small spoonful each. The chef calculated the amount to last all lunch-time but obviously hadn't bargained on the appetites of two greedy girls. Confronted by a pond of melted chocolate, we were insatiable. Not for us this genteel, pass-the-parcel style of eating. Like starving alley cats, we guarded the mousse, taking it in turns to scoop and eat, careful to ensure not even the most zealous waiter could prise our prize away.

Only being able to afford the cheapest hotel on the outskirts did not dampen our ardour for the city of love even if we were sharing our shabby room with a bidet.

On our final evening, Vera sweet-talked one of the waiters (an achievement in itself given she didn't speak a word of French) to bring us breakfast in bed the following morning. At eight o'clock, the young man dutifully delivered a French stick, some apricot jam and a pot of coffee. In bed together, the sheet pulled up modestly around our shoulders, we kidded ourselves we looked fabulous. Our two shiny faces framed by hair like dead rhododendrons, caused the waiter to back out of the room with the words,

'When yu 'ave fineshed, pleeze to leave yu trayer outsider yu door.'

His command of English was far superior to our grasp of French but that didn't stop us pretending we didn't understand a word and insisting he repeat himself over and over for our amusement. Fortunately, we were blessed with the one Parisian who shared our childish sense of humour and before long we were all laughing and reciting the now well-worn phrase in increasingly bad French accents. Even the waiter was hamming it up until he remembered his position, regained his composure and left, leaving us in hysterics. I just made it over to the bidet in time. Not one to let anything spoil her appetite, Vera made short work of her Continental breakfast. And mine.

This time, Tom and I will do it in style, an art deco hotel in the artists' quarter, maroon glacés eaten in pavement cafés and perhaps a picnic on the banks of the Seine with Camembert and white-flesh peaches, the sort with a lemony-pink bloom and a delicate perfume.

'Fancy going away next weekend, Tom?' I suggest excitedly.

'Sorry, love, no can do - got a big gig on Saturday night in Streatham.'

From the Seine to south London in a sentence. Reluctantly, I pack up my dreams and wave good-bye to romantic strolls along the boulevards. The Degas ballerinas will have to wait. Like me, they're not going anywhere. I look over at the gold-framed print mum bought me for my tenth birthday, depicting exquisite young dancers dressed in white tutus and satin pointe shoes tied with pink ribbons, performing their exercises at the barre. Like many little girls, I wanted to be the next Margot Fonteyn as I pounded around the living room in a white nylon petticoat, performing appalling arabesques every time I opened the door. 'Showing off' mum called it.

'I'm headlining so I'll be closing the show. I'll just crash at a mates. Bound to be someone on the bill who lives nearby.'

If he stays in south London, there's no way he'll make it back up here on Sunday and I won't see him all weekend.

'Surely you can get back?' I ask.

'It'll be so late, love. Easier for me to stay down there.'

'Oh, okay,' I say trying to conceal my disappointment. 'I'll probably catch up with Adam. There's a restaurant we both fancy trying in Covent Garden.'

'Adam?' he asks. 'What are you meeting him for?'

'Haven't seen him in a while. I can pick his brains about how to handle things when I go back to work. I'm not very good at office politics.'

He sits up, looking purposeful.

'Well, I'm sure I can sort something, either get a lift back or catch the night bus. And, I can grab a kebab on the way.'

I hug him; overjoyed he'll be home. But a kebab? How drunk is he going to be?

'Sorry about the trip, love, you haven't booked anything, have you?'

'No, but I have planned every last detail,' I think.

'We'll go another time,' he says sensing my disappointment. 'Leave it to me. I've got a mate who's a travel agent. He'll look after us.'

With Tom in my life, it's access all areas. I can go anywhere I want with Tom. From the Big Apple to Orange County, I've just hit the jackpot on the world's biggest fruit machine.

'Drink?' I ask him.

'Lager, thanks.'

I can hardly tell him I meant tea, he'll think I'm boring.

'Coming right up,' I say sounding all-American.

I need to get out more and stop watching so much television.

Opening the fridge door, my hand knocks against the pack of processed ham. It falls out and hits the floor, splattering watery fluid over my feet. Not only do they look like pig's trotters, now they smell like them too. I curse silently and vow to buy dry-cure next time.

The shelves are stacked with booze. When Tom stocked up at the supermarket, I had no idea it was just his weekend's supply.

I hand him a can and settle myself on the sofa, entwining myself around him like a cat. He's watching a cop drama, yet another American import. Give me a black and white movie any day. He has certainly got the hang of the video-recorder with programmes banked up until the Millennium.

'Comfy?' he yawns, leaning back and putting his arms around me, making me feel loved and wanted. ' Great sofa.'

So it should be, Chesterfields don't come cheap. This one, upholstered in dove grey velvet, was prohibitively expensive but didn't cost me a penny. It was made especially for a commercial I worked on for central heating. When filming was over, Peter arranged to have it delivered to my new flat. At the time, I thought he was being kind but now I know him better I reckon he wanted to help me christen it.

The first people to grace the settee were the jobbing actors I had cast as the two plumbers in the commercial. They have since gone on to greater things. I like to think the skills they acquired on a thirty second TV ad proved invaluable when filming their Hollywood blockbuster.

'Can you say, 'Stay warmer for less' with a little more feeling?' I asked Plumber No 1.

'Yes, but what's my motivation?' he replied.

Not many film stars can claim they can sing a jingle with their hand up a balanced flue.

Now Tom lights up another cigarette. Thank goodness the upholstery is fire-retardant.

'Fancy a coffee?' I ask.

He nods. I am mentally preparing the freshly ground coffee beans I bought this morning. Knowing my salary will soon start hitting my bank account again, I couldn't resist treats from the aromatic grocery store on Muswell Hill including a box of the finest French sugar cubes (the only brand Peter will touch, so they must be good) and a pint of organic milk which cost twice as much as a carton from the supermarket. I also bought a special mug for Tom with a smiley face on the front.

On my way home, my eye was drawn to the jeweller's window. Next to the heart-shaped, red velvet pads displaying gold wedding bands was a selection of second-hand rings. Amongst the garnets and opals was a silver ring set with the letter 'T'. It had to be Tom's even though I had no idea if it would fit or not. I bought it on impulse. It seemed the perfect way to say 'thanks'. Thanks for making me laugh when all I wanted to do was cry. Thanks for not being like my Dad, Peter, or Alan. Thanks for being you, Tom.

But I've only known him five minutes. What appeared to be the ideal present in the shop now smacks of desperation. The small, square box presses against my leg in my pocket. It probably won't even be the right size. I study his fingers then go into the kitchen. Taking a packet of chipolatas out of the fridge, I slip the ring on one. The perfect fit. I take it off and quickly rinse it under the tap before drying it on a tea towel and putting it back in its box.

I make a cafetière of Blue Mountain and a mug of herbal tea and look in the tin for some biscuits. I always have chocolate ones, on the off chance someone who is not de-toxing nips round for a cuppa. But I don't know anyone in advertising, apart from Adam and me, who isn't following some wheat-free, caffeine-free, carb-free, joy-free diet. I arrange everything on a tray, carry it in and set it down beside the sofa, before pushing down the plunger on the cafetière.

'Love! Get out the way,' Tom tuts. 'Oh, I've missed the ending now.'

'Just rewind it.'

He grabs the remote control and stabs randomly at the buttons, frantically rewinding, pausing and forwarding the tape.

'Where is it?' he shouts furiously as he continues to whizz the film indiscriminatingly, backwards and forwards.

'Here's your coffee,' I say anxious to appease him, stirring in milk and three sugar cubes, just the way he likes it.

I proudly hand him his drink in the new mug. He takes a couple of slurps, his eyes never leaving the screen.

'What the hell?' he declares thrusting the drink back at me in disgust.

Coffee washes over the side of the mug and spills on the sofa.

'It's fresh coffee.'

'I'll stick to instant. I don't want that muck,' he tells me wiping his mouth with the back of his hand.

He can make his own coffee next time.

'Like your new mug?' I ask.

'It's just a cup,' he says dismissively, dropping his fag end into the coffee.

I go to get a cloth to clean up the spill before it stains the sofa but he pulls me down next to him.

'Relax! Sit down,' he tells me. 'Sorry I shouted. Am I forgiven?'

He smiles. His eyes mesmerise me. I nod.

'Can I come to the club and watch you perform?' I ask.

'Sure,' he laughs. 'I'll put your name on the door. Just tell them you're with me. Tell them you're with Tom Tyler.'

I snuggle up to him.

'I'm starving. How about some pasta?' he asks.

I thought I was supposed to be relaxing?

'I'll do it in a minute. Let's see what happens next,' I tell him fixing my eyes on the screen.

I sip my camomile tea. I've left the bag in too long and it tastes like grass clippings. It doesn't smell too good either. Then I realise it's not my drink but Tom's feet which are resting on my lap, wrapped in the folds of my long silk blouse. I shift slowly along the sofa and as do I can feel the ring box in my pocket digging painfully into my thigh.

Chapter sixteen

Make comparisons

Brighton may not be Paris but it dances to its own tune. I like that. Besides it's not where you go, it's who you go with. And I'm going with Tom. I can't wait. It's only a day trip but I know it's going to be wonderful. Tom has a knack for transforming the mundane into the magical.

The ring I bought him is hidden inside my bag, zipped safely into the side pocket next to a packet of tissues. I have a headache and felt too lousy last night to go to Tom's gig but dosed up on aspirin, I am determined not to let it spoil our day. Unfortunately, the early morning start doesn't agree with Tom. I have no idea what time he got back; I was asleep when he got in. We had to be up and out by eight to catch the train so this must feel like the middle of the night to him. He puffs furiously on his fourth cigarette of the day, coughing dramatically between drags.

'Fancy a coffee, love?' he asks as we approach the ticket office at Victoria station.

I nod and join the queue. When I eventually reach the front, the man ahead of me is giving a detailed run-down of his health problems to the clerk who is looking sicker by the minute.

'Doctor said he's never seen one like it. It's huge and glows bright red. Wanna see?'

I look at my watch and sigh audibly. He runs out of ailments and moves reluctantly away from the window. I buy two, day-returns and feel excited just holding the tickets in my hand. Tom arrives back looking much brighter after his shot of caffeine.

'Sorry about Paris, love, but I must do the work when it comes up. You never know who might be at the gigs.'

'Well, you do. You told me there were four in the audience last night – two men and a young couple who mistook the club for the back row of the stalls.'

'Ah but those bookings are getting less and less,' he smiles. 'I'm going for the bigger venues now. Tom Tyler's going to be a star.'

For a moment I wonder who he means. It's strange to hear him refer to himself in the third person.

The train is waiting on the platform. We get in the first carriage.

'Got a fag, mate?' Tom asks a young bloke sitting by the window.

I know he's got an unopened packet in his pocket. I bought it for him on our way here.

'What's the matter?' he asks me.

'Nothing, Just this headache,' I tell him touching my forehead.

There is a great camaraderie amongst smokers and the man immediately gives him a cigarette and even lights it for him.

'Cheers, mate,' says Tom as he inhales like his life depends on it. 'Ella, what's wrong?'

I don't want to embarrass him by mentioning the cigarettes so I say the first thing I think of.

'I'm not looking forward to seeing Peter again.'

It's been weeks since I've had to think about that man. Now, when I close my eyes, I can't even picture him.

'Don't worry about it. He won't last long. He's screwed up too many times. They know you can do his job. That's why they've got you back,' Tom replies.

His confidence in me, gives me such a boost but he's a musician and not up on the malevolent machinations of Adland.

'Peter is too well-in for that. The clients love him. If he goes, they go and the board know it. The guy's got a job for life.'

'Tell them you can do his job for half his salary.'

'But I can't. I used to think this job was just all about being a good copywriter but it's all about being good with the clients. Not my strong point, I'm afraid.'

'You'll be fine. Promise,' he assures me.

I hug him. He starts to drum his fingers on his knees and tap his feet to a tune only he can hear. He starts humming.

'What's that?' I ask.

'Just a song I'm working on,' he smiles before stubbing out his cigarette.

'Sing it to me.'

'Oh no, it's not finished yet,' he tells me absent-mindedly.

'You're right, Peter is living off his past glories,' I say trying to get his attention.

'He's a has-been. He's jealous of you. You're worth ten of him and he knows it. He feels threatened. Come on, don't let that jerk ruin our day,' he says as he gives my hand a reassuring squeeze.

I sink back into my seat. Thanks to Tom, I can turn off the screen inside my head, the one that shows The Peter Richards Show, day and night. I rest my head on Tom's shoulder. I can't sleep but he dozes off. He looks gorgeous, his dark features perfectly neat and symmetrical. The perfect face. I lean over and kiss him. But my prince doesn't wake up. Perhaps, the fairy tale ending only works if he kisses me. Fat chance, I dribble on my pillow; I'm no sleeping beauty.

When we arrive, we walk out of the station hand in hand. With the sun shining and Tom on my arm, Brighton looks bright and beautiful. I'm doing that thing again. Smiling from the inside out. I want to run down the hill towards the sea.

'Ice-cream?' I suggest excitedly.

I love 99's. Eating one now, I'm a kid again. Enjoying the soft swirls of vanilla, then biting off the end of the cone and sucking the last of the ice-cream through the end of the cornet. Far more delicious than a few prissy scoops served up in an expensive restaurant.

'Fancy some proper breakfast?' Tom asks with his mouth still full of chocolate flake.

'Yeah. I know a little cafe, if I can find it,' I tell him mentally calculating how many inches a full English will add to my tugboat thighs. Oh what the hell, we're by the sea, they'll fit in nicely.

I remember overhearing Peter's secretary talking about a tea-room just off the sea-front. She described it as having a bow-fronted window full of home-made cakes. Sure enough, we turn left off the main road to see a woman setting up tables on the pavement outside a cafe. Much to my joy, the window is a vision of culinary delights with billowing meringues and mounds of sugar-coated shortbread piled high on old-fashioned cake plates. But I'm looking for the date and walnut loaf Peter's secretary raved about. She had even brought him in a slice; it looked gorgeous, dark and sticky and she gave it to him with his coffee. She had even held it for him as he bit into it greedily, mistaking its dark appearance for gingerbread. The nut proved a very expensive surprise and the ensuing dental work paid for his orthodontist's holiday to California, the home of the walnut. What sweet irony.

Now the delicious aroma of vanilla mingled with cinnamon hits me as I open the door. I wish Adam was here; he would love this. I wonder what he's doing? Probably having breakfast with his girlfriend.

'I thought we were going to a greasy spoon. I fancy a fry-up not a cake,' whines Tom.

A hash brown or a chocolate brownie? No contest.

'Look, Tom they do eggs with dry-cured Sussex bacon,' I tell him pointing at the menu.

'I don't care where it comes from; it's all pig,' he says following me inside.

After we've finished eating, he leans back in his seat, drumming his teaspoon against the rim of the saucer and humming the same tune as he did on the train. He smiles at me. Those eyes. Those beautiful blue eyes.

After we pay the bill, Tom grabs my hand and we head for the pier, where we play the slot machines, lose all our change before Tom wins it all back and doubles our money. He darts off and returns holding a pink cloud of candyfloss above his head. I jump up, accidently knocking the candyfloss out of his hand. We lean over the railings, watching as it sails towards the water.

'No worries,' says Tom replacing it with a shiny toffee apple from a nearby kiosk.

He crunches into it, shattering shards of bright red caramel over my shoes. Matching each other bite for bite we are soon left clutching just the core on a stick. Tom drops it between the wooden slats into the sea below before propelling me towards the ghost train.

We scramble into the first car. It lurches off and dives into the darkness. But it doesn't live up to its promise. Peter's concepts are more frightening than this. Next time I see him, I'll grab him by the ghoulies and start as I mean to go on.

Plastic skeletons jangle towards us, brushing their femurs against our faces. I jump when the siren sounds and Tom hugs me tightly as we hurtle back into the daylight. Laughing, we clamber out and race up the stairs to the top of the iconic red, white and blue helter-skelter, dragging squares of coconut matting behind us. Tom flies off first. I wait a few moments before following him down, feeling like I'm going to flip over the side, into the sea. But the date and walnut cake acts as ballast. Corkscrewing faster and faster, I see Tom sitting at the bottom and shout for him to move but he doesn't hear. He's too busy trying to light a cigarette, cupping his hand around the flame of the match to prevent the wind from blowing it out. I bash into him, banging my mouth against his shoulder. When I bring my hand to my face, my fingertips are smeared with blood.

'You took your time,' he laughs going to give me a smoky kiss and then changing his mind when he sees the cut. 'You okay?'

Not wanting to make a fuss and spoil the day, I nod.

'Come on then, I'm gasping for a pint. Race you to the nearest pub.'

He heads off, colliding with a little boy and knocking his ice-lolly out of his hand.

'Mind!' Tom screams at the child whose face is crumbling as he is watches his lolly melt through the slats of the pier.

The lads bursts into tears.

'You nearly had me over. Look where you're going,' Tom shouts.

The boy cries even louder causing his mother to stop laughing with her friend and turn around and confront Tom. Immediately, he grins at her. The mega-watt smile is brighter than anything lighting up the pier right now.

'Sorry, about that. Didn't see the little lad; he just flew out of nowhere. No harm done. Here, get him another one,' he says handing her a five pound note. 'And one for yourself. And your friend.'

Tom touches her lightly on the arm. She giggles and takes the money. He ruffles the child's hair.

'When you see me on telly, you can tell all your friends, Tom Tyler bought you an ice-cream on Brighton Pier.'

'Tom Tyler,' says the woman flirtatiously. 'I'll remember the name.'

Something about the encounter leaves a bad taste in my mouth. I lick my lips and taste blood.

'Tom! Wait!' I shout but he's run off and is too far ahead to hear me.

I panic, running back down the pier, darting in and out of the holiday-makers, unable to see him.

'Here I am,' he says jumping out at me when I reach the exit.

'You disappeared.'

'No, I didn't. I was over there all the time, watching you.'

He puts his arm around me. I shove him away, playfully trying to mask my embarrassment. I feel a fool getting so upset about nothing.

We walk towards The Lanes, looking in the shop windows, picking out outfits for each other.

'That's you,' I say pointing to a pair of tapering pink trousers and an Argyle sweater.

'You think so?' he asks with a grin. 'Well, I think that one would suit you down to the ground.'

After all the food I've eaten today, I turn expecting to see a kaftan or a workman's tent by the side of the road. But Tom is looking at a black silk sheath dress.

'I can just see you in that,' he tells me. 'Go in and try it on.'

The price tag is heftier than I am at a hundred and twenty pounds.

'Don't worry about how much it costs; I'll buy it for you,' he says when he sees me blanch.

I'm tempted but I can't let him. It's too much.

'No it's not me. It's too tight but thanks for the offer.'

'Okay, I'll have a word with Santa, perhaps I can ask him to put it in your stocking this Christmas.'

Christmas? He's obviously planning on sticking around.

In a haze as pink and fluffy as the candyfloss I just ate, I linger outside one of the many antique jewellery shops. Admiring a rose gold ring set with a diamond the size of a pigeon's egg, I spot the matching price tag. Tom has already disappeared inside the nearest pub. This is the longest I've known him go without a drink. I'm not about to spoil our day by nagging him. Let's face it - I'm no stranger to a liquid lunch, with an almond croissant chaser.

'Stick another one in there, mate,' he says handing over his empty glass to the barman. 'A large white wine for my girlfriend and whatever you're having.'

Girlfriend? That's the first time he's used the word to describe me. Never mind a haze, I am now floating on a pink candyfloss cloud. Delighted to be publicly elevated to girlfriend status, I puff out my chest. Obviously, no one notices.

Aware I am following in his former girlfriend's footprints, I know to tread lightly. Apparently, she fleeced him then left him for a pilot causing Tom to refer to her as a 'flight slag'.

Tom smiles at me.

'Sorry love, I've spent all my money,' he tells me.

I hand the barman a fiver and he sets down our drinks. I take a sip. It is typical pub wine, warm and acidic. But I don't care. I'm with Tom. I'm in heaven.

'Cheers love, here's to a great day,' he says.

'Thanks, it's been perfect,' I tell him.

Now, I think to myself, do it now. I take the small square box out of my handbag and hand it to him.

'What's this?' he asks suspiciously.

'Open it,' I urge, feeling like I did on Mum's birthday all those years ago, giving her the gift I'd saved up for weeks to buy. As presents go, the selection of expensive-looking perfumes I had bought from my school fete, stunk. Bewitched by the satin-lined gift-box and French-sounding name, I hadn't noticed the bottles were only half full and the scent had gone off.

'Oh love, thanks. Is it platinum?' Tom asks taking the ring out of the box and examining it closely.

'No, silver,' I reply suddenly feeling like a cheapskate. 'Try it on. Is it the right size? If not, I can get it altered.'

The only finger it fits is the third finger on his left hand. So much for my chipolata sizing guide.

'Congratulations, mate. When's the big day?' the barman laughs. 'I didn't realise it was a Leap Year. Never seen a bird propose to a bloke before.'

Tom laughs but seeing my face, puts his arm round me and kisses the side of my head. My cheeks flush.

'With this ring, I thee bed, eh mate?' leers the barman. 'Your lucky night, eh?'

'Enough,' says Tom in the same furious tone he had used to the guy in the car outside the unemployment office.

Immediately, the barman backs off.

Tom snatches up his glass and the ring clinks against the side, making an imperceptible noise, one I hope only I can hear. It resounds in my head like the peel of wedding bells ringing out all over Sussex.

I knew I should have waited until we were alone. I feel such a clown. And thanks to the wine, I've even got the red nose.

It's almost dark by the time we leave the pub and head back up the hill to the station.

'Don't worry about work tomorrow. You'll be fine love,' he says as we board the train.

'What?' I ask. 'How did you know I was fretting about that?'

'I told you, I can read your mind.'

No, he can't. For once, I wasn't thinking about work. I was thinking about him. My confidence has taken a knock thanks to Peter and now it's wonderful to have Tom by my side, fighting my corner. I lock my fingers through his and feel the silver band.

'I love you, Ella.'

My heart leaps. Perhaps he really can read minds. I turn to look at him. But I must have misheard. He's just staring out of the window, looking as vacant as the seat opposite us. I close my eyes so he can't see how disappointed I am.

'Well?' he prompts.

He smiles. Those blue eyes again. This gorgeous guy is mine. Lucky me.

'I love you, Ella.'

There's no mistaking those words. This is what I've always wanted but never believed I'd find, someone to love me and to love right back. I've experienced both, but never with the same person. Adoring Alan from afar was like driving the wrong way down a one-way street.

'I love you, Tom.'

'We'll have to go back to Brighton and buy you that ring you were eyeing up,' he says.

'Didn't think you noticed.'

'I notice a lot of things, always remember that, Ella.'

He is smiling but his tone has changed to something completely at odds with the moment.

'I love you, Tom,' I repeat desperate to get us back to where we were.

I go to kiss him on the lips but he turns away and I'm left nuzzling his cheek.

On the way home, we seem to have lost our way. Tom and I are both saying the same thing. The difference is I know I mean it.

Chapter seventeen

Show before and after pictures

The CBA receptionist is one of the least receptive people I know making her spectacularly under-qualified for the job. She usually manages a fleeting smile but today she is engrossed in inspecting her hair for split ends. She doesn't even look up when I approach her desk.

'Morning. This is Tom, my boyfriend. He's just going to give me a hand taking my stuff back upstairs. Do you need him to sign in?' I ask indicating the visitors' book.

She shakes her head, giving the box Tom is now balancing precariously on one knee, a cursory glance. He could have anything in there, so much for security.

The latest edition of 'Hello' lies unopened on her desk yet I know she regards getting her hands on that magazine as one of the few perks of her job. Today's papers are still bundled together inside the door where the courier has left them. The lift is also on a go-slow. I run up the stairs, two at a time, in an attempt to inject some vitality into the place. Tom plods up behind me. When we reach the third floor, even the three ceramic ducks on the wall, Peter's homage to his mantra, 'Get your ducks in a row', look desperate to migrate to the South Pole or wherever kitsch birds go when the going gets tough. There's no aroma of freshly-made coffee. Peter's not nice without his early morning shot of caffeine.

Chop! Chop!

'Where's Peter?' I ask his secretary as she tidies the inside of her designer handbag.

'He's not coming in,' she says examining a used tissue as if checking for deposits of gold.

'Ella! Ella!'

135

I turn to see Wally beckoning me into Peter's office.

'Hi Wally,' I say walking over and beaming at him. 'This is my boyfriend, Tom.'

'Hello, Wally. I'm Tom, Tom Tyler, pleased to meet you,' he says, putting the box down and shaking Wally warmly by the hand. 'Ella's told me all about you. It's nice to know she's got a friend here. This place sounds very cut-throat.'

'She's a good girl,' Wally says winking at me. 'They're lucky to 'ave her after what they done. Disgusting behaviour.'

'Ah, I've missed you, Wal.'

I hand him a large paper bag. He peers inside and takes out the chocolate croissant.

'Lovely,' he says biting into it and letting the shiny flakes drop onto his pullover. 'Listen, dunno what's going on, but it ain't good. Apparently, the board keep having meetings and come out with faces as long as tripe. Thank God I'm retiring soon. This used to be a great agency, not anymore. Watch your back, young 'un.'

For someone who only works nights, Wally is very clued up. If they gave him a day job, he'd be running the place within a week.

Tom steps forward.

'Don't worry, mate. I'm here now. I'm a singer, I'm about to sign a deal. I've got a few producers interested in me. I know...'

I listen in awe. Wally cuts across him.

'Right, young 'un, I'm off home. Thanks for the cake. See you tomorrow and remember what I said. Don't take no nonsense from no-one.'

He taps the side of his bulbous nose.

'A wee dram before you go, Wal? Toast Ella's first day back?'

To my horror, Tom has poured two fingers of Peter's single malt into a crystal tumbler.

'Not for me,' says Wally. 'Put that bottle down and drink up.'

Tom downs the whiskey and wipes his mouth with the back of his hand.

'Good whiskey that,' he says checking the label before replacing it on Peter's shelf.

'Why did you do that?' I hiss steering him past Wally and out of the room.

'This place can afford it. Peter won't miss it. The old boy was just being a dick.'

'No, he wasn't,' I tell Tom. 'He was just doing his job.'

'I'm going downstairs. Let me show you out, mate,' says Wally who is on the stairs, waiting for Tom to follow.

Bolstered by the whiskey, Tom swaggers towards him.

'See you later, love,' he tells me.

'Depends what time I finish. First day back, it could be a late one. Maybe best if you stay with a mate tonight.'

It's true but it's not the real reason. I didn't like him taking the whiskey, and I hated the way he spoke to Wally. Tom shouts something but I don't hear it as I walk upstairs to the account-handling floor. These people take work very seriously. You wouldn't catch them playing table football in the office or having casual sex on smoked glass tables. Nothing distracts them from climbing the greasy pole. They don't hang out with flighty creative-types in case our laissez-faire attitude is contagious. They don't want us breathing Chardonnay-breath in their faces, making it obvious we've been out to lunch since ten that morning and have no intention of doing any work that afternoon. Or any afternoon come to that.

Josh startles me by shooting out of his office, talking into his mobile very loudly but saying nothing worth listening to.

'Can I have a word?' I mouth.

He points to the phone as if I can't see it. The thing is the size of a Buick. I nip into his office and wait.

'Well?' he asks tersely.

'Thanks for putting out the welcome mat. What's going on? The place is dead.'

'You're at the wake,' he says, his chest moving up and down rapidly. 'High-Pro just fired us. The ship is sinking and this rat wants to leave.'

'I don't understand. We've only just won High-Pro,' I venture.

'Peter failed to develop your idea and tried to push through one of his own. The client hated it.'

I can't believe even Peter would be so selfish as to put the agency in jeopardy simply to satisfy his own ego.

'Tell me it's not the one with the gyrating girl with big hair and the line 'High-Pro – a Hair-Raising new idea!'

Josh nods, 'And the can that looks like a phallus.'

'But he knew how my campaign was supposed to pan out. Why did he have to ruin everything?'

'He wanted to do his idea. You know it's all about Peter and to hell with everyone else. '

'Where is he now?'

'Hanging by his balls from Big Ben, for all I care. His ex-wife showed up yesterday. Peter saw he was about to lose the one thing he truly loved and flipped. He wasn't about to give up his Porsche. There was a struggle in reception and she wrestled the keys off him. So he ran outside and lay down in front of the car.'

'Please tell me her foot slipped on the accelerator?'

'Sadly, not. She revved the engine. He leapt up. She jumped out to wallop him and he got in and sped off. Haven't seen him since.'

'Where does that leave us?' I ask.

'Shit Street.'

I assume the address doesn't have a Mayfair post-code.

'And Steve Winter has landed High-Pro,' says Josh, shaking his head in despair.

'How did he manage that?' I ask incredulously. 'He didn't have any creative work to present?'

'How do you know?' asks Josh rounding on me suspiciously.

'Someone must've mentioned it. I can't remember.'

'Steve impressed the client with his credentials and screwed a bargain basement media plan out of the boys. He was appointed on the strength of that alone.'

I stare at Josh in disbelief. Steve Winter had pulled it off but pulled the plug on us.

'This will be on the front page of 'Campaign' tomorrow and on the desk of every Creative Director in town. I'll be a laughing stock,' Josh wails.

No change there then, I think.

'And Peter?' I whisper, lest the mention of his name brings the walls tumbling down. 'Where will he go?'

'To hell,' replies Josh bitterly.

'Don't worry, knowing Peter, he's already there,' I tell him.

'The board suspended him while the dust settles. It's damage limitation. Officially, he's on gardening leave,' Josh says giving me a sly glance. 'I need to call my head-hunter and line up another job. I suggest you do the same. Kitty Rescue won't keep this place afloat for long. And you're back on the account.'

Somehow I make it downstairs to my office. Peter's secretary looks close to tears. I feel sorry for her. She's worked with him for years. She knows all his peculiarities, how he takes his coffee, how to calm his mood with just a smile and how to never discuss his numerous indiscretions.

'Don't worry,' I tell her. 'You'll be fine. You've got so much to offer. You're very good at...' I struggle to think what her particular skill might be. 'You're very good at washing your smalls.'

She bursts into tears.

'Sorry, I was only joking,' I tell her.

She ignores me and grabs her used tissue out of the bin, blowing her nose like a tiny trumpet, heralding the end of CBA as we know it. If Peter had a shred of integrity this would never have happened and we would all be laughing. Instead, his secretary is sobbing, Josh is hanging in rags and we are all going to be looking for work. At least one good thing has come out of this mess. If I don't have a job, I don't have to sleep with Peter to keep it.

Josh walks by and laughs, 'Reckon I'm safe. Just bumped into the MD. Think I've managed to convince him it was all Peter's fault.'

'I thought you two were friends.'

'Friends?' he asks as if I am speaking a foreign language – one of the few he hasn't got a degree in. 'Wake-up, Ella. This is business.'

Well, it certainly isn't pleasure. But I could learn to like it. This is my chance. I should grab it with both hands but I always like to keep one free to eat cake.

I stride into Peter's office, take my coat off and hang it on the back of his door. I've got work to do. Josh watches me as I sit in Peter's chair and lower the seat until my feet touch the ground.

'You don't believe in letting the grass grow, do you?'

'Just keeping Peter's seat warm for him.'

I sink down in his black leather ergonomically-designed throne, hold onto the arms and rotate 360 degrees. Twice.

'Don't panic Josh, play-time is over. Let's go to work. Get me a status update on all our accounts – I need to know what you know.'

He looks so relieved I think he might kiss me. Thankfully, his buttoned-up upbringing won't allow it.

'I knew I was right to get you back,' he tells me heading off to collect his files.

I'm in way above my head. I must get hold of Adam, with his experience as Deputy Creative Director he can help me avoid the pitfalls. In the meantime, I start as I mean to go on and follow Josh out to talk to Peter's secretary.

'Hi. I've been pretty rude to you. I'm sorry,' I tell her laying my hand gently on her arm.

She looks shocked and says nothing.

'It looks like we'll be working together for the time being. I should've asked a long time ago, what's your name? I can't keep calling you 'Peter's secretary'.'

'Apology accepted, Ella. I'm Jill,' she replies extending her hand for me to shake.

I smile with relief.

'Thanks, Jill. Please may I have a freshly squeezed orange juice and two croissants from Patisserie Valerie and whatever you'd like. Oh and a large double espresso for Josh.'

He'll need it. We're looking at a long day and an even longer night. And this is just the beginning.

Chapter eighteen

Make your client No 1

'I'm drowning,' I tell Adam as we walk through Soho towards Covent Garden, heading for our favourite fish and chip shop.

'Not surprised the amount of bilge that comes out of Josh's mouth,' he says diving into a Bar Italia and ordering two cappuccinos to take-away. He helps himself to a handful of Amaretto biscuits from a bowl on the side and offers them to me.

'I sit in meetings and haven't got a clue what they're talking about,' I tell him.

'And you think they do? It's all crap, Ella. Just do what Peter does. Make friends with the clients.'

He takes the coffees and hands over the money, offering me one of the polystyrene cups.

'Thanks, I'll get them next time,' I say taking my drink from him. 'Listen, I don't have anything in common with the clients. They're all middle-aged men who barely acknowledge me in meetings.'

'Get to know them as people, not clients. Find out what makes them tick. Find something you like about them. You're lovely. They'll soon see that.'

'You make it sound so easy, Adam,' I tell him as we cross Shaftesbury Avenue, darting behind a bus when the lights turn red.

'You're always going to get the odd awkward so and so but you can handle them. Just be twice as nice, it always works for me,' he says surging ahead.

'I'll give it a whirl,' I tell him, unconvinced.

'So, are you happy there? They say you should never go back,' he asks weaving through the tourists clogging the pavement consulting guide-books and maps.

'It feels like a different place without Peter. But I'm hopeless at office politics. I just want to do my job not keeping checking over my shoulder for stab marks.'

'Don't worry. Like I said, just befriend the clients. It's a tip someone gave me when I took this job. Trust me, it works. Even Jan is happy to socialise with some of them.'

Jan is Adam's girlfriend. They've known each other for years but I don't know much more about her now than I did when I first met him. He drops her name into conversation and I've never met her but have built up a picture of her as beautiful but unhappy.

We walk across Seven Dials and continue up past the cheese shop. We both hold our noses and laugh.

'I never touch the cheese board at dinner parties,' I tell him.

'Me neither. Why would you when you can have pudding?' he says hurrying by.

'Oh, that reminds me; we discovered a fantastic little tea-room in Brighton. Jill knows it. Delicious cakes. Tom wasn't keen. Preferred his fry-up.'

'Oh, yeah, Tom,' he asks vaguely. 'You're still seeing him then?'

I nod enthusiastically, trotting to keep up with Adam who has quickened his pace.

'Yeah, he's amazing. We had a great day. It was such a laugh and we ...'

I look at him. He must have heard every word but he's not listening. Not really.

'Adam, you okay?'

144

'Sorry,' he says looking at his watch. 'I've just remembered, I've got a meeting at two thirty.'

'Oh, okay, we can get a take-away and I can walk back with you.'

'No' he replies hastily. 'I can't turn up stinking of cod and chips. The client's a vegan.'

He laughs but he doesn't smile.

'I'll shoot off now and bell you later. We'll do this some other time, yeah?' he says as he turns to retrace his steps.

'Okay,' I say puzzled. 'I look forward to it.'

Chapter nineteen
Ensure the client's name is clear

I recognise the tune as soon as I walk in the door. It's the one Tom was humming on the train to Brighton. He is sitting on the sofa strumming his guitar. When he sees me, he starts to sing and motions for me to sit next to him. A bottle of wine and two glasses are ready and waiting on the table, alongside a vase of fresh flowers, tulips, my favourite. I pour us both a glass and settle myself on the chair.

I watch in awe as his fingers move effortlessly over the strings. Playing an instrument is like magic to me. I am not musical as the woman who tried to teach me piano a few years ago discovered. My ex-boyfriend had insisted I learn, even paying for the lessons. A few months later, I found out why. While I was doing up and down the scales, he was going up and down on another girl. I assume they were making sweeter music than I was.

'Welcome to your private audience with Tom Tyler. Unplugged,' he announces. 'Just, close your eyes and relax.'

I do as he says and after a brief pause, he begins to sing. His voice is beautiful, clear and pure.

As usual, in these situations, I get the urge to laugh. The more I try to suppress it, the worse it gets. I chew the sides of my mouth and think of something serious, like Patisserie Valerie running out of croissants before I get there tomorrow morning. It works a treat but Tom has stopped playing. Cautiously, I open my eyes as I mouth, 'sorry' to him. He presses against his lips.

'Ssch!' he tells me with a wink.

I loosen my collar. In an attempt to look creative and wacky, I am wearing a shirt and bow tie. What am I thinking? I could only look more ridiculous if the thing lit up and spun.

Leaning back in my seat, Toms starts again, from the top. I close my eyes again and let the words wash over me, my foot tapping to the beat. The tune is catchy. But it's the innocent, sweet-sounding lyrics I really love. A line leaps out at me. When I open my eyes, Tom is staring at me, grinning.

'Ella, you mean more to me than you'll ever know. I want to make angels with you in the snow.'

He leans forward and sings the final lines to me.

'Ella, you mean more to me than you'll ever know. I'm never gonna let you go.'

I reach out to him but he ends with a flourish, bringing his right arm up and over his head, rock star style. He even throws his plectrum in the air before taking a bow.

'That was fantastic. I love it, thank you,' I say clapping excitedly.

'My pleasure.'

'It's brilliant. When did you write it?'

'This morning. I've had the tune in my head for a while but the lyrics are thanks to you.'

He looks at me and I melt.

'Ah, that's so lovely, Tom.'

'Well, you bought me the ring, I just wanted to give you something special too.'

'No-one has ever written me a love letter, let alone a song. I was dumped by Post-it note once but that doesn't count.'

He laughs and I throw my arms around his neck and kiss him.

'Play it again, Tom.'

Shame he's not called Sam.

He takes centre stage and sings the song again. When he's finished, I get to my feet and applaud. In my ridiculous get-up, I'm less rock chick, more rock chicken. Plucked and trussed.

'How long did it take you to write?' I ask him.

'Not long. I got the hook and the rest just followed.'

'That was such a lovely thing to do. Can you tape it for me?'

'Sure, no problem.'

'What's it called?'

He takes a mouthful of wine and gulps it down.

'*Love Ella.*'

'Oh! Tom! I really do love you.'

'I know.'

Chapter twenty

Build your brand

Tom and I are having a Quiet Night In or *QNI* as he likes to call an evening in front of the telly with a bottle of wine and a bowl of pasta. It's not very rock and roll. But it's our favourite way of spending an evening, just the two of us, on the sofa, a decent bottle of wine and a video. Bliss.

These days, he's usually the headline act, which means he closes the gig and invariably misses the last train. I would rather he stayed put, rather than spending a fortune on a cab or getting into a car with someone who has had a skinful.

Tonight, he's made us chilli con carne. He hasn't got a sweet tooth so that means no pudding but it doesn't stop me from stopping off at Maison Bertaux on my way home and indulging in a slice of meringue.

'Hungry, love?' he asks expectantly as he dishes up the meal.

'Starving,' I tell him. 'Haven't eaten all day, just some raspberries.'

Omitting to mention the other ingredients in a raspberry Pavlova: eggs, sugar and cream.

'How was last night's gig? I've never been to Cardiff, is it nice?'

'Didn't see much of it. They'd shut off a section of the motorway so we were late getting there. Dave drove like the clappers. His acoustic set went down quite well but then I went on and blew the place apart. They love Tom Tyler.'

He tastes a mouthful of chilli from the pot and smiles approvingly. He ladles the sauce into two bowls, dribbling a trail of shiny brown droplets across the cooker. The gas hisses in protest. Tom doesn't notice.

'Good crowd though. Had a queue of people waiting for my autograph.'

'Get you, that's great. You must be tired. What time did you get back this morning?

'Dunno but I'm knackered and my back's killing me. We ended up sleeping in Dave's car. I had the gear stick stuck up my ...'

'Tom, the rice!'

I grab the pan and haul it, at arm's length, into the sink. Tentatively, I lift the lid on the acrid stench and the steam acts as a facial sauna. A circle, like white tarmac coats the bottom of the saucepan.

'Doesn't matter. We can eat it without. I need to lose some weight,' I tell him with a grin.

'You look alright to me. More than alright.'

He kisses me. In full view of next-door's tabby who is peering at us through the kitchen window.

'Look, a peeping Tom,' he says chuckling at his own joke. 'Does he remind you of Marmalade?'

'No, he just showed me his bottom, I'd say he was more like Peter.'

'You really don't like that guy, do you?'

'Nope,' I say taking a mouthful of chilli.

It's hot. I run to the tap and gulp some cold water.

I hand Tom a bowl and spoon and he eats, leaning against the worktop.

'So you definitely think he'll be back? Dunno why they don't just get shot of the guy and put you in charge.'

'They won't do that. He's in with all the clients. He's probably got some dirt on some of them too. Besides if they fire him, half the clients will go with him. The board can't risk losing that sort of money.'

'Bet you're dreading him coming back,' he says, beads of sweat erupting on his forehead.

'My plan is to make my mark and prove myself before he gets back and ruins everything. At least then the board will know what I can do.'

'Must be horrible having to work with a dick like that.'

'Needs must when the devil drives. And Peter's definitely at the wheel.'

I shrug. Tom scrapes his bowl with his spoon and the noise makes me shiver.

'Your Mum wouldn't want you having to put up with all this crap. She'd really worry if she knew what they put you through.'

'She doesn't need to know. I'm a big girl. I can handle it.'

'I'm doing a gig over her way soon, I'll pop in and see her before the show, take her some shopping.'

'Yeah, she'd like that. Thanks, I'll let her know.'

Snuggled up on the sofa, we finish our food and I hide my bulging stomach under a cushion hoping he doesn't notice.

'Ah don't worry love. I've already had to unbutton my jeans. Since we've been together, I haven't stopped eating. Look!' he lifts his T-shirt to reveal a protruding belly.

Less of a six-pack and more a result of drinking too many six packs. Like the way cream cheese turns to cottage cheese on my bottom.

'I'm here most of the time these days. Why don't you let me help out more? The mortgage repayments on this place must be crippling you. What's the interest rate now, nine, ten percent? It's crazy. I met a bloke the other night who had his house repossessed. I think he worked in advertising too, funnily enough.'

'That's not funny, that's tragic,' I tell him. 'Anyway, I'm getting paid soon, so don't worry.'

'I just want to do my bit and give you some space to find another job.'

I would love to get out from under Peter but I need to have something better lined up. Besides, I am happy for him to pay his share but I don't want him going over the top and paying towards the mortgage. I am not comfortable taking that sort of money. Mum has always told me to pay my own way and not rely on anyone else.

'Buy me dinner sometime. It's more romantic than paying bills,' I suggest.

'Sure, I'll take you to dinner whenever you like but you know what I'm saying, don't you? Or do I have to spell it out? I want to spend every moment I can with you. Go to bed with you. Wake up with you. Well, on the nights I'm not gigging obviously. But I want us to live together, forever, Ella.'

'Really? We're happy as we are, aren't we?'

'Yes, that's why I want to be with you. You're the one, Ella.'

He takes my hand in his and kisses me. He is lovely and he wants to look after me. I've spent so long taking care of Mum, I find it hard to accept help. I look around, his guitar is propped against the wall in the corner of the room, his tapes are stacked in neat piles on the shelf and his feet are most definitely under my table. I can smell them. It's a manly smell. I like it. It makes a change from overpowering pot pourri.

He holds me in his arms in one of his big, reassuring hugs and lets out one of his infectious laughs.

'Do you remember that time in Brighton when the candyfloss blew off the pier? Your face!'

If he wasn't here, I would miss the sound of that laugh.

'I love you being here too,' I tell him.

'Then let me help. The last thing we want is for this flat to be repossessed,' he says, smiling.

Repossessed. The word hits me like a bullet to the brain.

'Don't say that. I'm working. It's not going to happen. I won't let it,' I tell him defensively.

'Sorry, love. I didn't mean to worry you. Anyway, why should you fund my lager habit?' he laughs.

'With me here, life will be so much easier for you. Maybe you can even think about saving up for a deposit for a flat for your Mum and help her escape the landlord's clutches. Wouldn't that be something?'

Mum and landlord. The double whammy. How could he know the effect those two words would have on me? My veins flood with adrenalin and my heart pumps faster.

'Mum's fine. She's happy.'

'That lot at CBA screwed you once; they'll do it again,' he replies lighting up a cigarette and accidentally blowing smoke into my face. I cough. He walks away. I can't help wishing this was more romantic and based on more than just money.

'Tom. It's early days. Perhaps we just stay as we are. Why risk spoiling everything?

'Are you saying you don't love me?'

'No, of course not, I'm saying I do love you. Very much which is why I don't think we should rush into living together.'

'Let me know when you think the time is right, Ella' he says bitterly.

'Oh Tom, I didn't mean...'

He takes a final drag on his cigarette and stubs it out in the ashtray. I look into his eyes, hoping to see some warmth.

'Forget it, Ella. I only wanted to help,' he says coldly.

'And you do. You make me laugh, you make me happy,' I tell him running over to him and holding him. It's like trying to hug a fridge.

'Yeah and you make me happy too,' he says looking more miserable than I've ever seen him.

Chapter twenty-one
Have the Big Idea

I hate being late for anything. Let alone Tom's big night. With his picture and a great review in this week's *'Time Out'*, he should attract quite a crowd. A group of girls push past me. I follow them into the pub. One night a week, the back room turns into a smoke-filled sweatbox, one of the hottest music venues in town attracting some of the most talented new musicians around. I edge into the packed club and hand the girl on the door the few quid entrance fee. In return, she rubber-stamps the back of my hand. I can hear Tom singing his latest number, *'Don't tell me you love me and expect a reply. Don't tell me you love me and expect me to lie.'*

I remember him telling me it took him minutes to write. The lyrics came to him when he was having his lunch. Very rock and bread roll.

He looks gorgeous on stage, in a white shirt and blue jeans. He has a great voice, a talent that makes him all the more attractive. Judging by the smiles on some of the women's faces in the audience, I'm not the only one who fancies him. Even a couple of the men look enamoured. I weave through the crowd, bouncing off beer bellies and trying not to knock into drinks and the red hot tips of cigarettes. The smoky air stings my eyes and someone jabs their elbow in my face. I spot a space at the side of the room and edge into it. Immediately a tall girl with spiky blonde hair positions herself in front of me, blocking my view so even when I stand on tip-toe, I can't see Tom.

'Thanks very much. I've been Tom Tyler and you've been great. Goodnight.'

Whistles and applause fill the room. Slowly, he makes his way towards the back of the room and he is now close enough for me to see the sweat glistening on his forehead. He lifts his arm and wipes his face with his shirt-sleeve. I reach out for him but the crowd surges forward, closing the gap between us. Everyone seems to want to shake his hand and pat him on the back like they think his talent might rub off on them. I want to rush forward and hug him but I force myself to hang back; this is his time. Someone steps on my toe. I look up to see the blonde. She may be model-thin but she's no light-weight. No shrinking violet either. She manoeuvres herself into pole position, thrusting her double DD chest into Tom's doubly delighted face.

'I love your act and I love you,' she gushes, taking hold of his shirt collar and gently pulling him towards her. She kisses him on the cheek with lips as bulbous as her breasts. Big, wide and sticky with red lip-gloss, her mouth is like a couple of spare ribs coated in bar-b-q sauce.

'Can I have your autograph?' she simpers, in an accent that's pure Hollywood via Harlow.

She hands him a pen. She's organised, I'll give her that.

'No problem, blondie. Where shall I sign?'

His eyes follow hers.

'Take your pick,' she tells him, helpfully holding open the top of her shirt.

I want to slap her or at least button up her blouse. But I want to see what Tom does next.

'Eeny, meany, miney, mo,' he says, unaware I am watching as his index finger moves from left to right like a metronome.

It comes to rest on her left breast.

'What's your name?' he asks.

'They don't have names,' she giggles making her breasts bounce.

'I meant your name. But, I like that, it's funny,' he looks at her approvingly and laughs.

No, it's not. Not remotely amusing. I am about to tell her to leave him alone. But when I open my mouth nothing comes out. It feels like I've been punched in the windpipe.

'I'm Cara. C-a-r-a. Call me,' she says, sliding her business card into his pocket.

'Whoa! I'm trying to keep a steady hand here,' he laughs leaning forward. '*To Cara with love Tom x*. There you go.'

'Yes, and there you go,' I think pushing through the crowd until I am beside her.

I thrust out my chest, like two drawing pins in a notice-board.

'Thanks Tom. I'm never going to wash Eeny and Meany again. Call me, yeah?' she says ignoring me.

I am now close enough to him to smell the drink on his breath. His eyes are like saucers and his pupils dilated.

'Ella! I didn't know you were here.'

Obviously.

'Tom, why ...' I begin but he cuts in.

'Did you see me? They love me. They all love Tom Tyler.'

'I noticed,' I remark sourly.

'They like the love songs,' he says reliving the applause and the adulation.

'Really?' I ask, my ego getting the better of me and hoping I'm the inspiration. 'Written any new ones about me?'

He nods.

'Which ones?'

He turns away to chat to another fan, one of the girls I saw outside. She paws him, hanging on his every word. Her two friends run over and together they swamp him underneath copious amounts of bare flesh. One kisses him. The others follow suit as they laugh and egg each other on. My heart plummets from the place it soared to only seconds ago. I feel humiliated.

'Don't let them do that,' I tell him.

'Calm down, love. It's my job. It's not about you. Not everything is about you,'

That stings.

'Let's go, Tom – we can talk about this at home. I've got an early start and...' I say to the back of his head as he turns to smile at a bloke who hands him a pint.

'You go. I'm staying,' he tells me raising the glass to his lips.

'Drink that and let's go,' I tell him firmly.

'Don't tell me what to do.'

His tone is aggressive but he's still smiling for the fans.

'But we need to talk, Tom. Who was that girl?'

'What girl?'

'The one with the boobs. The one who put her card in your pocket.'

He shrugs his shoulders and scans the room, looking for someone to rescue him.

'Her name's Cara,' I tell him. 'I heard her tell you.'

'Tom Tyler has got lots of fans.'

He may be talking about himself in the third person but he's putting himself first. He waves his left hand dismissively at me.

'Where's your ring, Tom? You're not wearing your ring.'

'Oh that,' he says airily. 'It's best the girls think Tom Tyler is single.'

'But you're not a pop star. You can't...'

'I can do what I like. Just go home and have a cup of tea with one of your fancy chocolate biscuits.'

Why is he talking to me like this? I'm Tom Tyler's biggest fan.

'Don't be like this, Tom.'

'Just go!' he hisses at me, still smiling at the girls.

I stumble out of the door. I want to be sick. My insides bunch together making me feel light-headed. A gang of women push me out of their way, dressed in skimpy tops and short skirts.

'Oh, look Tom Tyler's on tonight. Did you see his picture in *'Time Out'*? I wouldn't kick him out of bed,' says one spotting his publicity shot outside the pub.

'Let's go in and find him, perhaps he needs someone to hold his microphone,' leers another.

'Fight you for it,' say the other two birds of prey as they all link arms and go into the club.

He's not theirs to lust after. Their Tom Tyler is not my Tom Tyler. I breathe in and wait for the night air to anaesthetise me. Far from numbing the pain, it freezes it into a ball that sits like a toxic toad in my guts.

Suddenly, I see a movement in a nearby doorway. I step forward.

'You're Cara, aren't you?' I ask her in a voice I hardly recognise.

She seems shorter, less striking. Even her chest seems smaller.

'Get away!' she cries, her voice now more East End than West Coast.

I don't know what possesses me but I yank open her shirt.

'Ah yes, here we go, 'To Cara with love Tom x'. Tom is my boyfriend, not yours.'

She wraps her jacket around her chest. Shame she couldn't have been this modest earlier on.

'Your boyfriend? He's a performer. He's public property,' she snarls.

'Leave Tom alone. He'll have forgotten you already. Trust me, he won't even remember your name.'

'Cara!' shouts Tom his voice filling the door-way. 'Cara, you okay?'

To my horror a small group of loved-up fans gathers behind him. Cara obliges them with an Oscar-winning encore. She is every inch the drama queen.

'She attacked me, Tom,' she says in her best American drawl, squeezing out a tear.

Looking him in the eye, she lets her jacket fall open. Her bust is centre stage with Eeny and Meany appearing as a double bill.

'Please, come home, Tom,' I plead.

'You go,' he shouts.

'Go on, then, go!' I say to Cara as she stands her ground.

Then I realise Tom was talking to me.

'Sure you're okay?' he asks Cara as he puts his arm around her and guides her back inside.

'Tom, please,' I say unable to comprehend how the evening unravelled so disastrously.

'Go! You've done enough.'

This is my fault?

I wondered who had been the inspiration for the lyric, *'Don't tell me you love me'*. Now I know.

Chapter twenty-two

Do your research

'Who's the girl?' asks Adam his head swivelling to follow the plate of warm croissants being carried to another table by one of the waiters.

'I don't know her. But she wants to know Tom. He was like a different person. So nasty.'

'Had he been drinking?' asks Adam.

'No more than usual. But he was very odd. I didn't know him.'

Adam drums his fingers on the table and looks me in the eye.

'Does he do drugs?'

I am so shocked I don't answer.

'Sorry, I just thought if he was acting strangely, it might explain it.'

Then I remember Tom's pupils, huge and dilated.

'You don't think he ...?' I ask.

'I don't know,' Tom snaps. 'Sorry, I haven't got long. I'm in a new business meeting at nine. Who arranges a meeting that early? At least, we'll have bacon sandwiches,' he says eyeing up the chocolate éclair on my plate, having polished off his own in two mouthfuls.

'Have it,' I say, pushing the pastry towards him.

Only Adam would have afternoon tea for breakfast.

'Sorry you were saying, you got to the club and saw her with Tom?'

'Yeah, she was so pushy but he didn't seem to mind. Then again, he looked off his face.'

'Very rock 'n roll,' he says dryly. 'Anyway, I'm sure he didn't mean anything. It just goes with the territory, I suppose. At least she didn't throw her knickers at him.'

'She probably wasn't wearing any.'

Adam brightens at the thought.

'That's not the point, Adam,' I tell him. 'He treated me as if I meant nothing to him. He was only talking about moving in a couple of days ago.'

'What? You've only known the guy five minutes,' says Adam before shifting uncomfortably in his seat and changing the subject. 'How's the job going? Bet you love the power?'

'You're kidding. I'm going to do what you suggested and befriend the clients. But I worry about every decision I make. If I get it wrong, we could lose a client and then people lose their jobs. How do you do it?'

'I'm lucky. I don't make any big decisions; the Creative Director does all that,' he smiles.

He nods at the waitress who knows to bring him another cake, anything, as long as it's chocolate.

'We've lost High-Pro. The agency is on its knees and everyone's worried about their jobs,' I tell him watching the queue for take-away Italian coffee snake out of the door.

'Agencies lose accounts all the time. And they win news ones. If you want to cheer the staff up, take them on a team-building event. I did it with my lot last year. It worked wonders.'

'What? Like everyone building a raft out of raffia? What's the point of that?'

'You can do whatever you like so long as you work as a team. I can give you the number of the company that organised ours if you like.'

'No thanks, we can't afford it.'

'I bet you can.'

He looks at me intently as the waitress places a thick spiral of fresh cream chocolate roulade down on the table. He offers me a forkful but I can tell he wants it all to himself. Besides, I've no appetite after Tom's performance. And I don't mean his act. I shake my head obligingly and Adam tucks in.

'That girl's really got to you, hasn't she? Don't let her upset you,' he says, wedging in more cake.

'She's got massive tits and legs up to her neck,' I say feeling increasingly flat-chested and fat-thighed. 'Bloody Cara.'

Adam jabs the air with his fork.

'Cara? Tall, skinny with sticky-up blonde hair?'

He talks with his mouth full. If anyone other than Adam did that, I'd leave the table. I nod and lean forward, anxious to hear more. He catches the eye of a passing waiter and orders a glass of water.

'Go on,' I say impatiently.

'Phoney American accent?' he asks.

'False, like her boobs,' I reply.

I listen carefully, wanting to know all about my nemesis.

'If it's the girl I'm thinking of, I worked with her last week on a jingle. She's a session singer. Really fancies herself. She was all over anyone she thought could give her a leg up.'

'Or a leg over. Sounds like it could be her but there are tons of leggy blondes in London,' I say.

I slump back in my seat, defeated.

'Not with her accent, there aren't. And that place is just where she would hang out, desperate to be spotted. She'll do anything to break into the business. She's a real gold-digger.'

He eats three mouthfuls of cake in quick succession. Each bite fuels another attempt to discredit her.

'When I worked with her, I thought she said her name was Karen. So I kept calling her Karen. 'My name's Cara, C-A-R-A.' she would say. The more annoyed she got, the more I wound her up.'

Adam mimics her perfectly. He laughs then stops suddenly.

'Did Tom stay at yours last night?'

I blink at him.

'Yes.'

He looks at me uneasily and raises an eyebrow.

'He woke me up crashing about in the kitchen,' I tell him. 'Must've been about six, it was almost light. God knows what he was doing. Eventually, he came to bed stinking of booze. I pretended to be asleep.'

'Not frightened of him are you?' he asks.

He watches me closely. I look away. His serviette is in shreds in front of me. I don't remember doing that. I am holding the last piece in my hands.

'No, he would never hurt me,' I tell him.

I put the pile of white tissue paper to one side and toy with the sugar bowl, pushing it in circles with my hands.

'He already has,' he replies. 'What will you do now?'

This must be serious; Adam has put his cake down.

'Get on with my work. I can't afford to mess up. With Peter away it's the perfect opportunity to make my mark.'

'And Tom?' he asks.

I don't know what to say.

'What d'you think I should do?'

'I don't know, Ella. You've got to talk to him, I suppose.'

'I'm not sure there's anything to say after last night.'

He shrugs his shoulders.

'I'm sure he regrets it now. He must know he's lucky to have you,' he says with the gentlest of smiles.

'Try telling him that.'

'I will if you want me to.'

I shake my head, vehemently. He jabs his finger into the last of the chocolate cream on the plate and licks it.

'Better than sex,' he says.

'Really? So how is your girlfriend?' I ask relieved to change the subject. 'Do I detect trouble in paradise?'

Suddenly, I feel much brighter.

'I've known Jan since grammar school, we're at the comfortable stage.'

'Like an old pair of slippers?' I smirk at him.

'Yeah, but that's fine, isn't it?'

I am not sure if he's asking me or telling me. Either way, is it fine to be in your early twenties and in a relationship that's so cosy it's comatose?

'How's her job?' I ask. 'Still can't believe you're going out with a doctor.'

I have never met Jan but from what Adam tells me they don't have much in common. She sounds very serious and sensible. I can't imagine she'd know what to do with a jug of cream.

'You saying I'm stupid?' he asks good-naturedly. 'Yeah, it's going okay, I think. I hardly ever see her. She's on nights at the moment. Be better when she's doing day shifts again.'

'So are you living together now?' I ask feeling like a piece of flint has lodged inside my heart.

'Yeah, a house in Clapham, just off the Common,' he tells me looking away.

A house? He'll be telling me she's barefoot and pregnant next.

'She's mentioned starting a family but I'm trying to talk her out of it. Not ready for sleepless nights yet.'

Thank goodness for that.

'When did you move in together?' I ask, trying to sound casual.

'A few weeks ago. Her Dad gave her the money for a deposit. Think it was a tax dodge or something. Anyway, he's obsessed with getting her on the property ladder.'

My guts knot together. I try to force a smile.

'You okay?' asks Adam, putting his hand gently on my arm.

It feels warm and reassuring. I pull away.

'I'm fine, but I must go,' I tell him. 'Meeting with Josh. That man's so boring. The minute he opens his mouth I switch off.'

'I remember,' says Adam chuckling. 'I fell asleep in his Dreamie Beds presentation. Luckily, the client thought it was some sort of witty homage to his product. He even gave us more business because of it.'

'Oh yeah, Jill's told me that story. It's a good job she's in there with me, taking notes. I never thought I'd say this but she's great; I'd be lost without her.'

'Does she still wash her smalls in the office?' he asks with a knowing grin.

'Now she's working for me, she hasn't got time,' I say smiling.

He jumps up and hugs me good-bye. It feels wonderful. I jerk backwards and run out of the door. Then I stop, look over my shoulder and wave. He doesn't see me; he's at the counter paying the bill. I quicken my pace and dart into the newsagent for some chewing gum. I need something to keep me awake during my meeting. The queue is half way down the shop and full of impatient people like me, all wanting to be served first. I catch sight of this week's *Campaign* on the shelf.

'High-Pro Fires CBA,' screams the headline.

Now it is official, the whole of Adland will know we've failed. I walk towards the agency down-hearted but when I arrive in the creative department I switch on my bright and breezy-mode.

'Morning, Jill, how are you today?'

'Fine thanks, Ella. You look tired. You okay?'

'Yeah, didn't get much sleep last night, stressing out about the meeting,' I lie and then wish I hadn't.

Good job I never pursued my dream of becoming an actress; I'm rubbish.

'Never worry about work or men. Life's too short,' she advises with a wink.

'Instead of taking notes in the meeting, can you check out some information on team building events, venues, activities, that sort of thing? Just get some ballpark costs? Thanks.'

'Sure,' she replies following me into my office. 'How exciting.'

Reluctantly, I replay the events of last night in my mind, trying to make sense of what happened. Now, standing here amongst the calm opulence of the agency, vases of orchids and vast white walls lined with awards, I can almost pretend it never happened. Did Tom really tell me to leave? Stop. I'm here now. I must focus.

'What's this, Jill?' I ask pointing to a white paper bag on my desk.

'Don't know. Someone left it in reception for you about five minutes ago.'

I peek inside and see an enormous chocolate and hazelnut croissant. Well, that's lunch sorted. Thanks, Adam.

Chapter twenty-three

If it doesn't work, tear it up and start again

'Can we afford it?' asks Josh when I suggest the idea of a team-building event at the end of our dullest meeting to date.

'Can we afford not to?' I reply. 'Everyone is on their knees. Business is bad. People are worried about their jobs. It's worth a try.'

I pick at the croissant Adam gave me. Each mouthful reminds me I have a friend, even if I no longer have a boyfriend. Tom crossed a line last night. I couldn't bear to be like Mum, living for years in hope things would get better, one day.

'I'm not convinced an agency jolly is the answer,' Josh says. 'Waste of money, if you ask me.'

He has a way of dismissing me with a glance. I eat the last piece of the croissant, the crunchy end. It's made me feel a bit less jittery, must be the sugar rush.

'Sweet thought, thanks for that, Adam,' I think.

'Josh,' I say. 'We both know you spend more on lunch than the whole team-building budget.'

He likes to show-off when he's wining and dining clients by outdoing the table next to him and running up an eye-watering bar bill before anyone has even seen the menu. He once spent over a hundred pounds on a bottle of champagne. Even Peter blanched at signing that one off.

'Nice try, but once the fun and games are over, how do you propose we get more business through the door? We're sinking fast,' he snaps closing his box file just before I can impale him on his ring-binder.

'You're going to get us on every pitch list going and we'll hire some young, keen, inexpensive creative talent,' I tell him confidently.

'You don't have time to wet-nurse juniors.'

'So, we'll hire freelancers to help with the extra work.'

'On their rates?' he asks.

'No, you're right. Looks like it's back to plan A. I'll get onto the headhunter to send in some junior teams and ...'

The phone interrupts me. I answer it.

'Sorry to interrupt, Ella,' says Jill. 'I've got someone on the line for you.'

She knows I never take calls when I'm in a meeting. One slip-up, that's all it takes.

'I'll ring them back,' I tell her.

Josh pretends to be checking his papers but I know he's listening. He always is.

'It's Tom,' says Jill. 'He's insisting on speaking to you. He rang earlier. Sorry, I forgot to tell you.'

'Excuse me,' I mouth to Josh as I turn my back to him.

No doubt Tom has rung to apologise. About time.

'You made a scene at my work. So I thought I'd make one at yours,' he says, his tone edgy.

'I can't talk now, Tom.'

My default smart-arse comments can't save me know.

'You couldn't stop last night.'

This isn't like one of the films Tom and I watch, full of sharp, scripted responses. This is real life. My life. Tom's words are more powerful than any advertising slogan I have ever created.

'I'm in a meeting. I've got to go.'

My voice, small and uncertain, echoes how I feel. Josh is watching, barely recognising this weak, whispering woman.

'The same meeting you were in earlier when I rang?' Tom asks cladding each word in sarcasm.

That's rich coming from him. How dare he infer I am up to no good? I unfurl my crumbled body and hang up.

'Everything okay, Ella?' asks Josh. 'Can I get you a glass of water?'

Not unless it is holy water and you fancy flinging it over the spawn of Beelzebub, I think.

'I'm fine, thanks, Josh,' I lie because I can't afford to show Josh any sign of weakness.

'Sure, you look a little shaken.'

'Where were we?' I ask, sounding like my Mum.

She wasn't always a shadow of a woman. Once upon a time, dressed to the nines, in her sixties black and white silk polka dot dress, wearing a matching bandana and winged sunglasses, she could have passed for a film star. Her mile wide smile dazzled my father, for a while. But when their relationship died, so did her spirit. She cut out the joy in her life. Just like that.

'Oh yes, away days, they're fun, aren't they,' I say.

Funny word 'fun'. Not sure I know what it means anymore. A huge mental effort and I am back in the room.

'We can do this later,' suggests Josh eyeing me suspiciously.

'No, I'm fine,' my voice echoes uncomfortably inside my head.

I will not let Tom drag me under. I haven't known him long. And it seems I never knew him at all.

'Okay, so who's going to organise this so-called team-building event? And, don't look at me.'

'Jill,' I reply automatically. 'She deserves a chance.'

My mind presents me with an image of Tom's face, his achingly handsome features distorted with anger, just like they were last night. In that moment, I didn't know him. I didn't want to know him.

Josh's mouth is moving, his lips parted to reveal perfectly even teeth, the result of years of expensive orthodontic work.

'Ella for God's sake, focus! How do we persuade the board to sign this off? We can hardly bill the clients for our company jolly, unless we invite them too.'

'We're not billing the clients.'

'Not directly, but as good as.'

'No way, we're paying for this. Everything upfront and above board, for a change,' I reply. 'Smile! It worked wonders for Adam Hart's agency.'

'Adam Hart's agency is twice the size of ours and they've got money to burn. Didn't they all stay in a castle and do a spot of archery?

'It was clay-pigeon shooting but it's not what we do, it's doing it as a team that counts,' I tell him.

It's a direct quote from Adam and provides me with the ammunition to quash Josh.

'And we all know what our lot would like to do together,' he says raising his perfectly waxed eyebrows at me.

'They're adults, Josh,' I snap. 'I want solutions not problems.'

He is speechless. He has taken the bullet meant for Tom.

'Sorry, Josh, that wasn't fair. Please use your charm to persuade the board and I'll ask Jill to get all the facts and figures for you.'

'She is just a typist. Sure she's up to this?'

The word 'just' gets to me. I have heard it all my life. 'Just a girl.' 'Just a woman.' 'Just a mum.' I can't imagine the opposite: 'Just a boy.' 'Just a man.' 'Just a dad.'

'One minute you're saying a team-building event is nothing more than a glorified piss-up, the next it's too important for Jill to organise. Make up your mind. Do it yourself. Or give Jill a chance. I'm sure she'll surprise you.'

'I doubt that very much,' he says as Jill wafts past the open door, buffing her nails.

'I happen to know Jill's mum owns a huge property portfolio. Perhaps she can arrange for us to all stay in one of her country piles,' I suggest, knowing he'll warm to that idea. It would be like going home to Josh. His sister went to the same school as Lady Di.

'Really? Sounds amazing. Okay, Ella. You win. We'll give it a go but make sure this away-day doesn't turn into a whey-hey day. We can't afford the paternity suits.'

'Oh Josh, you cracked a little joke there. Well done.'

'Let's just hope the joke's not on you, Ella.'

Chapter twenty-four

Avoid superlatives

I have always felt a fraud. I wait for the hand on my shoulder and the voice telling me, 'You've had a good run, Ella. Now, off you go, there's a good girl. Close the door on your way out.'

Faced with interviewing a junior team fresh out of college, I remind myself I know more than they do about advertising. I re-apply my lippy and check my hair in my compact mirror. A stray curl sticks out to one side. I slap it down with the palm of my hand. It flies up again. The door opens.

'Ella. I've got Chloe and David for you,' says Jill.

I nod and she ushers them into my office.

'Hi there, I'm Ella, pleased to meet you. Come on in,' I say, one hand welded to the side of my head, as David manoeuvres their huge black portfolio onto the table.

They come highly-recommended. Adam loved their work but he's not hiring so he passed them onto me. I leaf through their ideas. They look beautiful but are inconsistent. I listen carefully, as the Art-Director, David talks about colours and typefaces. Chloe says nothing, just stares at me intently. Dare I risk moving my hand away from my head or will the wayward curl defy me? Perhaps she has noticed my roots need doing? I haven't had time to get to the salon. Is my lipstick too red? She's younger than me; she must know Ruby Berry is last season's shade. She holds my gaze for a moment longer than is comfortable. My other hand flies up to conceal my dark roots. She raises her eyebrows at me. Slowly I lower both my hands and sit on them as she outlines the first campaign in the portfolio.

'The headline fits with the brand's tone of voice and talks to the audience,' she explains.

I'll have to be all about with this one; she writes like a creative but thinks like an account handler, a rare but brilliant combination.

'And what was your input, David?' I ask.

'Me? I'm the art-director so obviously I drew it, duh,' he laughs.

He thinks he's being smart trying to make me look dumb. How stupid.

'I meant what was your input on the idea?' I ask.

He looks at Chloe. She shakes her head. He says nothing. Now I know who is pulling the strings. I look through their ideas. Most of them are ingenious but a few lack this raw brilliance.

'Some of this work shows real flair but other stuff is weak. Look.'

I flip back through their portfolio until I find an example. They exchange a nervous glance.

'But you've got talent. I'm going to give you a chance and offer you a short trial. We'll pay your expenses and give you some pocket money. How does that sound?'

The door opens and Alan Ferguson stands there.

He's wearing a new jumper, a slim-fitting green woollen polo neck. Perhaps it was a gift from the Italian waitress at the patisserie. I heard they're dating. It shouldn't bother me but it does.

'Hi, Ella, sorry to interrupt,' he says smiling at Chloe and ignoring David. 'Just need you to autograph this.'

He holds out a layout for me to sign-off.

'Can you give me ten minutes?' I ask.

He looks good. Green suits him.

'It's got to go now. Pete approved the concept before he left. I've done the tweaks he wanted. It just needs your signature,' he says.

He puts the storyboard in front of me. I want to like it but I don't. It's not on brand. I know the client won't buy it.

'Is there a problem?' he asks.

He flicks his hair away from his eyes and grins at me. For once his charm fails to work its magic.

'I can't sign this off, Alan. We both know it's not right.'

'Just initial it so I can get it biked over to the client,' he tells me coming out in an unattractive red rash on his neck. It clashes with his hair.

He is insistent, even offering me his pen and letting his hand brush against mine. Chloe is watching me closely.

'It has to go now. Just sign it off, please Ella,' he simpers. 'Pretty please.'

He winks at Chloe.

'No,' I tell him.

I've just said 'No' to Alan Ferguson. I give myself a pat on the back. His cocky smile fades.

'You need to redo it. Simplify the layout.'

'Come back, Peter, all is forgiven,' he mutters as he slams out of the office.

I've never seen him lose his temper before. Even angels have dirty faces in this business. I turn back to the team. Chloe is watching me from under her fringe.

'Okay, are you up for giving it a go?'

'Would we be working directly with you?'

'Yes, for the time-being, I'm acting the acting Creative Director.'

'Then, we'd love to,' she tells me, her face lighting up. 'I really like your work.'

She goes on to list my best campaigns in detail.

'Thanks,' I say stunned by her enthusiasm.

'If we do well, are we guaranteed a permanent job?' David asks, his tone pure steel.

'Wait and see. Someone better might come along tomorrow. Sorry if that sounds harsh, that's the business you're in. But you'll be working on live briefs. Who knows you may even get a television commercial out of this. It would look great on your showreel.'

They need to know this is Adland not a charity. That reminds me - Kitty Rescue.

'Chloe, how do you feel about being a cat?'

She slides a sheet of paper from the back of her folder and hands it to me. This girl really has done her homework. It's a letter she has written from Marmalade to me suggesting I give her Kitty Rescue to work on. It is brilliant, better than mine.

'Marmalade approves,' I tell her.

'Marmalade approves'? I can't believe I just said that.

'When can we start?' she asks her face lighting up like a Christmas tree.

I open the door.

'We have a new team, Chloe and David,' I tell Jill. 'Please put them in my old office.'

I pick up the phone and call Adam. His answer-machine kicks in. Shame, I'd have loved a chat but I settle for leaving a message.

'Just taken on Chloe and David, thanks for sending them over. They're great. Okay, talk to you soon. Thanks again. Bye.'

I replace the receiver and go to pour myself a large gin and tonic to celebrate. I enjoy the intoxicating smell of quinine. My hand is on the gin bottle when I opt for fizzy mineral water instead. New blood may be just the shot in the arm CBA needs right now but I need to stay sharp and be careful not to cut myself.

Chapter twenty-five

Avoid waffle

I'm dreading going home to Tom and put off leaving the agency for as long as possible by sorting through memos and signing-off art-work. Alan saunters in having re-worked his story-board. This time he doesn't smile, just hands me a pen to initial the layout he drops on my desk. The work is better but not his best.

'You haven't worked your magic,' I tell him flatly.

If looks could kill, I'd be flat on my back with his pen, driven like a stake, through my heart.

'Ella, it's on brief. We don't need to reinvent the wheel on this one. The courier's waiting, please sign it.'

'You're paid to be creative. If you can't do that you shouldn't be here.'

'It's a bloody trade ad. Nobody's going to care.'

'I care and so should you. That's what you get the big money for. Tell the courier to wait and redo it.'

I hand the board back to him and he snatches it from me. As he walks away, I see face has turned a violent shade of red. It clashes with his hair. For once, Peter's right, Alan is ginger. I wonder what I ever saw him.

I go into the corridor to find Wally chatting to Jill. He is about to start his night-shift. I invite them into my office for coffee. He insists on tea with milk and two sugars.

'Jill tells me you're taking us on holiday,' he says with a smile, displaying a full set of ill-fitting dentures.

He makes himself at home on the couch, luxuriating on the leather.

'I could do with some sea air,' he says.

'Jill's being very secretive. Even I don't know where we're going,' I tell him.

'So Jill, what's this one like as a boss then?' he asks her with a wink.

'Better than Peter,' she laughs, pouring herself a coffee.

'That's not hard,' I say.

'He's a naughty boy - only got himself to blame for the mess he's in,' says Wally slurping the last of his tea. 'He got too cocky. Thought he could get away with it but ...'

'Oh, God is that the time? I've gotta go. My evening class starts at seven; can't be late,' Jill says putting her cup down and heads off.

'Wally, can I ask you something?' I ask sitting down next to him.

'What d'ya wanna know, young 'un?'

'You met Tom. Just wondered what you thought of him?'

'Only saw the bloke for five minutes. I don't know him,' he says getting up and putting his mug on the table.

'Please Wal. First impressions.'

'Well, he's a charmer, I'll give him that.'

'And?' I prompt.

'Put it this way, if you were my daughter, he wouldn't have got his feet under your table so quick.'

'He doesn't live with me.'

'And where is he when he's not with you?' Wally asks.

'He crashes with a mate.'

'Believe him?'

I want to believe him but it's not the same thing.

'I don't know, Wally.'

'Yes, you do, young 'un. Yes, you do,' he says handing me a bar of chocolate. 'It's gone a bit soft but it'll still taste nice.'

I try to give him half but he's having none of it.

'You enjoy it,' he tells me. 'What's wrong? You look worried.'

'Nothing.'

I don't want to worry Wally. I'm not his problem.

'Tom can be so kind but ...' I tell him watching his face for a reaction.

'He can also be a right ...'

Wally is too much of a gentleman to say what he's really thinking.

'Listen, none of my business but Jill said she was worried about you. She's seen a difference since you've been with him.'

'Jill said that, really?'

And there was me thinking I was pulling the cashmere wool over everyone's eyes. I'm touched Jill even noticed.

'Sometimes the hardest thing to do, is the right thing to do,' Wally says giving me a salute as he backs quietly out of the door. 'Just do it.'

With Wally's fatherly words of advice still uppermost in my mind, I walk up my path and see the light on in the living room. My heart sinks. I should never have given Tom the key to my flat or my heart. Once, I longed for his arms around me after another stressful day but not tonight. When I open the door, the smell of stale smoke mingled with sweat hits me. Eau de Tom. When his fans get too overbearing, he can use it as crowd control.

'Hi love,' he says cheerily, turning down the volume on the television in my honour.

He's got a cheek after what he did last night and this morning.

'Sorry, I was out of order,' he says, hoisting himself off the sofa and walks over to me. 'Forgive me?'

'You can't talk to me like that,' I tell him steadily.

'I know. I'm sorry. It was the drink.'

And the drugs, I think.

'Presumably you weren't drunk this morning when you called me?' I say angrily.

He reaches out to put his arms around me. I step back.

Slowly and carefully, he raises his fist and just for a moment I see my father standing there, ready to strike me for getting between him and Mum in yet another argument. Now, I back away and knock against the table. Tom unfurls his fingers to reveal a gold heart pendant in the palm of his hand. He suspends the necklace from his forefinger. The heart swings back and forth like a pendulum and I am hypnotized by its rhythmic swinging. He loves me. He loves me not. But this heart is not the real thing; it can't be broken.

'Ella, I was out of order. I am sorry. The gig stressed me out. I'd had a drink. Everyone wanted a piece of me.'

I want to laugh in his face. He's Tom Tyler. Not Boy George.

'Let me make it up to you, please. Just give me time.'

'I haven't got that long,' I tell him. 'We're over. You need to find somewhere else to stay between gigs.'

'You don't mean that, Ella. I am so sorry. It's the drink. I'm not that person. I'll stop drinking, I promise, anything, just don't do this, please,' he says softly as he goes to fasten the fine gold chain around my neck.

I pull away and we both watch as the necklace falls, the heart slipping between the floorboards, pulling the chain down with it, the thin thread of gold slithering like a worm, out of sight. Tom stamps his foot to try and stop it from disappearing but it's too late.

'There goes last night's wages,' he says unable to disguise his annoyance.

'Well, if that's all you're worried about,' I snap.

'Sorry, I didn't mean it like that. Please Ella.'

He reaches out to me but he sees my face, taut with anger and disappointment and thinks better of it. My eyes dart to the crack in the floorboard. I wonder how long the necklace will languish in the dust, out of sight.

'You can't buy back my heart with a heart,' I tell him.

I turn round to look at him but he has one eye on the television, his hand reaching for the remote. I stand between him and the screen.

He tuts and throws the remote on the floor. The back snaps off and one of the batteries springs out and rolls under the sofa. I can't believe he can even consider watching a film. I am incensed and turn off the television at the set. He stomps over and flicks it on again just as the closing credits roll.

'Thanks! I've missed the ending. Happy now?' he grabs the flex and yanks the plug out of the wall.

The same sickening knot tightens in my stomach, the same one I felt when Adam told me he was living with his girlfriend. I need to know the answer to one question.

'Tom where did you sleep last night?'

He looks nonplussed.

'In a Photo-Me-Booth,' he replies without missing a beat.

An implausible answer but preferable to the alternative: Cara's place.

'Y'mean, one of those kiosks like they have in Woolworths for taking passport photos?'

'Yeah, a Photo-Me-Booth,' he tells me matter-of-factly, wondering why I need to define it.

I just need to be clear he's not confusing a Photo-Me-Booth with Cara's bedroom. It would be an easy mistake to make. I bet she's got a swirly seat that goes up and down too.

'Did you take your photo?' I ask.

'What?' he asks as if it's the most ridiculous question he's ever heard.

'Did you take your picture in the Photo-Me-Booth?'

'No, I was asleep.'

Of course, you were. Fast asleep, dreaming of Cara.

Tom is the archetypal bad-boy with exactly the right mix of narcissistic, Machiavellian and psychotic tendencies to make him irresistible to women who like that sort of thing. Add in the good looks and it's a potent cocktail. Delicious, dangerous and damaging, one too many and you're under the table and under him. Time to sober up just like Mum eventually did when she left Dad. Shame there's not the equivalent of the AA for people addicted to love.

'Hello, I am Ella, and I am a loveaholic.'

The first step to recovery is recognising I have a problem. The second step is walking away from the problem.

185

I wonder, was I madly in love or just mad about the boy?

Chapter twenty-six

Keep the concept relevant yet unexpected

'The Honeydrop client, Clive, will be here in twenty minutes and we know he's always on time. Josh was two minutes late for our last meeting and he wouldn't let him in. Quickly, show me your storyboard, Chloe.'

The brief Peter had said was perfect for me, ended up on Chloe's desk. She may not be a mum but she clearly knows how they think. Smiling confidently at me, she puts the work on my desk. The visuals are clear and simple. David's drawings are brilliant; they could sell the idea without any help from me.

'David has excelled himself,' I tell her. 'So have you.'

'Thanks, Ella. I'm so glad you like it,' she says following me as I walk away to speak to Jill.

'Chloe and David have done some fantastic work. Can you set up the boardroom for the presentation?'

'All done,' she tells me. 'Reception just rang through to say the client's here. Shall I go down and get him?'

I nod and check my hair. I got up early this morning to have it cut, coloured and scrunched. I pay a top stylist to make me look like I've just got out of bed.

'Morning, Ella, been jogging?' asks Clive.

He focuses on my hair as he bounds out of the lift like one of his father's over-enthusiastic gun-dogs.

'Lovely to see you, Clive,' I say making incredulous eyes at Jill behind his back and reminding myself to be nice, like Adam advised.

Clive looks at his watch and adjusts his cufflinks before taking off his overcoat and handing it to Jill.

'Sorry, ladies, I'm a tad early. Travelled up last night and spent a very interesting evening in a club full of girls who turned out to be chaps. Most disconcerting.'

I daren't ask how he discovered their true gender.

'You see all sorts in Soho, Clive,' I say steering him into the boardroom just as Josh arrives. 'I know a lovely restaurant, I can book it for us all next time you're down.'

'Oh, I'd like that,' he smiles.

Adam was right. Being friendly with clients is easier than I thought.

'Clive, how are you?' asks Josh shaking his hand and working his public school-boy charm. 'And your wife? Enjoying the new house? Marlborough isn't it? Beautiful place.'

'She's fine. We're both very excited to see what our architect has come up with. He's drawing up plans for a loft extension, should add a bit to the value of the property.'

'Fantastic. Good journey?' asks Josh.

I enjoy watching him work. It's a master-class in schmoozing. I can learn a lot.

'I was just telling Ella, I found myself in this amazing club last night. You might know it, Josh. Gorgeous girls, legs up to their necks and I'm thinking, 'Play your cards right, Clive and you'll be in here.' No such luck, a few bottles of incredibly expensive bubby later and it turns out they're all chaps. Even the one with the enormous...'

'Eyes?' I suggest motioning him to sit at the table. 'We've got some great stuff to show you so shall we make a start?'

Clive nods but I can tell his head is still in the nightclub, nestled in some bloke's cleavage, a latter-day Carmen Miranda, all falsies, feathers and forbidden fruit.

Josh clears his throat.

'Honeydrop Cough Syrup. Great brief, thanks Clive. Hope you like what we've done with it.'

Josh knows how to sell work to Clive, fortifying every word with credibility and integrity.

'We're positioning Honeydrop as the first thing mums reach for when their kids get sick. They need to trust the brand. We've come up with something very exciting. Instead of doing just a press ad, we have, for the same budget, created a TV commercial.'

Clive looks thrilled, like a small boy on his birthday who expects a goldfish but gets a puppy. Good old Chloe, I knew he would love it.

'Fantastic. Good thinking, Josh,' he says grinning broadly.

It was my idea, Josh, I think. You could give me some credit and glance my way occasionally.

Josh whips out the storyboards from underneath the desk.

'Picture this,' I say as I begin to outline the commercial. 'It's night-time, we hear a child coughing. He is trying to sleep but can't and is keeping the whole family awake, including the dog. Then, we see a big close-up shot of Honeydrop, thick and golden, being poured into a spoon. As if by magic, the kid stops coughing and the dog's eyes close. We even hear it snore. Big packshot, logo and finish.'

'Terrific, chaps. I love it but just one problem – you've got two actors in this commercial, the mum and the son. It's going to cost us a fortune in repeat fees.'

'No, it won't. The star of the show is the dog. We focus on his lovable face, awake then asleep. We never see the kid – just hear him coughing. And we never show the mum either – we only see her hand pouring the Honeydrop. We don't need an actress just a hand model,' I reassure Clive.

Clive is smiling – I've won him round.

'TV lets us hear the cough and then hear the silence,' I explain.

'I don't think you can actually 'hear' silence, Ella,' says Clive laughing.

He looks at Josh for approval and he obliges by joining in with the joke.

Josh stops laughing and for no reason, suddenly changes tack.

'Your budget is very tight, Clive. Maybe this would work better as a press ad?'

What is Josh up to? We've sold him on the idea of a TV commercial. It's much better value for money.

I look at Clive's face. He's that little boy again; bewildered as he watches the exciting puppy he's fallen in love with turn back into a boring goldfish. Josh is deliberately sabotaging our strategy. We've gone from a prime-time, thirty second TV commercial to a press ad in less than half a minute. How did that happen? I don't know what Josh is playing at but it's game over.

'We're not talking a cast of thousands. Just one dog,' I say, feeling the ground slip from under me.

'Directors don't come cheap,' says Josh. 'Plus there's the expense of the studio and the crew. We're talking a two day shoot, at least.'

If I had a gun, I'd shoot Josh myself. I retaliate by firing off ideas like rounds of ammunition.

'We'll use a new director, someone brilliant but hungry,' I say. 'I know someone who'll do it for cost and I can get the media boys to do a deal with breakfast TV. We can do this.'

I'm running on adrenalin and meeting myself coming back. Josh is getting jittery. And that's before he has even touched his coffee.

'By all means get your man to quote,' says Clive, paying lip-service to my suggestion.

'The director's a woman,' I explain. 'Her name's ...'

'I've only just got used to the idea of you working on my account, let alone a lady directing my ad.'

'Don't worry, Clive. I know just the chap for the job,' says Josh sniggering as Clive explodes with laughter.

'Just joking, Ella. Personally, I'd love to go the TV route. If you can get me a quote today, I can run it up the flag pole and see who salutes,' guffaws Clive. 'How does that sound?'

Like patronizing bullshit, I think.

'I'll bike the storyboard over to the director now,' I say biting my lip.

I give the Honeydrop layout to Jill.

'Those two are like school boys,' I tell her.

'Yes, but not ones you'd want to keep in detention,' she says rolling her eyes.

She's one step ahead of me and has a courier on stand-by. I ask her to get our TV production department to negotiate a good quote with the director. Just as I am about to walk back into the boardroom I hear Clive whispering.

'Will Peter be back to take this on, Josh? If we go the TV route, it will be a mega campaign for us. Ella may not be up to handling a project this size.'

Size isn't everything. A mantra I imagine Clive has no choice but to comfort himself with most nights. His poor wife must be easily pleased. I cough loudly and walk back into the room.

'Sounds like you need some Honeydrop,' jokes Josh in a rare moment of levity.

I ignore him but smile at the client.

'Thank-you so much for coming, Clive. I'll get back to you as soon as possible with that quote. And please give my regards to your wife,' I tell him.

We shake hands and Jill ushers him towards the lift. He'll be home in time to put his feet up with a nice cup of tea before a spot of hanky-panky with his Sloane-Ranger wife. I imagine she makes love wearing only a string of pearls and a tiara. Now I know Clive is safely out of ear-shot, I take a pot-shot at Josh.

'In your efforts to undermine me, you nearly lost us that one. Poor Clive didn't know what was going on.'

He snaps his file shut.

'Nothing personal, Ella. You can't expect me to encourage the client to spend money he hasn't got. Just doing my job and being honest with him.'

'Well, that's a first. Integrity isn't usually a stumbling block.'

'I'm not sure your judgement is as sound as it could be right now. You've obviously got some issues in your personal life.'

He looks away and straightens his tie. I can't believe he wants to turn my crisis into his opportunity.

'I never bring my home life to work,' I tell him.

'Ella, I was there when you took that call from your boyfriend. Admit it, you've taken your eye off the ball.'

I've got my eye on two balls. His. For now, I settle for giving him one of my looks, the one I reserve for Peter, Darren and Cara if I ever see her again. Josh picks up the negative vibe and scuttles off. I take the plates of untouched biscuits and plonk them on Jill's desk for people to help themselves. That's over a thousand calories saved. Now I need to be as resourceful with the client's budget.

'Adam called. Said to tell you he's running late and he'll see you at the restaurant,' Jill tells me, looking up from her typewriter. 'I put a note with the storyboard for the director asking if we could have the quote by close of play, hope that's okay?'

'Today, that's not giving them much time, is it?'

'Sorry, I couldn't help overhearing you arguing in the meeting and just thought if we act quickly, while Clive's still excited about doing TV, we might be in with a chance. I've chivvied up our TV department to liaise with them this afternoon.'

'Good thinking, Jill. Thanks.'

She really is firing on all cylinders today. Oh dear, I'm only supposed to have stepped into Peter's shoes not adopted his idiotic idioms.

'You're interviewing another team at three. And then I'd like to run some of my ideas past you for the team building event.'

'Great. We'll talk later,' I say running for the lift before the doors close.

By the time I arrive at the restaurant Adam has chosen what he wants and is buttering a chunk of bread.

'I'm having the steak. What d'you fancy? Quick, grab the waiter,' he says between mouthfuls of seeded granary.

I order the cod then reach across, pick the poppy-seeds out of his bread and eat them one by one.

'Have it all. It's too healthy for me. How's it going?' he asks scoffing the last white roll.

'Usual Josh crap. He tried to pull the rug from under me, in front of the client,' I tell him.

'No change there then. Nothing you can't handle,' he smiles. 'Are you doing what I told you and remembering to smile at the client?'

I grin at him by way of reply.

He laughs.

'Once more with feeling? Anyway, how's the new team doing?'

'Chloe's brilliant at the ideas and David draws them up like a god,' I tell him as our food arrives.

His sirloin steak looks delicious. Reluctantly, I push aside my creamed potatoes and spear a flake of boring but low-calorie fish.

'Don't you want that?' Adam asks eyeing up my mash.

I shake my head and he helps himself. Lately, there have been too many opportunities to eat too much and too little time to work it off. I caught Darren looking at my legs the other day. He was no doubt thinking, 'Look at the size of those thighs.' Or something equally complimentary. I must ask Jill to renew my gym membership and get me a new leotard, something with a bit more give. My waist measurement has increased in direct proportion to my new, over-inflated salary.

The restaurant is packed. Waiters move gracefully around the room, running to and fro tending to their customers' fragile egos. If they can't have the pay rise they want, at least they can have their steak cooked just the way they like it. Adam's eyes dart around the room, checking out the plates of other diners making sure no-one's got something bigger and better. He seems satisfied that he's chosen well and eats his meal quickly in big, rapid mouthfuls.

'Is that good?' he asks pointing at my food.

I nod. He takes it as an invitation to sample my meal. I put my knife and fork down. I know when I'm beaten.

'Chloe does all the Kitty Rescue stuff for me. It's great, I don't have to pretend to be Marmalade anymore,' I tell him wondering if he'll eat the deep-fried courgette flower.

I really want those potatoes now. Too late, Adam has polished off the lot.

'So Chloe is Marmalade! What did she do to deserve that? Seriously, you're giving her other stuff to work on too?'

He's chewing on the courgette floret and pulls a face.

'Be mad not to. The Honeydrop concept was awesome. She's so sharp but I think David would make a better designer than an Art-Director. I still can't understand why Chloe's so wedded to David.'

'Because they're married,' he tells me matter-of-factly, spitting the offending mouthful into his serviette.

'What?'

'Well, as good as. They live together – didn't you notice they've got the same address?'

I hadn't even read that part of their CVs, no eye for detail, that's my trouble. That'll teach me to be all about the big picture.

'Doesn't matter, does it? Can't imagine they're lovey-dovey around the office. Chloe struck me as a cold fish when I met her,' he says handing his empty plate to the waiter and simultaneously giving detailed instructions about what he would like for pudding.

'Chocolate cheesecake, please, a nice big bit,' asks Adam. 'With double cream instead of crème fraiche. Hate that stuff, tastes like it's gone off.'

'Cold fish? I don't get that impression. She reminds me of me when I first came into the industry.'

'You? But you're lovely,' he says showing me the dessert menu.

His words dance happily inside my head.

I could kill for an almond and pear tart. My blood sugar is so low I could take candy from a baby. But that's the trouble with Soho, it's a kids-free zone. No young mums with sticky toddlers. No elderly people either, just greedy young professionals, all fighting over the icing on the cake. Perhaps I should take a bite of the cherry instead, fewer calories.

'Why didn't they tell me they lived together?' I wonder.

'They did. It's on their CV. First thing I noticed.'

'That reminds me I'm seeing another junior team at three – gotta run.'

Or waddle, I think as I hand Adam a twenty-pound note. He refuses.

'My treat. Can I have your pudding?' he asks.

'I haven't ordered one.'

'I was going to have the Raspberry Pavlova for you.'

'Be my guest. Thanks for lunch, Adam.'

'Oh yeah, I forgot. We're going to have a house-warming party soon, nothing special, just a few people over for dinner. I'm dreading it. Jan's planning on inviting some of her new doctor friends. I know they're all be thinking, 'What is she doing with him, some jerk in advertising.'

'You're as good as they are.'

'They think I'm thick because I went to art school not University. Anyway, I'll let you know the date nearer the time but it may have to be midweek to fit in with their shifts. Hope you can make it. Bring Tom if you want. Everything okay?' he asks when he sees my face.

I've gone from smiley to sullen in a heartbeat.

'Not exactly. Think I've been suffering from Bad Boy syndrome but I think I'm on the Twelve Step Programme to recovery.'

'What?' he asks confused as to why I'd make a joke about something that's not funny.

'Don't worry. I'm fine. We can talk about it later. I've got to go now.'

I ease myself out from between the tables, my bottom skimming the soup of the person next to me.

'Promise you'll come?' he pleads.

'Promise.'

He smiles. I'm not sure if it's at me or at the glorious sight of his pudding that has just arrived.

'Here,' he says seeing my look of longing. 'Try this. Heaven on a plate.'

I take no persuading and open my mouth as he spoons in a mound of meringue and cream.

'Food of the gods,' I tell him as I run out of the door.

When I get back to the agency, I find a memo on my desk from Josh. Looks like Jill's quick thinking saved the day. The director, like everyone at the moment, is desperate for work and came back almost immediately with an unbeatable quote. Jill also persuaded Mr Media to drop everything to cut a great deal on air-time. Even Josh couldn't fault the final figure. We won't make much of a profit but the kudos we'll gain from this one ad will do wonders for our reputation.

I run into Chloe and David's office and feel just like I did the day I passed my eleven-plus, elated, knowing everything was about to change for the better.

'Honeydrop has approved the budget. Congratulations! You're going to make your commercial. Shoot starts next week so clear your diaries.'

Chloe stops what she's doing and glances at me as if she is mentally plotting her next three moves.

'Thanks for giving us this opportunity, Ella,' she says.

'It was your work that impressed the client. Thank you,' I reply.

'You'll be on the shoot too?' David asks me nervously.

'No, you'll be in good hands with the director and her crew; she's great. I'll get her to pop in and have a chat with you about the script. She loves it and can't wait to start working on it.'

Chloe seizes the moment, 'Do we have a permanent job then?'

'Oh, we need to talk,' I say the excitement I felt just a moment ago evaporating.

She watches me from under her fringe, saying nothing. I plough on desperate to fill the silence.

'Have you enjoyed your time here?' I ask.

'Are you hiring us or not?' she persists. 'Only Steve Winter has asked to see our work.'

She lets her word hang between us like a cobweb. And Steven Winter is the big fat spider in the middle, ready and waiting to snatch the prize away from me again.

'We'd be delighted to offer you a full-time position, Chloe,' I tell her.

'And David?'

'We'd be delighted to offer you...' I repeat.

'But we're a team,' says David angrily.

'I know and it's hard for you to accept this decision because you're in a relationship.'

This is a nightmare. If making other people's lives hell is what being a Creative Director is all about, Peter Richards is the man for the job.

'That's our final offer. If you're interested, I've seen a very talented Art-Director who would be perfect for you, Chloe.'

'I am still here,' hisses David.

'David, you're a great designer but you're not an art-director.'

'In your opinion,' he adds.

'Let me ask around for you,' I say flustered. 'There may be something going in our studio.'

He is studying me, making me feel uneasy.

'Chloe, please, think about what I've said. You're brilliant. This is your career we're talking about,' I tell her as I head back to my office.

I need to keep them both happy. That way, Chloe's more likely to accept my offer. If she works for Steve at KO'd, she'll be a lethal adversary in any pitch. I buzz through to Jill.

'Ask Darren to pop up.'

I should rephrase that. It sounds ghastly.

'Ella, I hear you want me,' says Darren appearing in the doorway.

Someone should tell him Kitty Rescue neuter randy alley cats like him for free.

'Knock, next time,' I tell him curtly.

'How's your boyfriend? He's a singer, isn't he? Bet he plays you like a guitar.'

He laughs, I don't. I saw that one coming. Darren is never troubled by original thought.

'I need a favour, Darren.'

'I don't give my favours away, unlike some people,' he says pointedly.

I remember that night, with him in my bed and feel sick.

'These comments need to stop. They're not funny. You're not funny.'

'And you're not my boss. You're just playing at it until I Peter gets back.'

'I am acting Creative Director for the foreseeable future and I've got the board's full backing.'

'Oh, touchy! Time of the month, is it?'

I try to imagine what sort of a woman a man like Darren would attract. No, can't think of one.

'Do you need anyone in the studio?'

'Who are you trying to off-load?'

'David. He's brilliant.'

'If he's so brilliant, you keep him. Chloe and David have only been here five minutes and you're already trying to split them up? That's one mighty big ego you've got there, Ella.'

I refuse to let him get to me.

'David's talented, much better than anyone you've got in the studio. Give him a break.'

'I don't have the budget. I'm struggling to hold on to the people I've got.'

'Okay, well, if you hear of anything, let me know, yeah?'

'Don't hold your breath, no-one's hiring. By the way, I saw your boyfriend's picture in *Time Out,'* Darren starts to laugh, a weasely wheeze. 'Tom Tyler, isn't it? He knows my mate, Cara.'

'I know, Darren,' I tell him. 'I know.'

Chapter twenty-seven

Check for errors

'Jill, why is there a half-used lipstick in my drawer? Where is my Blue Mountain coffee? And what have you done with my French sugar cubes?' shouts Peter as he barrels around his office disgusted by the last vestiges of my reign.

'Sorry, Peter no-one told me you were coming in today,' shouts Jill.

She doesn't look up but continues to type. Her shiny pink candy nails dance up and down the keys. Peter races over to her and rests his knuckles on the desk.

'Get your ducks in a row and get rid of this crap,' he yells.

'Leave her alone, Peter. Your stuff is in the cupboard,' I call as I approach the office.

Very slowly, I go in and gather up my things. He flings his coat across the back of the chair and hurls his leather brief-case on the sofa, narrowly missing my shin. He spots the white lilies, a thank-you present from the Honeydrop director.

'These stink!' he exclaims.

He carries the three-foot glass vase at arm's length across the room scattering pearl-shaped petals in his wake and sets it down on the floor beside her desk.

'Jill! Get Wally to dump this monstrosity before it kills someone,' he orders.

He looks down and blanches at the sight of the yellow pollen stain on his otherwise pristine shirt.

'Go to the shop on Jermyn Street and get me a new white shirt. They know my size but it'll need to go down one because I've lost weight.'

He examines his slightly less paunchy profile in the mirror.

'Jill's too busy to run errands for you,' I tell him. 'She's preparing for our hand-over meeting. I assume that's why you're here?'

'You two running the show now?'

He looks from Jill to me and sneers.

'We've been keeping things going in your absence,' I tell him.

'Thought I'd been fired and you could fill my shoes? You forget, they're very big boots and I've got friends in very high places.'

He opens a pack of cigarettes and offers me one.

'You know I don't smoke.'

'Thought the stress of your new role might have driven you to it. Or your new boyfriend might have got you hooked.'

He takes great pleasure in my horrified reaction. Who told him about Tom?

'Nothing escapes me, Ella.'

I try to defend myself by putting him on the back foot.

'Did you finalise the divorce settlement, Peter? Did your wife get custody of the pool boy?'

He ignores the jibe and calmly slides a silver lighter from his pocket, putting it on the desk for me to admire.

'I take it I still have a creative department? Guess there's only so much damage you could do in the time.'

'The board has no complaints,' I say.

203

Jill is standing beside me buttoning up her coat, her purse in her hand.

'I've got everything ready for your meeting, Ella. Just nipping out for your croissant. Can I get you anything, Peter?'

I smile and hand her a fiver.

'Oh, so you two are on first name terms now, how touching. I thought you couldn't stand each other,' says Peter.

'Get Peter an almond croissant, my treat,' I call to her as she waits for the lift. 'His blood sugar must be low to be so grouchy.'

'Not for me. I'm detoxing. I've lost so much weight. You should try it,' he suggests.

He gives me a sideways glance. By some unfair trick of osmosis, I appear to have gained the seven pounds he's lost. I look at him. The weight-loss doesn't look good. It ages him.

'Like what you see, Ella? For years, I was too busy to look after myself. Now, this is my time.'

'Is there any other, Peter?' I ask.

Peter is the most self-obsessed man I know. I wonder what he knows about Tom.

'When I took my brief sabbatical from this place, I was climbing the walls with boredom at home. No wonder all housewives are hooked on drugs.'

Not all housewives, I think, only the one crazy enough to live with him. His wife took tranquilisers when they married and took him to the cleaners when they divorced. She never has to see or hear him again. Unlike me, I seem to be wedded to him for life.

'I decided to join the gym in Highgate. Drive there every morning.'

It's two roads away from his house; he could walk it faster. And burn more calories.

'It's where I met a potential new client. We got talking on the treadmill and he was feeling neglected by his agency. He was very impressed by my credentials.'

'Wearing those tight shorts again were you, Peter?' I ask as a wave of nausea hits me like a broadside.

'You can laugh but he as good as offered me his business. I told the board and they bit my hand off.'

'So you bribed the agency to take you back?' I asked.

'I was taking a well-earned break,' he says. 'And my skill-set is irreplaceable.'

'If you say so, Peter.'

He checks the contents of his drinks cabinet before looking at me. Far from undressing me with his eyes, he mentally covers me up with a big baggy jumper.

'You've put on weight! Get a personal trainer. I've got one, Daniel, ex-Royal Marines and ex-Olympic coach.'

Add your ex-wife and you've got a full set, I think.

'He devised a personalised work-out strategy and an individualised nutrition programme for me.'

'You mean he put you on a diet?'

'He came to the house and cleared my cupboards of toxins. No processed crap. I've bought a juicer and just throw in whatever's hanging around – wheatgrass, alfalfa sprouts, ginseng.'

He lights up a cigarette. Guess he also pays Daniel to tell him nutrients cancel out the harmful effects of the nicotine. He sees me looking.

'I've cut down from forty to twenty a day. Daniel says it's good to maintain a balance. My new health regime means I can afford one or two pleasures.'

And the instructor can afford whatever he fancies. With Peter in such bad shape, Daniel's got a job for life. Peter draws on his cigarette and pulls his belt in another notch. He looks down and admires his flat stomach, at least that's what I think he's admiring.

'My counsellor says we should be transparent and not hide behind jargon. Looks like we need to get our ducks in a row and think outside the box.'

I raise my eyebrows. He pours himself a large whiskey.

'I've got an amazing therapist. For a woman she really knows her stuff; told me I've been blocked for years.'

'With all that roughage you've been eating, surely not?'

By keeping the flippant comments coming I avoid the real issue – what Peter knows about Tom.

'How much does she charge, Peter?'

'Best two grand I've ever spent.'

More money than sense, as Mum would say.

'Two thousand pounds? How many sessions have you had?'

'Enough to create the new me you see before you. And she makes herself available whenever I need her.'

'She must be on the phone to you day and night.'

'Ella, you need to work through your working-class hang-ups about money.'

I earn more in a year than Mum made in her life. It makes me feel guilty and Peter knows it.

'Heard you've been upsetting our golden goose. I don't want Alan Ferguson flying the nest because of you.'

'I need a word. When's good?' I ask.

He leafs through his Filofax, just in case a colonic irrigation appointment has slipped his mind.

'I'm free until this afternoon when I'm off to the floatation tank. It helps me get in touch with myself.'

If Peter was any more in touch with himself he'd be arrested.

'What do you want? I already know about the Honeydrop commercial and the new team.'

He pauses before delivering his next line, 'And I gather your boyfriend has moved in.'

'No, he didn't.'

'Oh come one, Ella, we all know a good looking guy doesn't have to find somewhere to live in London, just someone to live with.'

'Who told you about Tom?' I ask.

'I was in the pub, the one in Highgate village. Got chatting to some bloke. Had no idea who he was but when he mentioned his girlfriend, Ella worked in advertising, it fell into place.'

Peter loves having something on me.

'What did he say?' I ask, trying to sound nonchalant.

'Likes a drink, doesn't he? And the rest.'

He sniffs exaggeratedly and laughs, looking at me from the corner of one eye and checking my reaction. He stubs out his half-smoked cigarette and immediately lights another. We both know nicotine isn't his first drug of choice. When it comes to doing class 'A' drugs Peter is in a class of his own. Why else would he have clients lining up to work with him?

He inhales and blows two smoke rings in quick succession, moving his brief-case to one end and sitting down in the middle of the sofa, his arms outstretched along the back. He pats the space next to him and motions for me to sit down. I tentatively perch on the edge of the couch making sure I keep the maximum distance between us.

'We didn't sit around talking about you all afternoon, if that's what you think.'

I don't know what to think anymore. I'm still trying to figure out why Tom never mentioned meeting Peter.

'Sounds like Tom is going places. Obviously, our Little Arrangement still stands; you having a boyfriend doesn't change anything. It's not like you two are serious, or anything. So now your face has healed, we can make a date.'

'Our Little Arrangement' as you call it, expired the day you pretended to fire me. And, my private life is private.'

I feel my cheeks getting hotter.

'Really? Apparently you had a domestic in the middle of a meeting with Josh, hardly professional. I'm just thrilled you have a private life. Thought you were frigid,' he says.

I shouldn't have to take this lying down. No, totally the wrong metaphor.

'Peter, this has nothing to do with work. It's inappropriate. We need to discuss what's happening with the new team.'

He gives me a sly nod, content to have riled me.

'I want Chloe but not David and she's reluctant to cut him adrift. They live together so that complicates things.'

He licks his lips and flicks ash into a nearby plant pot.

'I hear Chloe is a little fleshpot.'

As if she would be interested in him.

'Peter, let me show you the Honeydrop commercial. It's Chloe's idea.'

'Haven't I taught you anything, Ella?' he says reaching over and stubbing out his cigarette in the Yucca pot. The leaves wilt. 'I wouldn't trust a kid straight out of college to hold my pencil.'

'That's not a euphemism, is it, Peter?'

'You don't give a rookie free rein on one of our most prestigious accounts.'

'They came highly recommended. Adam Hart sent them.'

'Adam Hart? What the hell does he know?'

'He knows what he's talking about,' I tell him anxious to stick up for Adam.

'Look, Ella, this can go one of two ways. Either, Chloe blows it and you carry the can. I don't fancy your chances with the board on that one. Or, she succeeds and covers herself in glory. That's 'herself' not you.'

'What's wrong with giving new talent a chance to shine? It reflects well on everyone.'

He leans forward and removes a stray hair from my jumper. I freeze.

'You've got a lot to learn. You let her do the hard work and then you take all the credit,' he says as he turns his head to indicate the raft of shiny awards lining the walls and shelves. 'How do you think I won all these?'

My mouth drops open.

'Oh don't look so po-faced, Ella. You're not pretty enough to pout.'

'If you've taught me anything, it's to behave with integrity and treat others like you'd like to be treated yourself,' I say allowing myself a moment of sarcasm to make myself feel in control.

'Watch my lips. This is Adland not a bloody charity. I'm not into altruism unless it means I get a knighthood. God knows I deserve one.'

This will remain forever a mystery between him and his maker. If a less deserving individual exists, I hope he beats Peter to the podium. I click on the video-recorder and press play. We're ten seconds into the thirty second Honeydrop commercial when he stares out of the window. The commercial has finished by the time he turns back to the screen.

'I'll rewind it,' I offer.

'Don't bother,' he says.

He clicks his lighter and wrestles with the inch-long flame threatening to shoot up his nostrils. Eventually, it dies down.

'Our Little Arrangement will have to wait,' he says ignoring what I told him about it being null and void. 'I'm celibate this month - I must restore my energy levels. I have to put myself first.'

I must have been away the day he put himself second.

'Staff morale needs a boost so we're organising a team-building event and Jill's heading it up,' I tell him quickly before I do something rash and hand in my notice.

'Jill? She's hardly the sharpest pencil in the box. I told her I'd had the stairs in my mother's bungalow painted blue and she believed me. She only got this job because I like having something nice to look at. No offence, Ella.'

I glare at him.

'She's sourced the venue and negotiated a very competitive rate so we can afford to go for two days.'

'An over-nighter? Sounds fun.'

He glances round the room and declares, 'This place needs Feng Shuing.'

'Wally got the cleaners to give it a good going over last night,' I say.

'Feng Shui isn't some sort of industrial jet-wash. It is an ancient art and science developed in China over 3,000 years ago. 'Feng' meaning wind and 'shui' meaning water.'

Piss and wind? Sums you him up perfectly.

He eyes me slyly.

'To hell with it! Let's just pencil Our Little Arrangement in for next week. That'll give you time to lose weight, Ella,' he says as he flicks open his Filofax.

'Fire me but you can't keep me here under threat.'

'Perhaps you'd like to reconsider. After all, your mortgage won't pay itself. And interest rates have just gone up. Now, have you got an opening on the twentieth?'

'Not if I can help it.'

He looks at his diary again.

'Oh no can do. I'm strengthening my sacral chakra that night.'

'Your what?'

'Sacral chakra. My chakra practitioner says it is under-active and I need to remain open to intimacy.'

The last thing the universe needs is for Peter to be any more open.

'How about next Friday?' he asks.

'And your vow of celibacy?' I ask desperate to hold him off.

'Vows are made to be broken. Shall we firm it up now?'

'No, let's not firm anything up,' I say feeling sick at the thought.

'There's no need to tell your boyfriend. Think of it as evening-up the score card.'

'Meaning?' I am past caring about Tom but I still want to know what he got up to behind my back.

'Ella, if you imagine he hasn't so much as kissed another girl, you're more stupid than you look. Of course he sleeps around. He's a musician; it's what he does for an encore.'

I knew about Tom flirting with Cara. But I thought that was a one-off. I thought that was his one mistake. One he was sorry for and would never repeat. I thought he loved me. Looks like my love for him enlarged my heart and shrunk my brain. No wonder Tom often slept over on gig nights. Thanks for the wake-up call, Peter.

Chapter twenty-eight

Use the word 'you'. Lots.

I am a working girl, professional and independent. So why am I considering giving Tom a second chance? Since I told him to leave, my mind is never free of him, one minute thinking how much I love him and the next wondering what the hell I want with someone who claims to have spent the night in a Photo-Me-Booth.

I've never taken the safe option. I work in advertising

To begin with Tom was exciting and hot. He swept me off my feet which was a feat in itself given I was at least half a stone over weight. But then he changed. He became someone I didn't know or like. But I can't quite let go of the notion, he might change back into the Tom I fell in love with.

Like an addict looking for the next fix, I tell myself I'm okay. I can handle him. Just one more night with him won't hurt. My mind hunts out the good, not the bad or the ugly in him. But, I am my Mother's daughter and eventually I find the strength to discover the truth. That's why I've agreed for him to come to my place and talk things through. I've got Adam on standby at the end of the phone just in case things get awkward.

My palms are sweating as I see Tom walking up the path. I rush to open the door. He looks amazing in a new black leather jacket and jeans. I step away from him. Like any recovering addict, I can't risk getting too close.

'Sorry, they didn't have any roses,' he tells me handing me a bunch of carnations.

I still don't quite trust him. I can't help wondering why he has chosen one pair of jeans over another. Is it because the black ones are tighter than the blue or because the zip is quicker to release than the button-fly?

He smiles at me. I look away. I am too vulnerable. I can't let him back in just like that. I remind myself this is the man who autographed another girl's boobs. Of course girls throw themselves at him. He is gorgeous. He is also a performer making him public property. If I couldn't accept it, I should have settled for an ugly man. Darren springs to mind, ugly inside and out, just to make doubly sure. I can't believe I am spending next weekend with him.

'How's work?' he asks.

'We're off on an agency jolly this weekend. Oh and Peter's back but I always knew that was coming.'

I study Tom's face. Not so much as a flicker of recognition at the mention of Peter's name.

'Is that okay? Having Peter as your boss again?'

'Not really. Anyway, you haven't come here to talk about Peter, have you?'

'No,' he shifts his weight from one foot to the other.

'Fancy a coffee?' I ask as an excuse to leave the room. The tension is too much.

'Yes, please, thanks.'

His politeness unnerves me. I go into the kitchen and make two cups of instant coffee. When I take them into the living room, he is standing by the mantelpiece checking out his reflection in the mirror.

'Oh, great, thanks,' he says, spinning round.

He takes a sip and can't resist watching himself as he swallows.

'I've really missed you Ella. Being away from you has been hard for me. I don't want those silly girls who throw themselves at me at the gigs. I want you.'

I say nothing but, like an alcoholic uncorking a bottle, there's no going back now. I'm hooked. He looks vulnerable, broken almost. He looks up at me with soft, imploring eyes.

'How are the gigs?' I ask.

'Great, yeah, they love Tom Tyler. I've written some new songs and yeah, it's all good.'

He runs his hand through his hair and I can picture him on stage, the crowd at his feet.

'You're wearing your ring,' I say surprised and happy as I catch sight of it.

'Yeah, of course. I never take it off.'

I smile.

'Oh Tom,' I say, letting him take me in his arms and hold me like he never wants to let me go. " I have missed you so much.'

The phone rings.

'Leave it,' he whispers as he covers my face in kisses.

'No, I better get it. It might be Mum.'

Reluctantly, he steps back and I run into the kitchen and pick up the phone.

'Hello.'

'Sorry I must have the wrong number,' says a surprised female voice.

'Who do you want to speak to?' I ask.

'Tom.'

'Tom?' I murmur buying myself time. I want to know what she has to say.

'I'm his girlfriend,' I tell her. 'Can I help?'

Obviously, I only mean the statement not the question.

'His girlfriend?' she asks unable to mask the disbelief in her voice. 'Lucky you. He's quite a guy.'

'He is?'

'Yes, he came to my rescue last week and lent me the money for a cab after I missed the last tube.'

Last week? We were still together then.

I torture myself imagining what they were up to that made her late for the train. Drinking? Snogging? Bonking? All three at once, probably.

'And he gave you this number?' I ask incredulously.

Why would he do that? If he had been up to no good surely he wouldn't have been so stupid? The number is ex-directory so there's no way she could have found it.

'I just wanted to thank him and arrange to repay him the taxi fare.'

'Don't worry about it. I'll let him know you got home safely. Bye.'

'You sure? It was fifty quid.'

Fifty pounds? Where does she live, Lands End?

'Goodbye,' I tell her.

'Thanks, tell him Jules rang. You're so lucky. You've got a good one there. He's a prince.'

I hang up and wander slowly back into the living room where Prince Charming is on his throne, cigarette in hand, with the beginnings of a beer belly beginning to show. I wonder if Jules would find him quite so regal now.

'Was it your Mum?' he asks.

'No, some girl who wanted to thank you for rescuing her,' I paused deliberately. 'Last week. Apparently, you were a real hero.'

I watch him. Lie to me if you have to, anything but break my heart again, I think.

'I don't remember.'

'You don't remember giving some girl fifty quid for a cab?'

'Oh, yeah, that's right. She got pissed and missed her train, big deal,' he mutters but knows I don't buy it.

It was clear from her tone she had no idea I existed. I tell myself it doesn't matter, that he did the right thing. It shows he's a good guy, doesn't it? Now I think about it, he rescued me the first time I met him. Is this his *modus operandi?* I doubt it. He doesn't look the sort to read Latin. Besides, he came back to me. He's here now, on my sofa. That must mean something. Nevertheless, the call has made me uneasy.

'I think you should go, Tom.'

'Ella!'

'Sorry, I've got an early start. Oh you left some dirty stuff behind. It's in the laundry basket. I'll get it for you.'

I go into the bedroom and pluck out his favourite pair of black jeans and white shirt. A handful of coins and some notes fall out of the pockets on to the floor. The amount of money Tom launders would put Ronnie Biggs to shame. I bend down to pick it up. It's not cash but it is currency. And, it says more about the bearer than a note ever can. These days, anyone whipping out a condom at the crucial moment looks like a new man, someone who cares. Someone you can trust. But, it means just the opposite when you find a condom in your partner's pocket when you're on the Pill. I go cold. I can't take my eyes off the repulsive thing. Its bright packaging can only be an inch square. How can something so small make such a big difference?

This is proof I have been lying to myself and Tom's been lying to me. He was never interested in me, just in somewhere to live. How did Peter put it?

'You don't need to find somewhere to live in London. Just someone to live with.'

'Found this in your trouser pocket,' I shout running back into the living room and brandishing the small square packet in his face.

'Calm down. Some drunk girl was coming onto me and my mate gave it to me for a laugh.'

'Ha bloody ha! I'm not that stupid. You don't need a condom, I'm on the Pill,' I yell.

'Don't be silly.'

'Silly to believe you.'

'You calling me a liar?'

'If the cap fits. Sorry, wrong contraceptive – if the condom fits.'

I throw it in his lap and it lands, appropriately enough, in his crotch.

'Keep it. You'll need it later because you won't be sleeping here tonight or any other night. Get out, ' I tell him, my eyes dripping with useless tears. 'And take your all bloody rubbish with you.'

'I can't help it if girls fancy me. I'm a musician.'

'And you've played me for a fool. All that crap about helping me with the bills. You just wanted to get your hands on my flat.'

'What this place?' he scoffs glancing around the room.

'It was good enough for you when you'd run out of sofa's to sleep on. Call Cara, you can share her bed.'

'Yeah, yeah, yeah. Cara, Cara, Cara. Blame her if it makes you feel better. But this is your fault. I'm going. I'll get my stuff some other time.'

He gets to his feet and heads for the door. We watched enough movies together; we both know this is the end. The door slams.

My life liquefies as I cling to the last vestiges of my love like left-over cereal in a bowl. I tell myself the Bad Boy was never good enough for me. I had been so desperate for love, I gave him all the power.

My stomach is raw and empty. I feel light-headed. Nothing alters the fact I loved him and making love to him completed me. Right now, I can't imagine my bed without him in it. Tom Tyler is going to be a hard act to follow.

No, I can't think like that. I am not Mum, forever holding a candle for Dad. I am Ella. I am in the spotlight now.

I bend down and pick up Tom's mug, anxious to cleanse the place of him. Two cigarette butts float in the greying dregs of cold coffee. I wash it under the running tap but the inside is still brown. I pour in a weak solution of bleach and let it stand for a couple of minutes. I work a squirt of washing-up liquid around the cup and give it a good rinse. The product works its magic, just like in the ads. The stain has gone.

Chapter twenty-nine

Be interesting

'What prat owns the Porsche?'

'Peter Richards,' I tell the driver of the red Routemaster bus as he tries to park on Shaftesbury Avenue where the agency is meeting for our team-building weekend.

'Want me to move your motor for you, Pete?' asks Wally.

Peter pushes past him, leaps in the Porsche, fires up the engine and immediately stalls it. Thank-you, God! What a great start to the day. We all get a laugh at Peter's expense.

Jill ticks names off a sheet as we board the bus. I am the first up the stairs, followed by Darren and his gang from the studio. One of them is carrying a sports bag. I would bet my flat on it not containing anything to do with any activity other than drinking. Sure enough, they immediately crack open the beers. Mr Media and Mr Planning sit together. Alan Ferguson is too cool to be here, no doubt holed up in his Notting Hill flat, drinking champagne, naked, with someone else's wife. Peter and Josh are amongst the last to board and sit in the only free seat, directly behind Chloe and David.

I look out of the window, down onto the pavement below. Wally's wife has come to wave him off. I can just see the top of her head. He holds her hand and kisses her good-bye. She hands him a carrier bag and gives him a final peck on the cheek.

'See you tomorrow, love!' I hear Wally say as he hauls himself up onto the platform of the bus.

His head pops up at the top of the stairs.

'Room for a little one?' he asks.

I nod and he sits next to me. He delves into the bag his wife gave him and pulls out a flask and a Tupperware box. 'Egg sandwich? Help yourself. The wife made enough to feed an army.'

The smell of sulphur is overwhelming.

'Blimey! Who's let one off?' shouts Darren. 'Was it you, Ella?'

No-one takes Wally up on his offer of a sandwich. He makes short work of them and sips tea noisily from a plastic cup.

As we pull round Trafalgar Square, someone shouts,

'Are we there yet?'

The blokes laugh and wolf-whistle as Jill walks confidently down the aisle to the front of the bus.

'Good morning everyone and welcome aboard! Your team-building weekend starts here.'

She looks calm and confident. Darren and the boys start yelling questions at her.

'Are you wearing stockings?'

'Will you sit on my lap?'

'Fancy a quickie on the back seat?'

Wisely, she chooses not to respond, just glances at her watch.

'We should be there in about two hours. So sit back and enjoy the ride.'

'Bet you go like a train!' yells one of the lads.

Jill shoots him a look and goes downstairs.

As we head south, Wally takes the opportunity to make a fast buck by opening a book on our final destination with a five-star health farm being odds-on favourite and a French Chateau the rank outsider at 100 to 1.

Josh is laughing loudly at something Peter has just whispered to him. Chloe has closed her eyes and is listening to her Walkman. I notice Peter's hand gently brush against her hair as he holds onto the back of her seat. David turns to glare at him.

Wally nods off. Not sure how he managed that given Darren and the boys haven't stopped shouting. One of them pulls his trousers down and moons at a woman who works in accounts. She tells him to put it away before discussing a recipe for coq au vin with the girl sitting next to her.

I am just happy to be here, away from it all. Try as I might, my mind rewinds to Tom and I torture myself with memories of the happier days. I feel so alone, so singular. Making love to him made me feel loved. And he was my Guardian Angel when Peter put me through hell. Now I wonder where the devil is sleeping now. And who with. Perhaps his fans are forming an orderly queue outside a Photo-Me-Booth. I can't help picturing what they might be getting up to inside. Flash! Bang! Wallop!

I must move on. Just like Mum did eventually. She never wanted to walk away from Dad but she did it to protect me.

'I had to leave, for your sake. If it wasn't for you, I would still be with him,' she would tell me wistfully.

I was never sure if she was blaming me or grateful for the excuse. I have a sneaky suspicion it was the former. She never remarried. I wish she had found someone to love her and make her happy. When I was older, I encouraged her to go on dates but she was having none of it.

'I still love your father. It wouldn't be fair on another man,' she would say her face turned to the wall.

I am not going to be like her. I want to be happy. I deserve to be happy.

I join in the singsong started by the boys on the back row. Joy is contagious. I am smiling. Someone downstairs starts singing Boy George hits and we all join in with the opening lines and the chorus. I break a couple of squares off the bar of chocolate I bought and foolishly hand the rest around. I never see it again. I wish Adam was here, he'd have brought a hamper.

Once the novelty of being on a London bus outside of London wears off, a few people start moaning about how rickety and uncomfortable it is. We get stuck in traffic and the journey takes longer than expected. Thanks to the bottle of whiskey being passed around, spirits are high. Three toilet stops and one sick bag incident later, the bus pulls off the road and we head towards a sumptuous-looking country hotel set in its own grounds. We slow down at the large wrought iron gates and we all get up, expectantly.

'Sit down, please. We're not quite there yet,' Jill tells us.

We don't have long to wait before we arrive at our destination.

'No way!' exclaims Josh as the bus pulls up outside a desolate compound, fenced with barbed wire. 'You can't seriously expect me to stay here. It's a holiday camp with chalets, bingo and third-rate entertainment.'

'Don't be a knob,' shouts Darren.

'Did you just call me a 'knob'?' asks Josh.

'No, a 'snob',' lies Darren.

Poor Josh. His annual holidays in Provence, filled with vineyards and olive groves, are a long way from a packet of crisps and a pint of lager. I can't wait to see him in the knobbly knees competition. With those legs, he'll walk it.

We all file slowly downstairs. Darren and the rest of the boys are laughing, convinced this is one big rouse and we'll soon be whisked us off to a five-star resort. The less inebriated know this is it and stand on the pavement like refugees with their luggage littered at their feet. Jill herds the stragglers off the bus like a crazed sheep dog. Dressed from head to toe in a pink gingham playsuit, she is embracing the 1950's holiday camp vibe. Turns out her mother is quite the entrepreneur, having

223

had the foresight to spot the trend for retro and snapping up a job lot of dilapidated holiday camps at auction five years ago. I should never have put Jill in charge. I should've smelt a rat when she insisted on keeping her plans a secret. Obviously, anyone who washes her pants at work is more knicker-drawer than top-drawer. It may be eighty degrees in the shade but no amount of sunshine can brighten this day. The only way things can get any worse, would be for Tom Tyler to top the bill tonight. It's just the sort of seedy hole he would feel at home in.

'Bagsy, the one with a double bed. Girls, form an orderly queue,' shouts Darren running towards the chalets.

He cuts a lonely figure sprinting across the concourse.

Peter descends from the top deck, looking bilious. I can only guess what chaos his chakras must be in without access to his herbalist, nutritionist and therapist. He looks like he wants to kill me. Or pay someone else to – after all, he wouldn't want my blood on his new shirt.

'What the hell?' he exclaims when he sees the full extent of Jill's mother's pathetic property portfolio.

'Peter, please not in front of the children,' I tell him indicating the kids from the campsite who have gathered to gawp open-mouthed at his linen suit and Panama hat.

'This is a fiasco. If we must be detained in this hell-hole we should've insisted on exclusive occupancy.'

He indicates an over-weight sun-burnt woman lounging on the grass eating ice-cream and chips. In the same mouthful. At least she'll be spared his advances.

Jill calls Darren back, and armed with a clip-board allocates the chalets. Some people are delighted with their house-mates especially as Jill has decided to have a bit of fun and mixed girls and boys. I will be sticking to my single bed and wearing two pairs of pyjamas, just in case Peter decides this is the time to consummate our Little Arrangement. Others are equally shocked at the prospect of their prospective partners and start trading. Darren opens the bidding.

'You can have Wally if I can have Jill.'

Poor old Wally, no-one wants him snoring in their chalet.

'Wally can share with me if he wants,' I tell Jill.

'Eh, Wally, Ella wants you bad,' leers Darren.

'I should be so lucky,' replies Wally.

I sling my bag over my shoulder and carry Wally's case to our chalet, number 41. It's pure nostalgia with candlewick bedspreads and linoleum flooring. There's even a patch of green mould inching up the wall.

'You take the big room, Wally. I'll have the small one. And no funny business; I've got my eye on you,' I tell him with a wink.

'I wouldn't dream of it; you're practically a married woman.'

'Not any more, Wal,' I tell him heaving his bag onto the bed.

'You told him to clear off? Good girl, you're learning.'

'Yeah, he ...'

I stop myself. Wally doesn't need to know about me finding the condom.

'You were right, Wal. And to think I was going to let him move in.'

Wally shudders and shakes his head.

'Narrow escape, if you ask me, young 'un. You won't make that mistake again. Forget all about him and enjoy the weekend,' he says taking a handful of coins from his pocket. 'Just nipping to the phone box to ring the wife and let her know I got 'ere safe.'

'I'll come with you,' I say, running after him, before remembering I have no-one to call. 'I can just get the lay of the land.'

The man in the call-box has settled in for the afternoon. Every three minutes he takes a coin from the tower he has piled on top of the telephone directories and pushes it into the slot. When Wally bangs impatiently on the glass, he turns away. Eventually, he replaces the receiver and we move forward in anticipation. Then the phone rings, he picks it up and carries on his conversation. When he finally hangs up, Wally steps inside only to emerge moments later, crestfallen.

'She must be out getting her hair done. I'll try again later. Just nipping to the loo – too much tea on the bus,' he says, heading for the toilet block.

Don't know why he didn't just save himself the trouble and go in the telephone box. Everyone else does. When I was younger my friends would tell me about fortnights spent with their parents at places like this. Beauty competitions, swimming pools and nightly cabaret shows, it sounded like holiday heaven. But this place is hell and now boasts its very own devil in residence. Peter.

Now he staggers towards me looking angry.

'Give me a hand with my bags. This heat is very debilitating,' he wipes his forehead with the back of his hand and nods at his set of matching, monogrammed luggage.

'Have you really been hanging about, all this time, in the hope someone would carry your cases?' I ask.

'Is this dick-head with you?' asks a well-built man, holding a small boy by the hand and pointing at Peter.

'Why?' I ask guardedly.

'He just offered my kid fifty pence to carry his bags to his chalet. Is he some sort of pervert? You can tell him from me, if I see him anywhere near my family again, I'll 'ave him.'

'Sorry,' I say.

I help Peter carry his stuff. Typically, he has pulled rank with Jill and got a chalet all to himself. The door is the only one painted a putrid shade of orange. He fiddles with the handle.

'You turn it and I'll push. No, not that way; turn it to the right, you fool. Oh, get out of the way and let me do it.'

He twists the knob as he shoulders the door. It flies open to reveal the interior in all its faded glory, a bed covered in a nylon counterpane and a faded rug on the floor.

'Wow, this is perfect for our Little Arrangement, isn't it, Ella? And the fact we're playing away from home adds a certain frisson.'

He can't imagine I would ever sleep with him, let alone in this room.

'Just going to freshen up. Make yourself comfortable,' he calls from the bathroom.

I slip out and wander across the camp-site. Children are leaping in the swimming pool as their parents sit limply in deck-chairs, sunning themselves. The place feels tired but everyone looks happy enough.

When I eventually arrive back at my chalet, Wally is soaking his false teeth in a mug on his bedside cabinet. His new blue flannel sits on the side of the washbasin, next to a fresh bar of soap and his dressing gown hangs on the hook behind the door. He puts his teeth back in to talk to me.

'My things are in the top drawer. You can have the bottom two. I know what you girls are like - pack for a fortnight when you're only away a couple of days.'

'Wally, that's very kind of you but I won't be offended if you'd rather share with a bloke.'

'Why would I wanna do that? I'm old, not stupid,' he says with a smile.

'I know. But it would be a shame to ruin a beautiful friendship for one night of unbridled passion, wouldn't it?' I say my tongue firmly in my cheek.

'You're right,' he says, playing along. 'Don't want to make Adam jealous.'

'Adam?' I ask taken aback.

'Yeah, I remember when you'd only just joined the agency and I used to catch the pair of you laughing in the kitchen when everyone else had gone home, polishing off the biscuits meant for the boardroom. Good job he left when he did or you'd have never got any work done.'

'Once we ate a buffet they'd prepared for a client lunch. Luckily, no-one knew it was us.'

'I did,' he said with a wink. 'And it was the pair of you what had the chocolate samples meant for the research groups. You two are made for each other.'

'Don't be daft, Wal. Besides. He's got a girlfriend.'

'Like you had a boyfriend, y'mean?'

Before I can reply, Wally goes into the bathroom and locks the door behind him. I hear him whistling to try to muffle the sound of him peeing.

I sit on my narrow bed, wondering where Adam is now. Wherever it is it must be better than my panoramic view of the car park. Now, I understand how Jill got such a great deal. The camp needs renovating. Our chalets don't look like they've been touched in the thirty years since they were built. I am startled by Jill's voice on the tannoy. I get up and go outside.

'Welcome CBA-campers. This is Jill, your Event Co-ordinator bringing you your weekend programme. Bingo starts this afternoon at 3.30. Dinner is at 6 followed by Marvellous Michael and his Magic Monkey at 8. Then, it's the disco at 9. Tomorrow, starts with keep fit on the beach at 10. Then there are mystery activities followed by prize-giving. Now, make yourselves at home. Lunch is being served in the canteen. Have a great weekend.'

Just as I am trying to decide whether or not I like the new-improved Jill, I spot David walking past.

'Hi, David.'

He quickens his pace, I run to catch him up, then trot beside him and try to make conversation.

'Poor Peter looked like he was going to have a heart attack when he saw the campsite. Not exactly the South of France, is it?

He stops abruptly and looks at me.

'Why am I here?'

'That's a bit deep, Dave,' I say, trying to lighten the mood.

'What use is a team-building exercise to me? I've got no future at the agency, thanks to you.'

'You're a designer. A brilliant designer. I've had a word with Darren in the studio and he's promised to keep you in mind if anything comes up.'

His breath smells of alcohol, he must have started drinking on the bus.

'Haven't seen much of Chloe, is she enjoying herself?' I ask.

He speeds up. I take the hint.

'Good. Well, I must find Jill. See you later,' I say.

I've walked further than I realised. All the chalets look identical. I'm lost. I remember the number because it's the same as my old house, number forty-one. I find myself outside Peter's chalet again. I recognise the orange door. The curtains are drawn which is odd. It's the middle of the afternoon. Perhaps he wants to shut out the horror of his surroundings – Peter doesn't do working-class. If he's relaxing after his shower, on that nylon counterpane, I hope he's dried himself properly and is not creating too much friction. I'd hate for him to get a shock from all that static electricity. Then I hear a woman laugh. Peter must be showing her his chakras.

When I finally find my chalet, Wally is waiting, washed, dressed and ready to party. He smells of soap and his wispy hair is combed neatly over his head.

'Hurry up, young 'un. Bingo starts in five minutes.'

I had hoped to miss the Two Fat Ladies but Wally is keen to look them up. He takes me by the arm and propels me out of the door.

The hall is empty except for an elderly woman with a middle-aged man who looks like she spat him out. Mother and son sport identical blonde curly perms.

'Wally, this is awful, can we go?' I whisper as I am handed a book of cards and a pen.

'Stick with me. We'll have a laugh.'

Gradually, the seats fill up. Everyone seems to take what is laughingly called a 'game' of bingo very seriously. I giggle when the caller says 'Legs Eleven'. It's a cliché but I've never heard it used in context before. At first I leap up and shout 'Bingo!' whenever I hear one of my numbers but thanks to the helpful tut-tutting of the other players I learn to button it. Thank goodness Alan Ferguson didn't come. I can't imagine Mr Cool with this lot. Wally certainly knows his way around the card. He calls 'House' so often he'll own half of Soho before the night's out. He wins the last game on number 13, unlucky for some. But not for him.

'Wish the wife was 'ere, she'd love all this. I better give her another ring. I can afford a nice long call with me winnings. Coming, young 'un? '

I stand outside and watch as Wally dials the number. His wife must have picked up straight away because he is beaming. I realise I'm intruding and turn away. Couples arm in arm and big, happy families go about their perfect lives. Right now, it's hard to imagine that will ever be me. My mum has always worried I would never settle down because I come from a 'broken home' as she calls it. But I can't blame the present on the past. It's up to me to create my own, one built on love and respect.

'What d'you fancy for dinner later?' asks Wally bursting out of the phone box like a short, balding Clark Kent. 'You must be hungry you only had them couple of bits of chocolate on the bus. I'm having meat-pie and chips but not too many, gotta watch me ticker.'

He pats his chest before we nip back to the chalet to get washed and changed.

When we arrive at the canteen it smells of school dinners. I spot the woman and her lookalike son from the bingo hall. Unable to choose between the myriad options on offer, they have them all. On the same plate. Peter swaggers in and goes straight to the front of the queue. He surveys the mix of pies, potatoes and puddings.

'This is carbohydrate-hell. Did no-one think to ring ahead with my dietary requirements?'

He flags down a sweaty lad dumping a tray of baked beans on the self-service counter.

'Excuse me, I notice you have tuna on the menu. I'd like mine lightly seared.'

'It's out of a can, Pete,' Wally informs him.

Peter flinches and opts for what he considers to be the least offensive item, tinned fruit salad. The shepherd's pie looks delicious. I spoon some onto a plate and load up another with pie and chips for Wally. I follow Peter to his table.

'Mind if we join you?' Wally asks him.

Without waiting for a reply he plonks himself down and I sit opposite them both. Wally tucks into his dinner. I copy him and blow on my food sending a small bobble of beef into the air. It lands in Peter's bowl.

'What the hell?' he yells leaping up and upsetting the dish into his lap.

Wally is wiping away tears of laughter.

'Very bloody funny! Look at me!'

It's hard not to. Slices of pear and peach cling to Peter's shorts and his legs drip with syrup.

'Well, do something!' he shouts.

One of the staff rushes over and, with the same damp cloth he's been using to wipe the tables, rub vigorously at Peter's crotch.

'Get off me,' screams Peter.

He looks like he's wet himself. He sits down, quickly.

'Have you any idea how many calories are in that?' he asks regarding my meal with disgust.

'Don't care,' I tell him, dipping the last of Wally's chips into the gravy.

'Right, young 'un, time to see a man about a monkey. Coming, Pete?'

'No, I'll get an early night,' he yawns.

I look at my watch. It's not even eight o'clock.

'Don't know what you're missing, mate,' says Wally.

'Oh I think I do - a man with his hand up a monkey's arse.'

Perhaps Marvellous Michael's blue velveteen suit fitted him back in the day but, in the intervening years, he has inflated. His jacket is now secured by one very over-worked button. Magic Monkey has just come out of mothballs. Not very effective ones either, judging by his patchy fur.

Surprisingly Marvellous Michael is magnificent, enabling Magic Monkey to conjure up nuts and bananas out of mid-air. When Tarzan, wearing nothing but a dangerously economic loin cloth, swings across the stage on a creeper and flies off with Magic Monkey, they bring the house down. Literally. Magic Monkey yanks the curtain, covering Marvellous Michael with a cloak of red rayon. The audience goes wild which seems fitting given the jungle theme. I turn to Wally, he dabs his eyes with his hands.

'Me and the wife honeymooned here. That monkey is older than I am.'

'Really?' I ask, moved by his response.

'No, only pulling your leg. For a hardened ad-girl you aren't half soppy sometimes.'

I nip back quickly to the chalet and change into my red silk New Romantic number and leggings. When I arrive at the disco, Darren is thrusting his pelvis in Jill's direction as she is carried aloft by the boys from the studio. Even Josh struts his funky stuff. I even think I spot a hint of eye-liner. David refuses to join in the fun, preferring to stare at the bottom of an empty pint glass. When the DJ slows the mood most people head for the bar but Wally spots me standing alone and takes my hand. For a few minutes, we're waltzing on air. I'm smiling, head up, shoulders back, I've never had a lesson in my life but I'm a natural. I was born to this. When the music stops Wally makes a little bow and I courtesy. Everyone is laughing.

Darren manages to say, 'Best entertainment of the night. Cheers, Ella.'

David is drunk but lucid enough to clarify the situation, 'They are laughing at you not with you. You've got no sense of rhythm.'

'You're the only joke round here, mate. Come on, you've had enough,' says Wally taking the glass from David's hand and hoisting him out of his seat.

'This place would drive anyone to drink,' slurs David, pulling away and accidently elbowing Wally in the ribs.

David staggers off. Wally collapses into a chair like a burst beach-ball.

'Alright, Wal?' I ask rubbing the papery skin on the back of his hand.

'Just winded; I'll be fine.'

I watch him closely and wait until I see the colour returning to his cheeks.

'Enjoy yourself, young 'un. I'm goin' to sit this one out,' says Wally when Status Quo starts blaring out of the speakers.

I devise a simple routine, basically the warm-up from my aerobics class and do that for about an hour. Having star-jumped my way through every record, I go to the bar for a drink. Out of habit I go to order a glass of wine then change my mind. I want water. When I turn round, Josh is leading some of the campers in a conga. Odd considering Abba is on the turntable.

I push my way through the drunken dancing queens and clamber on stage where I mouth a request to the DJ then I hunt for Wally.

'May I have the pleasure?' I ask him as Bob Dylan's voice begins to serenade us.

He takes my hand and I follow his lead, my feet barely touching the floor.

'You've got it, young 'un. That's it.'

I could dance all night but the music stops abruptly. I glance up at the mirrored disco ball shimmering above me, reflecting my happiness for a few moments. I step into one of the pools of light flooding the floor but it escapes, slipping out from under my foot like a sprite. I check my watch; it's nearly midnight. The DJ spins the final disk. It's a slow one giving sweaty couples the perfect opportunity to glue themselves together, tongues entwined.

'Time to go,' says Wally.

'Yeah. It's been a great night, apart from David's little outburst.'

I hold his arm with one hand and my sling-backs with the other and we make our way over to the chalet.

'Look, the Milky Way,' says Wally.

'Where?' I ask getting excited and automatically thinking of chocolate bars.

'There,' he replies pointing up at the shimmering haze set against the blackness.

I've never seen it before. It's beautiful. We stand, looking up at the sky, marvelling at the diamonds scattered against black satin. Reluctantly, we go into the chalet and close the door.

'Night, Wal,' I call from my bed.

'Night, young 'un,' he replies.

Then I hear his teeth drop into the glass. As I close my eyes, I am still smiling.

Chapter thirty

Use humour where appropriate

Having once woken to the sight of Darren's bare bum, I now start the day to the sound of Wally's snoring. I peak through the door and see the sheet, pulled up over his mouth, rise and fall with each puff. He won't mind missing keep fit; he's always telling me he had enough of it in the army.

There's a bang on the door, I open it to see Jill looking alarmingly bright-eyed.

'Everyone has overslept. Hurry up,' she booms.

'Ssch!' I whisper, pointing at Wally and closing the door behind me.

The other CBA campers stagger out of their chalets. Most of the girls have just rolled out of bed. With their unmade-up faces, they are unrecognisable and they have swopped heels for trainers making them all at least four inches shorter. The guys strut about with their T-shirts tucked into their shorts. Sportswear is a great leveller.

Peter jogs along the beach towards us wearing a pale blue and white tracksuit with matching trainers. He is sporting three sweatbands, one on his head and one on each wrist. I can't imagine him ever exerting himself sufficiently to perspire. He does a pointless little run on the spot before flopping over at the waist in an attempt to touch his toes. Jill marshals us into teams of two and puts me with Darren. Thanks for that.

'Good morning CBA-ers. I'm now going to hand you over to your lovely instructor, Sam.'

Sam's muscular body puts Peter's in the shade.

'You! Yes, you in the baby blue track-suit! Stop! Very dangerous manoeuvre,' Sam yells at Peter then continues to humiliate him. 'Okay, we all saw what Little Boy Blue did. Stupid and dangerous.'

Well, Sam's certainly got Peter sussed.

'You missed a brilliant night,' I tell Peter, mid leg-lunge.

'No, I didn't,' he says, straining to straighten-up. 'I went to bed early.'

He winks at me.

'Little Boy Blue! Back straight.'

'Listen,' Peter says. 'I don't know who you are or what qualifications you have in the fitness industry but I belong to a top London gym – platinum-membership. I know how to lunge.'

'I can vouch for that,' I tell Sam helpfully.

Peter hates him. But I love him and wonder how much Jill is paying to put Peter through his paces. It's worth every penny. Perhaps we should have a whip-round to ensure he achieves his full potential.

'That's me done. Doesn't do to mix training styles,' says Peter, clearly out of breath and jogging backwards up the beach.

With that, he reverses straight into the guy from bingo, the one who looks like his mum. Sam sprints over, ignores Peter and helps the other man who is not a bit embarrassed about his wig falling off. Satisfied the only injury is Peter's bruised ego, Sam tells us about the next event, a treasure hunt. He hands one person from each pair a padlock and chain, together with the first clue.

'I am locking all of you to a partner,' Sam says, chaining me to Darren at the ankles. 'It's a three-legged race.'

Manacled? This place really is a prison camp.

'Go! Go! Go!' shouts Sam.

Darren and I dash off in opposite directions and fall over. Reluctantly, we hold onto each other just long enough to get to our feet. Darren reads out the clue.

'What has a bark you can't hear?'

Cryptic is not my thing.

'Bark? Dog?' suggests Darren.

'A tree?' I shout.

'Yeah!' he yells before turning his head and throwing up.

'Filthy pig! We could've made it to the loo if you'd said,' I say feeling sick myself.

'Sorry,' he says putting his arm around my waist and breaking into a run before I can protest.

For the first time ever, Darren and I are in step and race to towards the copse where he spots the next clue pinned to a tree. He reads it before tearing it down.

'You can't do that. It's not fair on the others,' I tell him.

'It's not fair,' mimics Darren. 'You wanna win, don't you?'

'Not by cheating.'

He laughs, holding the slip of paper above his head as I try to grab it.

'You are such a pain in the arse, Ella.'

'Put it back.'

'No, you bossy cow.'

I hear the crunch of leaves underfoot and spin round to see Sam towering over us.

'Everything okay?' he asks.

'No. Unlock me,' demands Darren. 'She's a nightmare.'

'You'll be disqualified,' Sam tells him.

'Unlock me,' Darren repeats moving his foot forward and taking mine with it.

Sam kneels down and releases the chain.

'You can still compete but you're handicapped without him,' the instructor explains.

Really? You sure? This is Darren Davies we're talking about.

I catch sight of Josh and his partner frantically searching for the clue hidden in Darren's hand. I shoot him a look. I am about to take off when Darren grabs Sam's arm.

'Chain me back to her,' he hisses.

'Only if you put the clue back,' I whisper to him.

I nod and the instructor secures Darren's ankle to mine. As soon as Sam disappears, Darren secures the note back on the tree.

Surprisingly, we are a good team, what I don't know he does, and we quickly solve all the clues. We're into the home straight but Mr Media and Mr Planning are gaining on us. Those two will do anything to win, even sell their souls, if they had any.

We race towards Sam who unlocks us.

'You're in the lead so far,' says Jill noting times next to our names. 'Last leg, the hundred yard dash to the finishing line. Go for it.'

'We only did it for fun, Jill,' I tell her feeling obliged to bow out given how people lost time looking for the missing clue.

Darren opens his mouth to protest but throws up again instead. I sit on the grass and wait for the others to finish the race.

'I am so unfit,' Josh wheezes, collapsing next to me. 'You and Darren went like the wind.'

Darren wipes his mouth with the back of his hand and squats on the grass.

'Any more games later?' I ask, changing the subject.

'I think we're doing a presentation so I'm in with a chance,' says Josh.

'Presentation? Boring! Might as well be back at work,' says Darren, pulling out tufts of grass and throwing them at two sea-gulls scavenging from of a nearby bin.

Josh rolls his eyes at his partner who is lying in the recovery position.

'She's nice,' says Darren looking at her longingly.

I'm hot and need a shower. I get up and head back to the chalet.

'Did you win, young 'un?' Wally asks towel-drying his last few remaining strands of hair.

It doesn't take long.

'Not really, Wal. Any hot water left?'

'Plenty, I only had a strip-wash. Just did me bits.'

Now, I have an unfortunate image of Wally naked. I mentally log it alongside the one of Peter without pants.

'Wakey! Wakey!' Wally says waving a piece of paper at me. 'Someone shoved this under the door earlier. We've got to write and perform a sketch at 3pm in the hall.'

'Got any party pieces, Wally?'

'Don't ask me, you're the writer.'

I hate it when people say that. Nothing strikes fear into my heart like a leaving card waiting for my comment. It sits on my desk, silently mocking me until Jill comes to collect it and I'm forced to write something incisive and witty like, 'Lots of love, Ella x.'

Even Josh comes up with something more original than that.

Wally clicks his fingers in my face as I watch a spider shoot across the floor, like small black tumbleweed.

'Chop! Chop!'

'Wally you're beginning to sound like Peter. Hey, that's it. You be Peter. No, I'll be Peter and you be Jill.'

'I ain't having none of that,' says Wally at my affront to his manhood.

'Don't be silly. Sit down and let me do your make-up. What colour eye-shadow would madam like?'

'Blue to match my eyes,' giggles Wally.

He sits obediently on the side of his bed, feigning annoyance but secretly loving his new role, trusting me with his transformation. I brush the blue powder over his wrinkly eye-lids and blend it in with the tips of my fingers.

'Open!' I tell him.

He peers at me, like a terrified fledgling.

'Do this,' I tell him, opening my mouth and stretching my lips over my teeth.

He looks like Magic Monkey. I laugh and my hand shakes as I attempt to draw a Cupid's Bow on his thin lips. After sweeping bronzer over his frail cheekbones, I finish off with a dusting of face powder. He sneezes fitfully three times like an asthmatic cat.

241

'Finished?' I ask.

He sniffs and nods. I apply the mascara. He sneezes again causing me to poke him in the eye with the brush. He cups the side of his face with his hand.

'Ow!'

'Sorry,' I say handing him a tissue. 'Quick, let me do your nails.'

Even his wife wouldn't recognise him now. I show him his reflection in the mirror.

'I quite fancy myself,' he pouts.

I open the chalet door.

'Don't leave me! What if I have an accident and have to go to hospital looking like this?'

'The only accident you're likely to have is to chip your nail varnish. Now, sit still and don't panic, I'll be back soon.'

Ten minutes later, I return with the finishing touch.

'Get that thing away from me,' he protests.

'Hold still,' I tell him securing the bingo man's hair piece to Wally's shiny head with a blob of chewing gum. 'There, you look gorgeous, Wal. Or should I say Jill?'

He struggles into my blouse and skirt and I look away as he wriggles into a pair of my tights. I love Wally but there are limits. I give him my sling-backs. Luckily, he has small feet so my shoes just about fit him.

'Practice walking in them, Wally.'

He sets off across the room, his legs bowed. I laugh so much my stomach aches and I end up putting Wally's shirt on inside out. His trousers are a surprisingly snug fit. He helps me into the jacket before slicking back my hair with a dab of his Brylcreem. I put on the black leather lace-ups and Wally spits on his hanky before giving the toes a quick rub.

'There you go,' he says stepping back to admire his handy-work. 'But we ain't got time to write nothing now.'

'We'll improvise.'

'What?'

'Make it up. Just go along with everything I say,' I tell him quickly.

'Talk about living dangerously.'

When we arrive everyone has made an effort. Jill is on stage to introduce Darren and his room-mate who are both wearing swimming trunks. Unable to contain herself at the sight of not one but two six-packs, the receptionist wolf-whistles and throws her knickers at the boys. Just as Darren is about to reciprocate, Jill runs back up to lead the audience in premature applause. Then she announces Josh, type-cast as a public school boy and his side-kick who plays a Cockney. They attempt to have a conversation but struggle to understand one another. It's surprisingly funny and it's good to see Josh can laugh at himself. Especially, as the rest of us have been doing it for years. Peter produces such a turkey we can smell it from the back row. We all make clucking noises and he struts to the front of the stage.

'You lot are either too ignorant or too drunk to notice but we are performing. I don't expect you to understand the creative process - especially those of you in the creative department - just shut-up and let us get on with it!'

The booing and jeering erupts to such a level, the double act retreats double-quick. Meanwhile, I am still trying to come up with an outline for our sketch. No worries, I'll think of something during the next act.

'I'd like to introduce, Wally and Ella. Up you come, guys,' says Jill handling the microphone like a pro.

My blood chills. Wally takes my hand and gives it a reassuring squeeze. I can hear people laughing before we even start. That's a good sign. Wally is miming washing a pair of my pants – clean ones thank goodness. It's an in-joke; we all know Jill launders her smalls in the office. I can just make her out in the front row, hiding her head in her hands. Wally is sitting facing the audience his legs, deliberately akimbo. People cheer. Jill is watching through her fingers, giggling. Then he pretends to apply lipstick, exaggerating every movement and I stomp about looking priggish and angry, which seems to nail Peter for the audience. Wally plants a kiss on my cheek before leading me off the stage by my tie. The front row stands up, clapping and whistling. The rest of the crowd follow suit and get to their feet. It takes forever to get back to our seats - the men want to shake Wally's hand and the girls want to cuddle him.

'Well done! You were brilliant,' I tell him.

'Thanks, young 'un but Pete's not too chuffed.'

I turn to see him glaring at us.

'Alright Pete?' says Wally waving at him.

'Can I have my pants back, Wal?' I whisper.

'Oh yes, wouldn't do for the wife to find those,' he says handing them to me.

I stuff them in my pocket and we settle down to watch the end of the show.

Wally is the toast of our last supper. Bottles of champagne, a goodwill gesture from Jill's mother, are set out on the tables and we quickly empty them. Everyone is anxious to party, our final fling on the dance floor before the bus comes to pick us up. We finish the meal as Jill announces the awards. For once, no-one really cares. Tonight, we don't need accolades to make us happy. Only Peter looks lost without the trappings he has come to rely on in Adland. No Porsche, no hand-tailored suit and no fawning entourage. Most people are genuinely pleased when Wally and I are awarded 'Best Double Act'.

Tomorrow, I'll be back at my desk working hard at being a housewife. Or an astronaut. Or whatever else the industry demands me to be. Tonight, I am Ella and it feels good. I grab Wally's hand and we swirl and twirl as we perform our version of the jive.

'Thank you, young 'un. I'm...all...out...of...puff,' Wally says trying to get his breath. 'I'm going to have to love you and leave you; just gotta do me packing. See you back at the chalet.'

As the DJ announces the last dance, unlikely couples take to the floor and snog to the music. Josh is dancing with a girl from media. She is so tall, her chest is in line with his head. He's happy. A couple waltz past. It's Mr Media and Mr Planning. I catch a look between them, just a flicker of something. They made a great team on the treasure hunt. I hope they found what they were looking for.

Darren asks three girls in succession to dance. Each one turns him down.

'Looks like it's me and you,' he says slipping an arm like an eel around my waist.

It's the first touch from a man since Tom.

'No, thanks,' I tell him, moving out of his reach. 'It was bad enough being chained to you all day. Anyway, what made you change your mind and finish the race?

'I thought you were a stuck-up cow but you've got guts. And you can't half sprint!"

'Yeah, these thighs are good for something,' I tell him.

He's not sure if I'm joking or not.

'Promise you won't be sick on me?' I ask, stepping into his arms and reprising his line from that fateful night when he rescued me from Peter.

He laughs.

'Shame you grassed us up to Jill. We would've won that treasure hunt,' he shouts over the music.

'You cheated, Darren. Besides, it's not about winning, it's about taking part,' I yell in his ear.

'I'll remind you of that next time we lose a pitch,' he says good-naturedly, before adding, 'Sorry for being a prat.'

'You can't help it, Darren,' I tell him with a smirk.

Ensuring I keep at least six inches between us, we dance together.

He motions towards Chloe and David who are standing together but staring in opposite directions.

'Where's she been all weekend? The first I saw of her was this afternoon,' he asks.

'Dunno, haven't seen much of Peter either.'

We exchange a glance. The music fades and the crowd fades away. Darren offers to walk me back to the chalet and we set off across the grass. I am still wearing Wally's shoes. They are beginning to rub.

'I thought you were going to make your move on that girl at the disco,' I say.

'She's out of my league.'

He kicks a discarded can along the path and looks down at the ground.

'Josh is obviously more her type. I'd just be her bit of rough.'

'Don't do yourself down, Darren. Our receptionist seemed pretty impressed with you earlier.'

'I think she was taking the piss. Even if I get a girl, she ends up dumping me. Must be my winning personality.'

'So, Peter and Chloe, do you think they ...?'

'You know Peter. Remember that night I caught you and him?'

I recall it only too well. Darren looks like he's about to apologise again.

'Forget it, Darren. I have. Fancy a paddle?'

He looks relieved and shakes his head but follows me over the sand to the water's edge. I take off Wally's shoes and give them to Darren to hold. Then I carefully roll up Wally's trousers. The cold water numbs my feet. We stroll back up the beach, making up our own awards. Wally wins 'Best Man in Tights' and Peter sweeps the board as 'Worst Actor', 'Worst Script-Writer' and 'Worst Director'. Darren offers to walk me back to my chalet but the weekend has been full-on and I need to be alone for a while. He hands me back Wally's shoes and I slip my damp feet into them. It's a beautiful warm evening and I enjoy wandering slowly back through the rows of chalets, reflecting on the day. Tom will be getting ready to go on stage now. He's got an hour or so to kill. I wonder what he's doing and who he's doing it with. I remember Wally's wise words and stop tormenting myself.

'Well, if it isn't, Ella!'

Where did Peter come from? He's drunk. I can smell the booze on him.

'You're looking horny!' he tells me which is patently untrue given I'm wearing Wally's clothes.

I say nothing and go to dart past him. He puts out his arms.

'I couldn't take my eyes off you on that stage. And you're supposed to be me, so bonking you would be like having sex with myself.'

'Nothing new there then,' I tell him sharply as I walk on.

'Not so fast,' he says, grabbing me roughly by the shoulder. 'Time to fulfil the terms of Our Little Arrangement. You owe me.'

He laughs in my face. I try to pull away but he tightens his grip and forces himself against me. I open my mouth to scream but nothing comes out. My right leg shakes uncontrollably. I try to move my foot forward but it remains stuck, shuddering on the ground.

'Come on. I pay well, remember.'

He thrusts himself urgently against me, like a goat.

'I'm not that sort of working girl,' I tell him, my voice breaking.

'But you pride yourself on being such a pro,' he laughs, delighted with his double-entendre. 'Come on, Ella. You know you want me.'

He stumbles. I take the opportunity to pull away. As I run, I glance over my shoulder to check he's not following me. My toe catches on a lose paving stone and I lurch forward. I put my hands out to save myself but crash to my knees, skimming the pavement with my palms. I get up quickly and half-run, half-limp back to the chalet. My hands sting and the flesh is studded with grit. I look down and notice a rip in Wally's trousers. I burst into tears. These look like his best pair, bought with his hard-earned wages. Trust Peter to ruin them.

I am so relieved to see No. 41. I must tell Wally what's happened. He'll know what to do. I go in. The smell of his soap fills the chalet. I knock on his bedroom door.

'Wal? You there?'

When he doesn't reply I tentatively peer around the door. I can see him lying on top of the counterpane, dressed in a fresh shirt and trousers ready to leave. I don't want to disturb him but I have to talk to him before we go.

'Wally, are you awake?' I whisper, gently touching his hand.

It feels cold. Too cold.

Chapter thirty-one

Emotion can be more powerful than reason

I arrive home to an empty house but the smell of stale tobacco still lingers. For a moment, I wish Tom was here. I just need to talk to someone about Wally.

I slump to the floor, still wearing his suit. Jill gently tried to persuade me to change before we left but I refused, wrapping the jacket around me in a futile attempt to defy his death and keep him close. I stayed in the chalet with him, holding his hand, until the ambulance arrived. I hated that he died alone, without his beloved wife at his side. The poor woman must be inconsolable.

'He wouldn't have known anything about it,' Jill reassured me as she gently took my arm and helped me onto the bus. 'He didn't stop smiling the whole weekend. He had a wonderful last dance, thanks to you.'

Dear Wally was so much more than the night-watchman come caretaker, the go-to guy when something needed fixing. If you wanted a light-bulb changed or a fuse mended, Wally was your man. He would call you a cab after you'd worked all night and he would call you a fool for putting work above family and friends. He had it sussed, enjoying a simple care-free life with his wife. He worked to live, unlike me and the other success-obsessed drones in the agency.

Now, I slowly replay the film, forever archived in my memory. There we are dancing like we just don't care. There's Wally eating his pie like it is fillet steak. Now he's leaping up and shouting 'House!' And that's us getting ready for the show. Even in drag Wally is more of a man than Peter will ever be. This afternoon he left the stage full of life. Whatever killed him was waiting in the wings, for his fifteen minutes of fame to end before bringing down the final curtain.

Why did the man who showed me how to live have to die?

I can feel something in the pocket and discover my knickers, the ones he 'washed' on stage. Now I am crying and laughing. Sunshine and showers, there will be a rainbow soon.

I lean over and unzip my bag, emptying the dirty washing onto the floor. My tights and blouse, the ones Wally wore only this afternoon tumble out together. He must have packed them for me. I smile and untangle the clothes before hanging them carefully over the back of a chair.

'Stick with me, young 'un. We'll have fun,' he told me and he was right.

Despite being old enough to be my Grand-dad, Wally showed me how to be young. He proved it doesn't take a fat salary to be happy, just an old man in tights. I smile before bursting into tears again.

'What's wrong with you?' Tom asks.

Startled, I jerk backwards knocking my head against the washing-machine. It's only been a few days since he left but already he looks detached. I don't recognise his clothes and he's had a hair cut.

'Tom, what are you doing here?' I ask with a dry mouth.

He lights up a cigarette and flicks the spent match into the sink.

'I forgot something. Thought you were away and I could just nip in and get it.'

I remind myself to get the locks changed.

'Why are you crying?' he asks without caring. 'Still upset about me? You need to move on. I have.'

Tom Tyler's ego fills the room like methane.

'It's got nothing to do with you. I stopped loving you the night Cara showed up. I just didn't realise it,' I tell him.

He snorted.

'My friend died today. Wally died. Heart attack.'

'Wally? Who's Wally?'

'The caretaker, I told you about him. He was a lovely man.'

'Oh,' he says as if it doesn't matter, as if Wally doesn't matter.

'He was wonderful, my idea of a perfect dad or grand-dad and he …'

'Whose clothes are you wearing?' he cuts in, not listening.

'Wally's.'

I start to cry again as the pain I feel about losing him erupts.

'Calm down,' he scoffs. 'He was just the caretaker.'

'He wasn't 'just' anything. He was lovely.'

'Whoa!'

'Just go,' I tell him. 'Get out and give me back my keys.'

'With pleasure,' he says reaching into his pocket and throwing them on the table.

As he walks away, his hand catches the edge of the chair, knocking it to the ground and kicking it across the floor. My clothes fly into the air, the sleeves of the blouse and the legs of the tights lashing out at him before falling impotently, to the floor. He grabs the shirt with both hands

'No!' I cry picturing Wally wearing it. 'Don't!'

He rips it in two.

'There. We're done,' he declares as he walks towards the front door.

'You bastard,' I call after him.

He lets out a long, throaty laugh.

'You think everyone loves Tom Tyler? Well, I don't,' I scream.

Slowly, he reverses back into the kitchen, 'I'm having the best sex of my life.'

His words act like a dirty rag wiping away the last stubborn stain of what we shared. There's nothing left. For a moment, it feels like he's punched me in the stomach and I double-over, unable to speak. He has reduced our love-making to nothing more than a competitive sport. I think of us together and squirm. My dream, built on little more than a stranger's handsome face, evaporates. I fell in love with a man full of hate. Just like Mum, I equated good looks with goodness. Now I understand what the old lady in the supermarket meant by, 'Handsome is as handsome does.' Just because he's good-looking, doesn't mean he's good.

'Who?' I hear myself asking.

Why do I need to know? It shouldn't matter but it does. My mind rewinds and replays our film, the one of our time together. Even the moments I remembered as special are now sullied, like he's scratched the negative with a pin.

'No-one you know.'

I hunt for answers, snatching at threads of information like a fish darting for food.

'Cara! It was Cara, wasn't it?'

'No, not Cara. She wanted me but she's not my type. No, the girl I've been seeing is amazing,' he laughs. 'So is her dad, he's a record producer.'

This has obviously been going on while he was living here with me. I don't want to hear it but it will strengthen my resolve. Whenever I get weepy I will remember this.

Women are just notches on the bedpost and rungs on the ladder to him. I lean against the wall, defeated. Although Tom has only gone a few steps, he's already a million miles away from me. The front door slams behind him.

Some days, when it was good with Tom, it felt like the two of us, shoulder to shoulder against the world and with his arms around me, I felt special. Even his smile said, 'I love you'. Now I know it meant no more than a line from one of his songs, just words to manipulate me.

I jump up and rifle through the box of cassettes to find the one he made for me. Here it is. I pull out the thin brown magnetic tape. It spools onto the floor like a tapeworm. Then, I run into the bathroom. Where is his aftershave, that ludicrously expensive stuff he slapped on before every gig? He kept it right here on the shelf. I open the cupboard. His toothbrush and razor are gone too. I hate the thought he has been here while I was away. The flat feels dirty, violated. I run into the bedroom, my stomach lurching and fling open the wardrobe. It's half empty. My clothes hang like shrouds. His shoes have disappeared from under the bed and the diary he used for his bookings is no longer beside the phone. He's even taken his jar of 2p coins. At last, the penny drops. He planned all this, all along. He wasn't in love with me, just my flat and when I wouldn't let him move in, he moved on.

The phone rings. I hope it's not Tom, ringing with another revelation.

'Hello,' I say hesitantly into the mouthpiece.

'Before I forget, can you bring one of those fancy chocolate cheesecakes from Pat Val's to the dinner tomorrow night? Jan can't cook. She thinks she can but no-one likes it when she does.'

'Adam!'

I am overjoyed to hear his voice.

'Adam, d'you know what time it is?' I ask.

'Sorry, I didn't think. Jan's still on nights and has just left for work. She was talking me through the menu and ...'

'Don't apologise, I…'

He hears my tears before I know they're there.

'What's wrong?'

'Wally died.'

The words still don't sound real to me.

'Not Wally. He was good a bloke. He used to let me leave my BMW in the client car-park. I paid him in cake. His wife wouldn't let him eat stuff like that.'

'She was right. He died of a heart attack.'

'Sorry. That's terrible. I can't believe it. His wife must be devastated. I met her once. He had forgotten his flask and she had come all the way in from Leyton by train to give it to him.'

'Yeah, he really loved her.'

'Promise you'll still come to the house-warming? I'll make sure we have something nice to eat.'

'Thanks,' I say and burst into tears again.

'Come on, Wally wouldn't want you getting upset. Is Tom there with you?'

The tears race down my cheeks. When I open my mouth to speak, they drop in for me to swallow.

'No, it's over. He's been sleeping with someone else,' I sob.

'But you're lovely,' he tells me and his kindness makes me cry harder. 'I'm coming over.'

I hug the pieces of the blouse Wally wore last night to my face. It smells of his soap.

As I go into the bathroom to blow my nose, I look up and catch sight of my reflection, swollen eyes and face smeared with mascara. No wonder Tom left me. I wander back into the bedroom and sit down. I can see something small underneath the dressing table. I bend down and feel underneath with my hand. I pull out a cassette. The words 'Tom's songs' are written in ballpoint pen in his handwriting.

I know I shouldn't play it but I do.

'Stella, you mean more to me than you'll ever know, I want to make angels with you in the snow. Stella, you mean more to me than you'll ever know. I'm never gonna let you go.'

Even the song he claimed to have written especially for me, wasn't mine. It was Stella's, whoever she is. If my name hadn't rhymed with hers, I wouldn't even have got that.

I am expecting Adam but the knock on the door still startles me. As I walk down the corridor, I can see his outline through the etched glass.

'There you go,' he says holding out two carrier bags of shopping. 'I got a couple of packets of those really thick chocolate wafers, the ones you like.'

I follow him into the kitchen where he unpacks cake, biscuits and olives. Things he knows I like and hopes will tempt me.

'Sorry not much of a selection but it was all Mr Patel had left. I was surprised he was still open. Does that man ever sleep?'

'Thanks, how much...?'

'My treat,' he insists. 'Let me make you a cup of tea and we'll have a nice slice of cake to go with it.'

He potters about filling the kettle, finding mugs and getting plates.

The kinder he is, the more I cry.

'Sorry,' I sniff. 'It was just such a shock when I saw him here tonight.'

'Thought you said he'd left?' says Adam his mouth full of millionaire's shortbread.

'He has. He came back because he'd forgotten some stuff.'

'What was so important?' he asks offering me a caramel wafer.

I can't imagine. Then, I remember and run to the bedroom. I lift the lid on my jewellery box, look inside and let it slam shut. I go back to Adam.

'The gold heart necklace, the one he gave me has gone. We fished it out from under the floorboards. I don't think I even got to wear it. He must have taken it. Probably going to give it to his new girl.'

'Don't get upset. You don't want his heart. Anyone who prefers lager to cake, can't be right,' he declares. 'Here, try this.'

He slides a chocolate slice out of its box and feeds it to me.

I finish it in two bites. Instantly, its sweetness fills me with pleasure. And, just for a moment, I feel my heart beat a little faster. It must be the sugar rush.

Chapter thirty-two

Be different

'Ella, please don't go in there,' says Jill looking concerned and jumping up from her seat.

It's the first day back after the away weekend. It was heart-breaking knowing Wally wouldn't be here. I even paused outside Patisserie Valerie's window and picked out the cake I would usually have bought him. A chocolate croissant. My mind floods with wonderful memories of him and I am happy to let them blot out the toxic residue left by Tom. Too much has gone wrong recently, I just need to get back to normal. I need to work.

I open the door to my office to be greeted by Chloe sitting at my desk with her back to me. She doesn't even bother to look up when I walk in. My eyes sweep around the room. Immediately, I am disorientated. What's happened? The walls are stripped of my awards. The framed stills of my commercials, signed by the directors, have been removed and my collection of vintage press advertisements has gone. But this is my office. I recognise the view across to the private drinking club. My chair has disappeared and has been replaced with an ergonomically-designed number, all sleek black leather and polished wood. Chloe is sitting comfortably in it, typing. But I can't hear the familiar clack-clacking of the keys, just the faint whirr of her new, improved electric model.

I feel like I've been burgled and the thief has not only taken all my belongings but has moved in. I see my shocked expression staring back at me from the vast gilt mirror now covering one wall. Details for a Primrose Hill property, secured by a single red drawing pin, hang beneath it. I lean forward and tilt my head to read the asking price, £200,000. Chloe's only just left college. Where can she get that sort of money?

I turn to Jill hoping she can help make sense of all this. She meets my gaze and bites her lip, her hands knotted in front of her.

'What's going on?' I ask, although the answer is obvious.

'Oh, hello Ella. I didn't see you there. You're next door,' says Chloe, spinning round in her chair.

Her dark eyes are hard and her glossy black bob, immaculate. She is wearing a hand-tailored dress in white linen. It is a perfect fit even if it does make her look like an Egyptian mummy. She smiles faintly at me before turning away.

'Sorry, Ella,' says Jill. 'Peter wanted Chloe to have the bigger room.'

'Oh he did, did he? So much for team-building. What was the point of all that? May as well have not gone. Poor old Wally might still be here. All that exertion and excitement can't have been good for him.'

'Ella, please don't upset yourself,' says Jill taking my arm.

Not only have I lost Tom but I can't even keep hold of my office. It's like being on a cakewalk at a funfair but without the cake or the fun.

'And where's my stuff? My awards, my ...'

'Calm down,' sneers Chloe appearing in the doorway. 'Those certificates are so out-of-date now. Not worth the paper they're printed on.'

I want to mess up her sleek, smug hair-do. The two-faced madam. I gave her a chance, paid her good money and this is how she repays me?

'You haven't won anything,' I tell her.

Slyly, she slides a piece of paper across the desk towards me. It's an all-staff memo from Peter announcing that Chloe has been shortlisted for Best Television Commercial for Honeydrop Cough Syrup. My head swims. This was never meant to happen and certainly not this fast. One minute I'm giving her a leg up, the next Peter's got his leg over.

'Peter reckons I'll clean up in Cannes this year. He's so confident he's booked a table near the front for us so I don't have far to walk to the podium.'

Now she's pushed me over the edge and I'm clinging on by my fingertips. She steps forward and I feel like she's crushing my hands under her six-inch heel.

'Jill, can you get me an espresso, a large one. And a pain au chocolat? Thanks,' says Chloe.

The pain is sickening. She's not only stolen my office. She's raided my patisserie and purloined my secretary. Bile rises in my throat. My world is in freefall. Jill gently steers me back into the corridor.

'I'm so sorry, Ella. Peter said he'd told you about all this.'

I shake my head.

'Your things are safe. I put them in Wally's old office. You're in here now,' she says, flinging open the door to what used to be the photocopying room.

To disguise the fact there are no windows, she quickly flicks on the light. At least that works. The walls are painted charcoal but there is a patch of magnolia where the photocopier once stood. A desk and two chairs are pushed against one wall. Someone has dumped a pile of layout pads and pens on the floor.

'Really?' I ask. 'There's not room to swing Marmalade in here.'

'Morning, Ella. Like your new pad? It's 'bijoux' in estate agent speak. And they say advertising must be more legal, decent, honest and truthful,' Peter glides into view.

He can barely speak as his mouth is full of chewing gum. He throws the keys to his Porsche up in the air before catching them in the palm of one hand. He is wearing designer jeans teamed with a white shirt. Having hit forty, Peter is one of those men who look faintly ridiculous in denim.

'I'm your writer so it would make more sense if I share your office,' I tell him.

He walks away and calls over his shoulder, 'My writer? Hasn't Jill told you?'

I look at Jill hoping she'll make everything right but I couldn't be more wrong. She averts her eyes and stares at the floor. Oh Wally, I wish you were here. I turn to Peter. He looks even odder than usual. It's his hair. Once greying at the temples, it has turned a mysterious shade of blue-black overnight. At least it matches his heart.

'I'm working with Chloe now. We're a team.'

The odd couple.

It's cheered me up knowing he is having a crisis, mid-life crisis.

'What are you so upset about?' he asks as I start to cry again.

'Wally.'

'Wally?' he ponders. 'Oh yeah. Unfortunate business. At least he didn't peg out in the agency. Not sure we're be insured for that. That reminds me. Jill, here use my credit card. Send a wreath, white lilies, spelling out C-B-A, be great publicity for the agency when the hearse goes through London.'

Jill doesn't move. Even Chloe seems stunned by his callousness.

'You're unbelievable,' I tell him, too angry to cry. 'He was wonderful. Saved your life on more than one occasion. Now the poor man's dead. Show some respect.'

'I'll ask the florist to make up a bouquet. I'll call his wife. Find out if he had a favourite flower,' insists Jill, her voice metallic. 'And I'll start a collection. Everyone loved Wally; they'll all want to contribute.'

'Suit yourself,' he says swiftly replacing the card in his soft leather wallet. 'By the way, Ella, I've teamed you up with David. Opposites attract.'

They also repel.

'You've hired David? You are joking.' I say. 'Guilty conscience, was it? You've taken his girlfriend so you let him keep his job? You're all heart, Peter.'

'You are quite the curmudgeon these days, such a cynic. David is okay with the arrangement. He can learn a lot from you. And you can learn a lot from Chloe. I love her 'can-do' attitude.'

I bet you do.

Right on cue, she appears and feeds off the atmosphere like a bulimic vulture. When she sees how upset I am, her perfect porcelain-like face erupts into a smile. She sashays into Peter's office.

'I've got something to show you,' she coos.

'I can't wait to see it,' he sings.

He snakes the tip of his tongue across his top lip as the door clicks shut behind them.

I turn to Jill who is twirling her string of pearls nervously through her fingers.

'Can you believe that? What a bitch!' I say bitterly.

'I'm really sorry, Ella,' she tells me and I believe her.

'It's not your fault, Jill.'

'I had no idea what he was up to until last night. He doesn't tell me anything anymore.'

'They've done me a favour. I'll have to find another job now. I can't stay here,' I tell her.

I want to believe what I'm saying.

'Can't you just see how things go with David? He's been shafted same as you,' she says. 'At least you'll still get paid.'

261

'No, it wouldn't work. I've got to go.'

'Think about it. Jobs are thin on the ground. I get creative teams ringing me everyday begging to show Peter their portfolios. He just tells me to get rid of them. Unless they're girls, of course, and then he's only too delighted to meet them. So to save a few lambs from the slaughter, I tell them we've got no vacancies.'

I never knew Jill was so wily.

'Good thinking,' I tell her.

'Don't do anything rash, Ella. You've had a big shock with Wally dying and everything else. Not the best time to make big decisions,' Jill advises with genuine concern. 'Why don't you hang on here until you find something else? Use Peter like he used you?'

How the smoked-glass tables have turned. She was once a pathetic creature who pandered to Peter's every whim and considered laundering her smalls in the company's washer-drier a perk of the job. Now she's telling me what to do. She means well. And she has got a point. Try as Maggie may, she hasn't got the country back to work. There are no jobs to go to.

'Peter's really screwed me this time,' I tell her.

'You're not the only one Peter's screwed,' she says looking down.

I usher her into my cupboard. There's just enough room if we both stand sideways.

'Remember Peter's broken table? That was me,' she confesses.

I nod in wonder. Not only because I can't believe she would be so stupid as to have sex with Peter but also because I can't imagine how a woman who weighs so little could do so much damage to plate glass.

'Was he married at the time?'

'Yes, but there was a rumour going round the agency that they'd split up.'

'Peter probably started it.'

She looks embarrassed.

'It can't have been much fun when he was never around at weekends or Christmas.'

'I was in love, I put up with anything just for a few moments alone with him.'

I stare incredulously at this girl who has caste her pearls before a swine like Peter.

'Jill, I can't believe you fell for that pig.'

'At first, he treated me like a princess.'

'He treated you like a bit on the side.'

'You had a fling with a bloke you met outside the dole office, hardly the romance of the century.'

Her words eat into the part of me that's still raw.

'Sorry, I wasn't judging you,' I tell her. 'But you could have any man you want. Why him?'

'You know how it is. One minute it's a laugh, the next you're in bed and in love with them.'

I understand only too well.

'To be honest, I may have loved his Porsche more than him,' explained Jill. 'When he opened it up on the M4 it was such a thrill.'

I am repulsed at the thought of a turbo-charged Peter.

'He promised he'd leave his wife when she recovered.'

'I didn't know she was ill.'

'She wasn't.'

'I didn't think even Peter would stoop that low. I can't believe you fell for him and his corny lines,' I say.

'Don't so hard-faced, Ella,' she says as she leaves my office.

I follow her back to her desk.

'I didn't mean ...'

'Yes, you did,' she says. 'But it's okay. You're right.'

She has ended the confrontation and started me thinking. This business has changed me. For the worse. I can't remember when I last saw Mum, or even spoke to her. I have no time for my friends, unless I count Adam but even he is an ex-colleague. I seem incapable of holding down a relationship, let alone a job. Jill sees my face. She reaches down into the cupboard underneath her desk and takes out a bottle of red wine and two glasses. I raise my eyebrows as she pours us both a drink.

'It's Peter's secret stash. He won't even notice it's missing. It's the least he owes us.'

'Bit early, isn't it?'

'Well, I can't imagine you were planning on doing any work today. I'm not. Here,' she says handing me a glass as she sips from hers. 'Want to hear something funny?'

I nod and sit on the edge of her desk as I down half my wine in anticipation.

'Peter used to tell me I was more stupid than I looked. So one day, I decided to prove him wrong.'

'What did you do?' I ask desperate to hear about Peter's demise.

'I hid my knickers in his bed, in his car and in ...'

'His desk? So they were your pants? Small, clean and ironed, they had to be yours,' I say. 'That was a brave move. There was no going back after that.'

'I had nothing to lose. He had already accused me of trying to cause trouble after his wife had found another pair tangled in their sheets. The thing was they weren't mine; they were enormous. The bastard was sleeping with someone who had an arse the size of Soho,' she says.

'So he had three of you on the go?'

Turns out I needn't have worried about our Little Arrangement. With his busy schedule, he'd never have had the time to squeeze me in. Oh, that's a conjured up a horrible mental image. No sooner have I erased one picture of Peter in flagrante from my mind, another pops up. Then, I remember.

'Of course, it was Mrs Kitty Rescue, wasn't it?' I exclaim. 'Peter was sleeping with you, his wife and Mrs Kitty Rescue at the same time. Well, not together, obviously.'

'Please don't mention that woman's name,' she hisses.

Now I get it. Peter was the dirty dog and Jill the wily fox.

'You swopped the High-Pro tape we were meant to watch in the briefing for the X-rated video of Peter and Mrs Kitty Rescue, didn't you?'

'I don't know what you're talking about,' Jill says with mock innocence.

'It had to be you. Mrs Kitty Rescue didn't want her dirty laundry aired in public. And Peter's wife rarely came near the agency.'

'He asked for it. He was insatiable. He's got a thing for posh girls with blonde hair.

'Who else d'you think he slept with?' I ask.

'Lady Diana!' she squeals.

265

'But she's just got married,' I reply.

'Not the Lady Di. I mean the work placement girl with the blonde hair. Peter was always taking her to lunch.'

Of course, her Sloane Square pad was ideally placed for shopping at Peter Jones and sleeping with Peter Richards.

'Well, Jill, at least you didn't take it lying down,' I smirk.

Even if the joke is in poor taste, I think we both deserve a little levity.

'Very funny, Ella,' she says as we chink glasses.

Her face etched with pain. She's clearly reliving some of her more unsavoury moments with Peter.

'Trouble is, Jill, I think Peter saw the tape of him and Mrs Kitty Rescue more as a promo for his sexual prowess than as something to be ashamed of. He was completely mesmerised; couldn't take his eyes off the screen. Josh was about to implode.'

I'd go so far as to say it was a career highlight.

'I didn't plan it,' she tells me. 'I went into his office one day and caught him watching that video. He was so engrossed; he didn't notice me. But I saw him and that cow at it like a pair of fat rabbits. She's got tons of cellulite. You'd never guess she used to be a model. Anyway, I slipped out of the room, waited for him to go to lunch and then nipped back and took the tape. Then, all I had to do was bide my time and find the perfect moment to replay it.'

'Well, you certainly played a blinder,' I say raising my glass. 'Here's to you, Jill and all who sail in you.'

'Unfortunate turn of phrase, Ella. But thank-you,' she replies.

She picks up the bottle and swigs from it.

'He's got such a big ...'

She stops and waggles her little finger in the air.

'Ego!' she laughs. 'He was forever videoing himself. I just ensured the film reached a wider audience.'

We are both laughing hard now. Suddenly she looks aghast.

'My God, I wonder what he did with all those tapes of the two of us? They could be anywhere now.'

'I shouldn't worry, Jill. If I know Peter, he'd have been hogging the camera and you wouldn't have got a look-in.'

Reassured, she opens her desk drawer, pulls out a long white envelope and hands it to me.

'I don't care anymore. Peter can do what he likes. I've typed up my resignation. What do you think?'

I read the letter. It's word perfect - sharp but not cutting. She's been smart enough to ensure Peter gives her an excellent reference.

'It's good but like you told me, it's tough out there. Why should you lose out because Peter can't keep it in his pants?'

'I'm going to work for Mummy. I love that holiday camp. And I really get what she's trying to do with it.'

Prefabs that look like prisons. Not my idea of fun, I think. She reads my mind.

'I know it's not exactly Tuscany but I think there's a market for it. The whole retro thing could really catch on. People will love reliving their childhood memories with their kids.'

Relive my childhood? No thanks.

'Go for it but it won't be easy,' I say.

I can't help wondering how wise it for her to re-launch a clapped-out holiday camp during a recession when she doesn't know the first thing about marketing.

She grabs a couple of packets of crisps from her magic cupboard and rips one open. She offers them to me. I shake my head not fully understanding the concept of a savoury tooth. Why bother when you can just eat cake? She stuffs fistfuls of crisps into her mouth in the vain hope they will soak up the alcohol. She's swaying now. But at least, she's happy.

'Sitting in on meetings with you has taught me so much. And I've been studying marketing at the college. Just heard I've passed my exams,' she squeals raising her glass.

'Wow! Congratulations! You have been busy,' I say. 'No wonder you handled the weekend away so well.'

'When Peter did the dirty on me, I needed something to take my mind off it so I signed up for a marketing course.'

'Good for you.'

We hear Peter and Chloe laughing in his office. A match made in hell. At least with Chloe tending to his every need, it will take the heat off the rest of the girls.

'I give it six months, max,' says Jill reading my thoughts. 'She'll use him and move on.'

'Let's hope she breaks his heart,' I tell her draining my glass.

'Peter? Heart? You've lost me,' Jill laughs. 'Peter had me pegged as a dumb blonde.'

'He underestimated you; we all did,' I tell her.

I shudder as I remember how callow I had been when I first met her. I couldn't even be bothered to find out her name. She was just Peter's secretary. She senses my discomfort.

'At least you gave me a chance, Ella. At first I was terrified I'd blow it but I took to it like a duck to water.'

'No more f-ing ducks, Jill,' I say and we both laugh.

'D'you know he even used to tell me to 'get my ducks in a row' even when we were in bed together?'

'No way!' I exclaim.

'His favourite was 'Run it up the flagpole and see who salutes' when he took his pants off,' she declares through joyous howls. 'Seriously, we're going to need some advertising for the holiday camp. Fancy it? We'd pay you the going rate?'

'Well, I've already done the site visit and tested the product so I don't see why not!' I say.

I look away.

'You're thinking about Wally, aren't you?' asks Jill.

'How do you know?'

'Because you're smiling.'

Chapter thirty-three

Be prepared to make changes

'Hi, you must be Jan, I'm Ella. Sorry for barging in but the front door was ajar and I couldn't get your bell to work,' I say feigning a happy-go-lucky attitude as I walk into Adam's kitchen and introduce myself to the back of Adam's girlfriend's head. I used to be Tom's girlfriend. Not sure who I am anymore.

'Hi, nice to meet you. Any friend of Adam's and all that,' she says without turning round.

I stand behind her, not knowing what to say next. My mind is set on rewind. I think about Tom too much. All it takes is someone lighting up a cigarette and I feel like bursting into tears. There's no logic to it, just loss. Like all things, it will pass. Just not right now. But I am impatient. I want to fast-forward to the happy ending.

Unfortunately, I seem to be stuck in the middle of someone else's domestic bliss. Jan is moving effortlessly about the room, opening drawers and cupboards, gathering implements and ingredients while referring to a new cookery book open on the marble worktop. She lifts a willowy hand to her face and brushes back a strand of naturally blonde hair. No wonder she's in a happy, steady relationship, with a happy, steady guy.

She reaches for an opened bottle of extra virgin olive oil and slowly pours a thin stream into a pan on the stove.

I stand beside her still holding the bottle of Chateau Neuf du Pape, my contribution to the evening. Adam told me not to get the cheesecake; Jan had insisted on making dessert. She turns to get the salt.

'Thanks, just stick it on the side,' she tells me, referring to the wine. ' Sorry, at a crucial stage with the cooking.'

She runs her index finger down the list of ingredients.

'Courgettes, aubergines, fresh thyme,' she tuts. 'Thyme. Adam forgot the thyme. I ask him to get one thing and ...'

She flings open a cupboard hunting for a substitute and pulls out a small glass jar.

'...oregano? No, it's not the same,' she says, answering her own question and replacing the container back on the shelf.

She turns it until the label faces front, just like all the other tins and bottles.

'Adam never stops talking about you,' I tell her, hoping she might turn round.

It is a slight exaggeration but I think it's what you are supposed to say when you meet your best mate's partner.

'Have some wine,' she tells me waving her hand in the direction of a wine box on the edge of the work surface.

I look longingly at the expensive bottle I brought. Perhaps we'll drink it with dinner. Reluctantly, I hold a glass underneath the small plastic tap and press the button down. Nothing happens. I push harder. The box falls on the floor spraying red wine everywhere. Not content with being unable to operate her doorbell, I have ruined her state-of-the-art kitchen too.

'I'm so sorry,' I say.

I try to move but my feet seem to be nailed to the floor.

'Adam! Can you come? Your friend has spilt wine all over the kitchen,' she yells chopping shallots into regimented rings. 'Hurry up. It's gone everywhere.'

Adam rushes in wearing long baggy shorts and a tee-shirt. He is playing with a Rubik's cube.

271

'Sorry,' I tell him as I eye the pool of wine.

He continues to twist the coloured squares into rows.

'Look, I nearly did it,' he says proudly showing me one of the faces covered in red squares.

'What about the other five sides?' asks Jan.

Adam puts it on the table and steps over the puddle of wine before yanking open the fridge door.

'Ella, look, we've got chocolate roulade for pudding,' he says excitedly.

'Starter and mains first,' orders Jan. 'Hope you're going to change for dinner, Adam. What are you doing? Get the mop!'

Adam rolls his eyes and picks up the wine I brought. He eyes the label approvingly.

'Thanks. This looks good. Let's get it open.'

He pours us both a glass.

'I've already offered Ella wine, Adam.' asks Jan ripping open a packet of smoked salmon and arranging it in the centre of an oval china plate.

She rapidly slices lemons into quarters and nestles them around the slices of fish.

'Here, Adam stick this on the table,' she orders, handing him the food.

He salutes and marches into the dining room.

'So many people are vegetarians these days. It's hard to come up with interesting ideas for dinner party menus when people don't eat meat, don't you think?' she asks with her head in a cupboard.

'I wouldn't know. I don't cook,' I mutter.

'Don't forget to put the brown bread out, Adam,' she shouts.

I watch her as she layers sheets of pasta and sauce into a large oven-proof dish before grating Parmesan cheese over the top. Adam comes back into the kitchen and pretends to gag.

'Hate that stuff, smells like someone's been sick.'

'Grow up, Adam,' she says. 'Get the door - I think I heard the bell. '

Someone brighter than me has obviously arrived. Adam darts off down the hall chewing on a chunk of granary bread.

'Lovely house, Jan,' I say, looking around at the shiny kitchen crammed with the latest gadgets.

'That wallpaper's going to have to go. Adam can start stripping next weekend.'

I smile at the thought of Adam, naked in the kitchen. Jan is oblivious to her unintentional double-entendre and points, with a large metal serving spoon, at the yellow candy-striped walls. For the first time since, I get a good look at her. She's blonde and icy. She reminds me of someone but I can't think who.

'Adam chose the wine for this evening so blame him if it's rubbish. If you don't like it, just throw it down the sink,' she says like someone who has never known what it is to go without.

She squints at me, screwing up her clear blue eyes.

'I know you, don't I? I never forget a face. I remember! The hospital!' she exclaims.

Of course, that's where I've seen her. She was the trainee doctor in A&E that night. Now it's my turn to look away. I am so embarrassed. It was hardly my finest hour.

'That was ages ago. You must see so many people. Surely you don't remember me?'

'It was my first night in A&E, a real baptism of fire. There were lots of accidents because the weather was so bad. There had been a pile-up on the Marylebone Road. It was mayhem. Then the ambulance brought you in. You'd fallen down the stairs. Yes, that's right. One side of your face was all mashed up.'

She lifts my chin roughly with her fingertips. To my horror, she scrutinises my cheek, like an artist checking her brushwork.

'It's healed well. You were lucky,' she remarks before turning her attention to sniffing a round of brie on the table.

I realise I have been dismissed and shrink away, pretending to be interested in her collection of European cookery books. Out of the corner of my eye, I see a tall thick-set man walk in and hug her. He drops an expensive-looking bouquet of hand-tied flowers onto the table. She spins round and kisses him on the cheek.

'Hey Mark! They're beautiful, thanks.   You're early. Did Nurse Ratchet give you time off for good behaviour?' she laughs, suddenly animated.

'Hardly. It was another twelve-hour-yawn-fest in casualty. We lost two this evening,' he replies watching her every move.

'That was very careless of you,' says Jan with a grin. 'Hope you like veggie lasagne.'

The loss of human life is lost on them.

'No meat? Jan, please tell me you're joking,' he says helping himself to a bottle of lager from the fridge.

'Sorry, Markie. Boring but you know Karen won't touch anything with a face.'

'Oh God! I'd forgotten she was coming. Why did you invite her? I suppose she's bringing that loser, Gary? Why she wants to date a man that specialises in dead people is beyond me.'

'Geriatrics are not dead people!' she laughs spooning Greek yogurt into a bowl and attacking it with a balloon whisk. 'Just because she doesn't fancy you there's no need attack poor Gary.'

She dips her little finger into the bowl and scoops out some yogurt.

'Open wide, doctor!' she orders him playfully inserting her pinkie into his mouth.

'Oh, very tasty,' he tells her smiling broadly.

I look away and pretend to be interested in a picture of a cabbage hanging on the wall.

'Why are you pandering to Karen? She wouldn't cook you fillet steak so why make her veggie muck?'

He helps himself to an olive from a bowl on the side and chews it rapidly.

'Where's Adam?' he asks spitting the stone into his hand and throwing it into the sink. 'Don't tell me, selling lager to louts. Is that his car outside? It's even better than mine; I'm in the wrong job. He writes slogans, for God's sake. I'm the one saving lives.'

'He's a Creative Director, I'll have you know,' Jan says in mock awe. 'Well, Deputy Creative Director.'

They both laugh.

'Advertising is such a vacuous, self-serving industry. One day, it will implode, trust me,' he says opening a bottle of white wine and pouring them both a glass.

Despite wearing a rather violent shade of red I seem to have become invisible since his arrival. Jan catches his eye and nods towards me. He looks vaguely in my general direction.

'Oh, didn't see you there, I'm Mark.'

He extends his hand for me to shake. It's cold and oily from the olives.

'Hi, I'm Ella,' I reply, forcing a smile.

He looks nonplussed.

'Adam's friend, works in advertising,' clarifies Jan, neatly condensing me into just five words before calling out to Adam, 'Come and clear this wine up now!'

Mark turns away and helps himself to some brie. Jan playfully slaps his hand away as she tears up basil leaves and scatters them on top of a dish of sliced tomatoes. I want to say something smart. Something that will force him to revise his opinion of Adland but my mind is empty and vacuous just like he said.

'Anything I can do, Jan?' I ask.

I hope she declines my offer because I'm sure I could never do anything to her impossibly high standards.

'Take those glasses through to the dining room.'

Say 'please', I think as I watch her spoon clear honey over thickened yogurt with one hand and indicate a tray of champagne flutes with the other.

I carry them carefully into the dining room where I am surprised by a young couple locked in an embrace. When they eventually notice me, they dart apart.

'Hello, I'm Ella, Adam's friend.'

They smile briefly before their lips are drawn together again like magnets. Jan sweeps in holding a stack of dinner plates.

'Karen! Gary! You pair of lovebirds! I didn't know you were in here. This is Ella, Adam's friend works in advertising,' explains Jan as if I am a two-year-old and advertising is some sort of adventure playground where Adam and I mess around all day. She's not wrong.

'Adam!' she yells. 'Come and pour the drinks.'

I hate the way she orders him about. If she could see him at work, she would respect him more. Adam appears with chocolate at the corners of his mouth. Naughty boy. He's been unfaithful to her even if it is only with a chocolate cake. I can't let his indiscretion be discovered. I touch my lips then point to his. He looks quizzical then opens the champagne and pours it too quickly so it spills over the tops of the glasses. I repeat the mime, only this time I exaggerate every movement, touching my mouth and then reaching out to point at Adam's just as Mark walks in.

'Give it to me, Adam. You get back to your game of charades with your friend here,' says Mark snatching the bottle from Adam and glaring at me.

Adam shrugs and sits down. I notice he's still wearing his shorts. Another act of rebellion. He picks up a mound of smoked salmon and wedges it between slices of brown bread.

'Adam!' scolds Jan. 'Sorry everyone, please sit down and help yourselves.'

Jan has put me next to Mark. From the way she keeps looking over and smirking I guess this is her attempt at match-making. She should stick to the day job. There's more to mending a broken heart than splicing it back together with a scalpel. But at least it means she's not interested in him. I would hate to think she was doing the dirty on Adam. Karen and Gary play footsie under the table. I play with my food, painfully aware that everyone else in the room is more intelligent, better qualified and happier than I am.

'So, Mark what do you do when you're not saving lives?' I ask genuinely interested.

Mark, Jan, Karen and Gary look up, aghast.

'What's that supposed to mean?' Mark replies his fork just inches from his mouth.

'Nothing, I ...'

'He is doing a parachute jump for charity, aren't you, Markie,' says Jan. 'Why don't you sponsor him?'

She dabs at the sides of her mouth with her serviette.

'Did you have to do much training?' I ask.

'I've trained for seven years at medical school; I'm a professional,' he says.

He throws his knife and fork down and pushes away his plate.

'I think Ella means did you do much training for the jump,' explains Jan.

'What training did you do, Ella?' he spits my name out of his mouth like a lump of gristle. 'What qualifies you to sell people shit they don't need?'

'Hey, don't start on her,' says Adam leaning across the table.

'Did I touch a nerve?' sneers Mark, pleased to have provoked Adam.

Jan stands up, desperate to restore order but Adam hasn't finished.

"Markie' might be a god in your world, Jan but he certainly isn't in mine. How dare he come to my house and insult my friend,' says Adam.

'Jan's house, I think you'll find it's her name on the Deeds, not yours,' says Mark smugly.

Adam jumps up and rushes at him.

'Steady on, mate. Stress is a killer, y'know,' says Mark. 'I thought you got enough of that in your job. I had an ad man die on me only the other week. You wanna be careful.'

He leans back in his chair and puts his hands up to protect his face.

'I'm not your mate,' hisses Adam through clenched teeth.

'Calm down, Adam,' says Jan.

'Don't tell me to calm down,' he says walking off into the kitchen.

'Check the lasagne,' calls Jan.

She collects up the dirty plates as if nothing has happened. I take them from her as an excuse to see Adam.

'You okay?' I ask.

His head is in the fridge.

'Yeah, fine. Want some?' he asks.

He emerges with a spoonful of chocolate roulade and offers it to me.

'Shouldn't we wait until after the lasagne?'

'This is better, trust me,' he says, eating another mouthful.

He's right. By the time Jan comes in, there's none left.

'Oh! My God! You haven't, Adam? I've spent all afternoon making dinner and you two sneak in here and eat all the pudding like greedy children. Now, we will all have to make do with yogurt and honey. Explain that to our guests.'

She sounds like a school teacher. I want to giggle but no-one else is laughing.

'We did them a favour, that lot wouldn't want it clogging up their arteries,' says Adam.

He defiantly scrapes the plate clean with the spoon before popping it into his mouth.

Jan stomps off, disgusted by our lack of self-control. I go back into the dining room to find Mark slumped in his chair, a large glass of red wine in his hand, my bottle of Chateau Neuf Du Pape at his elbow.

'So what ads have you done?' he asks me aggressively, swigging back his drink. 'Anything I would know?'

It's the question every copywriter dreads. Mark is no more interested in my work than I am in the ins and outs of suppositories. I say nothing, I can hardly tell him about Marmalade.

'What you do isn't really proper writing, is it? It's very formulaic,' he tells me, helping himself to more wine.

I take the bait and feel myself sinking into the sea of effluent that most people think Adland pumps out.

'Don't dismiss advertising. You're dismissing it, aren't you? I can tell by your face. Don't. We work with budgets worth millions, every word counts,' I tell him.

'Sorry, I didn't realise it was art-form,' he tells me with a smirk.

'And science has all the answers, does it?' asks Adam as he walks into the room. 'Shame not one doctor knew enough to save my dad when he was dying.'

He slams the tray of lasagne down on the table and throws the oven gloves on the floor.

'Adam! My table. You've scorched my table,' cries Jan grabbing the dish with both hands. 'Ow! Shit! That's hot.'

She runs into the kitchen, through the puddle of wine, to the sink.

'Hold your hands under running water,' says Adam charging in and turning on the cold tap.

'I'm a bloody doctor; I know what to do. This is your bloody fault, Adam. Leave me alone. And clean up that bloody wine before someone breaks their bloody neck,' she shouts.

That's very bloody, even for a doctor.

Karen appears in the doorway, having managed to extricate herself from Gary. She gently examines Jan's red fingers before being pushed aside.

'It's nothing. Will everyone just stopping fussing!' implores Jan.

She snatches her hands away and looks shaken. I think about offering her a brandy for the shock. But I'm only a self-serving, vacuous ad girl, what would I know? Karen gently takes her by the elbow and guides her to a seat.

'Adam, listen, I think I'm going to make a move. I hope Jan will be okay,' I tell him.

'It's only nine o'clock. Please don't leave me with this lot,' he says.

'Look after Jan and thank her for me, yeah?' I tell him giving him a quick kiss on the cheek.

I get in my car and take the 'A to Z' from the glove compartment. Like most north Londoners, I am lost south of the river. I find Adam's road in the index and attempt to plot my way home. The route spans four pages. I trace my index finger up towards the river. The tiny print swims together blurring the street names. I can't even read a map now. Mark's remarks seem to have rendered me useless. Thanks to him, I can no longer justify my job let alone my salary. Perhaps he is right. What good do I do?

As I put my key in the door, the phones ring. I rush in and pick it up.

'Sorry about tonight,' Adam whispers into the phone.

'Dinner wasn't that bad,' I reassure him, wedging the receiver under my chin and getting in a tangle with the cord as I pull off my coat.

'I meant the people - full of themselves.'

'Like us, y'mean?' I ask.

'We're in advertising, we're allowed to be like that,' he says. 'They think they're better than us.'

'They are better than us. We sell cat food, they save lives.'

'What about all the cats who have had all their nine lives thanks to you?'

'Hardly the same thing. Why are you whispering?'

'Jan's asleep, don't want to wake her. I'm in enough trouble. What were we saying? Oh yeah, if you can help cats, you can help people. You should write fund-raising ads for good causes.'

'Adam, I need to go to bed. It's a bit late for all this,' I tell him.

I wonder whether I can be bothered to take my make-up off.

'Just saying, we're as good as they are.'

'We're not. Put it this way, if I have a heart attack, I want Jan manning the defibrillator, not you. How is she? Are her hands okay?'

'Yeah, fine, thanks. We're okay when we're on our own but when she's with that lot she's a different person.'

'Spend more time alone with her then.'

'She's always working and when she's not she invites the doctors over. The rest of the time, we're too knackered to even speak.'

'Less chance to row.'

'Less chance to do anything,' he says ruefully. 'Anyway, how are you? Heard anything from Tom?'

'Not unless you count the vile message he left on the answering machine. He told me I was 'unliveable' with.'

'Is that even a word?'

'According to him it is and I'm the definition of it. I'm 'controlling' too, guess that comes from telling people what to do at work.'

I laugh but I don't know why. It's not funny. It's tragic. My personality, honed by years of writing snappy copy for things people neither want nor need, has turned me into a snappy person no-one wants or needs.

'It's not your fault, Ella.'

'It must be. I'm a pain in the arse so everyone tells me.'

'You mean, Peter and Tom? Who cares what they think?'

'I loved Tom.'

'He loved himself.'

This last comment is true but hurts my pride nonetheless.

'I drove him away.'

'No, you didn't, stop this, please. You did nothing wrong. Everything will be fine, I promise.'

'You don't know that.'

'I know he treated you badly. Stop blaming yourself,' he tells me gently.

I rush to fill the silence but as soon as I have spoken the words I want to reach down the receiver and retrieve them.

'He didn't want to have sex with me.'

'Was he mad?'

I don't answer.

'I know lots of blokes who'd love to give you a good ironing-over.'

I let out a little gasp. The most sexually explicit Adam and I ever get is to discuss the sensual pleasures derived from eating a slice of The River Cafe's Moist Chocolate Cake.

'Sorry, I don't know why I said that,' he says apologetically.

'It's a new one on me,' I say laughing.

Secretly, I am thrilled he thinks of me in that way.

'You must've heard that one loads of times.'

Tom was never one for compliments. It's been a while since anyone has referred to me as attractive. When I don't reply, Adam changes the subject.

'Another biscuit?' he asks.

'Don't be daft, we're on the phone,' I laugh wanting to get back to what we've just been talking about.

For once, I'm not interested in food, preferring something much sweeter.

'I'll eat one here and you have one there.'

'Like phone sex,' I say and immediately wish I hadn't. 'Go on then. You go first. If it sounds good, I'll join in.'

'Okay. I'm eating a chocolate and caramel wafer,' he says crunching through the layers. 'It's gorgeous.'

With the receiver wedged under my chin, the flex uncoils just enough to allow me to reach the biscuit tin. I open the lid and select a plain chocolate ginger thin.

'Here goes,' I tell him, taking a bite. 'Oh that's good.'

'Better than sex,' says Adam.

For once, I agree.

Chapter thirty-four

Avoid repetition

'You've spent years being a cat, why is being a doctor so difficult?' asks Adam.

He will not let this one go. Every time we speak, he brings it up. I keep telling him it's not my thing; I can't do scientific stuff. My physics teacher made that very clear when he told me I was 'stupid' in front of the whole class.

'At least look at it. It's fund-raising, not for profit,' Adam persists.

This is a bit heavy. I would rather be having phone-biscuit-sex.

'Can I call you back? David will be in any minute,' I say looking at the door and willing it not to open.

David never arrives before ten-thirty. He dislikes working with me as much as I do with him. We are both stuck here, in the holding bay, taking the money until something better turns up. We spend as little time as possible together and work separately, coming up with ideas on our own before the torture of sitting in the office together, deciding what to present to Peter. I take out a new felt tip pen, pull the top off with my teeth and start doodling.

'Let's do this later,' I tell Adam. 'They've moved my office; can't talk now.'

'I need to brief you. The client wants it yesterday,' he replies.

I can hear him eating something on the other end of the line. I wonder if it's another caramel wafer.

'Adam, being Marmalade was hard enough, let alone trying to get inside a doctor's head. And the one you've asked me to work with is so smart she just happens to be a research scientist in her spare time,' I whisper.

I jerk my head, straining to hear if anyone is outside, listening,

'You can help her save lives,' persists Adam. 'Gotta be better than selling bog-cleaner.'

'You're not wrong,' I say.

I lean back in my chair and open the drawer.

'Come on, Ella, it's easy,' says Adam. 'You write a fundraising letter from her and people will give money to help her find a cure for heart disease.'

'It's that simple?' I ask wishing it really was that easy.

The door opens. I jump. It's only Jill seeing if I want my morning cappuccino from the Italian coffee bar. I nod enthusiastically. She gives me the thumbs-up, closes the door and leaves.

'If they'd had the money to carry out ground-breaking research a few years ago, my Dad might still be here.'

And Wally, I think. Dear Wally. What a senseless waste of a wonderful life.

I remember Adam was still grieving for his father when he joined CBA. Peter was surprisingly sympathetic; he had lost his mother the previous year to a massive coronary. It's strange to think he wasn't always such a monster.

'So, are you up for it?' persists Adam.

I know how much this means to him but I'm not convinced I can help with his quest, however worthy.

'No, I don't know anything about medical stuff. And this is far too important to mess up.'

I can hear David talking to Jill in the corridor. I must get off the phone.

'Don't put yourself down,' says Adam. 'I wouldn't ask if I didn't think you could do it.'

'I've got to go. Dave the Rave is here.'

Adam takes no notice.

'The doctor will explain everything and then you can write it in a way that people can understand. You're good at that. Then just interview one of her patients to prove what she does can work.'

The telephone flex will just reach far enough to allow me to reach out and ensure the door is shut.

'It sounds too complicated,' I say.

I accidentally pull my phone onto the floor. It makes a terrible jangling noise, like all the workings have come loose.

'What's that?' asks Adam.

I hear him swallow whatever he was eating in one almighty gulp.

'Nothing, just dropped the phone,' I say.

I haul the receiver up by its flex and step over the wire. 'I know it's for a good cause but if I did it and it's a big 'if', will I get paid?'

'Of course. I can pay you as a freelancer.'

'Fine, let me speak to the doctor, if I can understand what she says, I'll do it,' I tell him. 'Then you can give my fee to the charity.'

I carefully set the phone back down on my desk.

'That's great. Thanks, Ella. You'll love her. She's very down to earth. I met her when Dad was ill.'

I've never done anything vital in my life; unless I count keeping the patisserie at the bottom of the road in business.

287

'Same skills, different product. It's still about emotion and persuading people. But it's persuading them to do some good for a change.'

That sounds good to me.

I hurriedly replace the receiver when David comes in. He regards me with suspicion, unzips his jacket, hangs it on the back of his chair and sits down. We don't bother with pleasantries so I know a 'Good morning, how are you?' greeting is out of the question. True to form, he takes a handful of layouts from his bag and slaps them on the desk.

'Here are my ideas. What have you got?'

I look down at my pad. It's covered in hearts.

Over the next few evenings and lunch-breaks, I research heart disease, its causes and its cures. I read articles and talk to people who are living with the condition. Our cleaner's husband has angina and she is more than happy to tell me all about it in the hope I might be able to help him. I leap on any piece of information that unlocks the new world I am about to enter. When I've gleaned as much knowledge as I can, I feel confident enough to talk to the doctor. She is every bit as approachable as Adam said she would be and explains what I need to know clearly and simply. I note down her every word and my hand aches by the time she's finished speaking. Then I phone one of her patients, an elderly man who puts me to shame with his bravery. He answers my questions with dignity. He sounds just like Wally. I slap my hand over the mouthpiece so he can't hear me cry. He is so calm and upbeat. It's amazing; Peter can't cope if he's served the wrong brand of coffee.

Thanks to both the doctor and the patient being so open, the copy writes itself. I fax it over to Adam in my lunch-break and he phones me minutes later.

'Love it,' he says. 'It's honest.'

'I remember Peter telling me to be 'honest' about Marmalade's emotions. Nice to know I've finally cracked it.'

'You waited until it really mattered, using your talent to help people. Fancy dinner tonight at L'Escargot, my treat to say 'thanks'? I took a client there last week. Great chocolate mousse – three types on the same plate, plain, milk and white.'

'Sold. See you at the restaurant about seven. Sure Jan won't mind?'

'Why should she?' he replies defensively. 'She's on nights this week.'

'That must be hard.'

'Not really. She does her thing. I do mine.'

'You sound more like flat-mates.'

'In more ways than one,' he replies.

'What d'you mean?'

He laughs.

'Can't remember when we last had sex. Oh yes, I can. She'd passed an exam and had had a couple of glasses of wine to celebrate. She couldn't remember anything about it the next day. Very flattering.'

'Oh,' I mutter not knowing what else to say.

Why am I delighted to think they don't make love anymore?

He ploughs on.

'Whenever I looked at a piece of cake or a bar of chocolate, I'd get a lecture from her. 'Don't eat that. It's bad for you. Full of fat. You'll collapse.' The more she moans at me, the more I want to eat everything in sight.'

'And you do,' I laugh.

'How do you know?'

'I know you, Adam.'

'Well, I bet you don't know this. We've split up,' he tells me matter-of-factly.' Lucky my flat didn't sell. I'm back there now.'

My stomach flips. Not once but twice. It feels good, like I'm smiling on the inside.

'When?' I ask trying to keep the excitement out of my voice.

'Couple of days ago.'

'Why didn't you tell me?'

My mind is racing. So is my pulse. What's going on?

'Felt stupid, I suppose. It's been brewing for a while and by the end neither of us could be bothered to make the effort. And I didn't like who she became when she was with her doctor mates. Gradually, that side just took over. She changed. We both did.'

I think back to the dinner party and how she grated on me, the way she treated Adam like a cross between a servant and a child.

'You okay?' I ask still unable to believe what he's telling me.

'Fine. I'm not heart-broken or anything.'

Well, that's promising, I think.

'But you were together years,' I say.

I silently calculate the alarming speed relationships can end. One minute you're in love, the next, you're in therapy trying to figure out where it all went wrong.

'We weren't going anywhere. We were more like flat-mates by the end. It was too easy.'

'An easy relationship? That sounds great.'

I think about my split with Tom. I didn't so much ignore the warning signs as refuse to see the flares Tom was sending up. Photo-Me-Booth? Shag-Me-Senseless, more like. What was I thinking?

'Anyway, how are you, Ella? How's work?'

'Well, it's not the same without Wally, obviously. I keep telling myself he's on holiday, it's the only way I can get through it.'

'Bless him. He was a good bloke,' says Adam. 'They'll never find another one like him.'

'No, he was special. The funeral's next week, just close family,' I say and stay quiet for a moment. 'His wife doesn't want flowers just donations to a heart charity.'

'Good idea,' says Adam.

We are both quiet for a moment. I break the silence. 'Oh, Jill's leaving. Going to be Marketing Director for her Mum's holiday camp. She thinks retro is the next big thing.'

Talking to Adam is the best I've felt since Wally taught me the Fandango. Well, it might've been the waltz; the way I danced it, no-one could tell.

'Don't you mean the last big thing?'

'Very funny, Adam. She wants me to do their advertising.'

'That's two freelance jobs you've got now. You'll be setting up your own shop next,' he teases.

'Don't know about that,' I say. 'Oh yes, scandal, Peter's teamed up with Chloe. In every sense.'

'So you've been ousted?'

'I don't want to work for Peter anymore,' I tell him. 'Meet you at L'Escargot later.'

I quickly replace the receiver. There's something I must do.

I think about the patient I spoke to, despite all he is facing, he has guts. His belief in the doctor is unshakable because she gives him hope. And we're all entitled to that, no matter what.

For the first time ever I am proud of what I do. For the first time, my work can make a difference. If writing copy raises funds for research into heart disease and helps save lives in the process, that's wonderful. Mum will approve. I just wish Wally could have hung on long enough to benefit.

I may have sold my soul to the devil the day I agreed to work for Peter, at least now I can buy it back.

I sit down and write my finest work to date: my letter of resignation.

I rap sharply on Peter's door and walk in. Luckily Chloe is at a recording so I can confront him alone. He sees the sheet of paper in my hand and the look on my face. Before I can say anything he is on his feet applauding.

'At last! You finally took the hint. This agency ain't big enough for the both of us. You are definitely handing in your notice and not just getting my hopes up, aren't you?' he says.

I want to tell him how sad he looks in those jeans with his middle aged bottom sagging sadly like two blue chickens in a sack.

'I have found something better, Peter. Something worthwhile. I'll soon be out of your hair. What's left of it.'

'Great, you can go today. I'll give you three months money. Very generous all things considered,' he tells me.

'How do you sleep at night?' I ask him.

'It's not 'how' I sleep but who I sleep with,' he leers.

'Give it a rest, Peter. Hopefully, other people will see you for what you are and follow me out of the door.'

'Chloe and I are re-inventing the creative department and filling it with hungry lads fresh out of art school. They won't be bursting into tears every five minutes or getting pregnant.'

He glances at my stomach.

'You're not are you? Oh, no, I guess not, you would have had to have had sex to be up the duff.'

He laughs so much at his own joke that he coughs uncontrollably. He decides the best remedy is to light up.

'And I bet you'll have them working for nothing?' I ask.

'They're getting invaluable experience working for me, in a top London ad agency. I'm not paying them as well,' he says.

'Peter, times are changing. This place is set to implode. You'll never find another job. How attractive will Chloe find you then?'

'You keep telling yourself that, Ella.'

He laughs in my face and I dodge the smoke he is blowing in my direction.

'And surely she'll want a baby one day? Your baby?' I ask.

'Not a maternal bone in her beautiful body, too busy with her career to want a brat throwing up everywhere,' he says. 'Anyway, what does she want a kid for when she's got me to love?'

'She's got the killer instinct. Watch out for the knife in your back, Peter.'

'She worships me.'

'You think so? She shafted David.'

'And now she's with me. David's history,' he snips.

'And you thought I could work with him?' I ask.

He grins.

'Ella, darling, you can work with anyone.'

'Too true, I put up with you for long enough. Anyway, I'm sure you and Chloe will be very happy together.'

'Yes, she cuts the mustard in more ways than one.'

He runs the flat of his hand over his head and sucks in his stomach, stubbing out his cigarette in the cut-glass ash-tray.

'So I gather, Peter.'

'Meaning?'

'You're a dirty old man. How old is she? Twenty?'

'Get out,' he screams.

'You can't push me, I'm jumping!' I tell him as I leave the room.

'Did he just fire you?' asks Jill.

I shake my head.

'No, I left.'

'How will you manage? Sorry but you've got a very bad almond croissant habit to feed.'

Good question. How will I cope?

'I can get a lodger to help pay the mortgage, if I need to,' I say.

I make a mental note to buy the Evening Standard on the way home. I can look through the flat-share section.

'You'll get by without the expense account lunches and your company car?' she asks.

I nod reluctantly. I wish she'd change the subject. I can't deal with this now. She senses my unease.

'And what about Adam Hart?' she asks. 'Perhaps he could be your knight in shining armour? I hear you're both free agents now.'

How could she possibly know? I had no idea Jill knew I was that friendly with Adam. I nip any gossip in the bud. Snip. Snip.

'The only passion we share is for chocolate.'

'Are you mad? He's gorgeous. If you don't want him I'll have him.'

She means it as a joke but her comment unsettles me.

'We're both having a break from relationships. Who needs the hassle, eh?'

'Well, if you two fancy a weekend away, they'll be a chalet ready and waiting for you. Separate beds, of course.'

'Only if I can have the room with the ivy creeping through the roof.'

I walk across the corridor to my office. David has arrived and is sitting at the far side of the desk, sulking. He has lined his tubs of marker pens and pencils up like a barricade between us.

'Very professional,' I tell him.

'That's an interesting word, coming from you,' David says flexing his ruler and letting his words hang between us.

'What's that supposed to mean?'

'Nothing. Just didn't know we worked on a heart disease charity.'

He has been busy snooping.

'Not that it's any of your business but I did the work at home and just typed it up here in my lunch hour,' I tell him.

'It's still moonlighting.'

'Have you been going through my things?' I ask.

I open my drawer to check if anything is missing. David says nothing.

'Did you tell Peter?' I ask.

'Of course,' he replies.

He thinks he's won.

'You've got a lot to learn, David. Advertising is a small industry. Be careful who you attack.'

'Is that a threat?' he asks.

'No, it's a fact. Anyway it doesn't matter now,' he says looking down at the floor. 'I've lost everything. Chloe was my team-mate and my girlfriend. How do you think I feel watching her with that piece of shit?'

'Crap.'

He slumps back in his chair.

'Why don't you leave here and move on?' I suggest.

'Clever Ella,' he sneers. 'Got it in one. I'm setting up a studio with Darren. He's got the contacts and I've got the money I was saving for a deposit on a flat with Chloe.'

'Good for you,' I say genuinely pleased for him.

'We've found a space to rent over in the Docklands. It's not exactly Soho but it's got potential. 'Up and coming' if you believe the estate agents. '

The Docklands is the back of beyond. I can't imagine any clients trekking out there to do business but I try to sound positive.

'You should be happy then,' I tell him.

'I am.'

'You don't look it.'

'My dream was to be an Art-Director like Alan Ferguson. I couldn't believe my luck when we landed a placement here with him. The man's a genius.'

'Alan plays to his strengths. And that's what you're doing by becoming a designer.'

He smiles and rearranges the pencils in his desk-tidier.

'Sounds like we've both got an escape plan. I've just handed in my notice. No hard feelings?'

He shakes his head and removes the battle line between us. Then he walks to the door and shouts loud enough for the whole creative department to hear, 'To hell with Chloe.'

'Don't worry, David. She's sleeping with Peter. She's already there.'

Chapter thirty-five

Have the light-bulb moment

Wally's widow is waiting for me at the gate when I arrive. She is warm and inviting.

'Hello, Ella,' she smiles. 'Thanks so much for coming. I'm Cathy, pleased to meet you. Come on in.'

'Hello, Cathy, it's lovely to meet you.' I mean it. It's a real honour to meet Wally's wife.

I follow her into her neat terraced house, the home she had shared with Wal for the past forty-three years. It smells of polish and roses.

'Shall I take my shoes off?' I ask seeing the pristine cream carpet in the hallway.

'No, of course not. Come on through to the living room. Tea or coffee? Or would you prefer something stronger? I've got some wine left over from the ...' she pauses, then bursts into tears. 'The funeral.'

'Here,' I say taking her by the arm and helping her to a chair.

'I can't believe he's gone. Keep thinking the silly sod's goin' walk through that door any minute. The last thing he said to me was, 'I'll be home for me dinner',' she says crying and dabbing at her eyes with a tissue. 'I never thought I'd never see 'im again. I miss him so much. I'm sorry you ain't come all this way to listen to this.'

'Please don't apologise,' I tell her. 'We all loved Wally. I am so very sorry.'

She sits and sobs quietly for a few moments. The circular clock on the wall ticks away the minutes, putting space between Wally and us when all we want to do is bring him back.

'He was so excited about that weekend,' she continues. 'I lost count of the number of times he packed and unpacked his flipping suitcase. I said to 'im, 'Wal, you're going for two days not two weeks.'

She laughs and blows her nose.

'When he rung me he was so happy. Said the camp was the same one as we'd been to when we was first married.'

Now it was my turn to cry. So he wasn't joking. He really had stayed there before.

'We hadn't had a holiday in years. With Wal having the sandwich bar, we could never get away. Then when he got the night job at your place, he was so tired to go anywhere.'

She stops talking and looks at me.

'He loved teaching you dancin'. Said you picked it up just like that.'

I smile at the memory.

'He was a good teacher,' I say.

Her eyes slowly move around the room and come to rest on a silver framed photograph of the pair of them on their wedding day. She walks over, picks it up and places it in my hand.

'Look! He had the beginnings of a comb-over even then,' she said pointing at Wally's slick hairstyle.

He's looking at her like his heart could burst.

'He phoned me just before, just before …'she pauses as a tear rolls down her cheek and she catches it with her forefinger. '…just before he went back to his chalet on Sunday afternoon. Told me you two had been awarded Best Act. He was well pleased. Said he was dressed in your clothes? And he was the secretary? I didn't have a clue what he was going on about but he was laughing his head off. Wish I could've seen 'im.'

She is half crying, half laughing. And I am happy because now I know she was the last person he spoke to. He didn't die alone, not really. His wife was right there with him, in his heart, their telephone conversation fresh in his mind.

'So, I just wanted to thank-you, Ella. He knew it was you what got him the job at the agency. He never forgot that and he wanted to repay you somehow. Thought the world of you. To some people, he was just the caretaker, they never gave him the time of day.'

'Cathy, he was my friend. He got me through some hideous times at the agency,' I tell her holding her frail hands in mind.

She twists her gold wedding band, thin and worn from years of wear.

'It was his Mum's.'

Suddenly, through her tears, she laughs.

'Tell me he didn't eat them egg sandwiches on the bus?'

I nod.

'He must've stunk you all out. I told him to wait 'til he got off.'

We both laugh and then fall silent. The sideboard with its barley-twist legs has been lovingly polished, likewise, the display cabinet crammed full of memorabilia from their life together. A ship in a bottle, a pair of miniature clogs, a souvenir pottery plate from Malta and a framed photographs of the pair of them. I walk over to take a closer look.

It must have been taken twenty, thirty years ago, they are both sitting on the grass, a huge Chestnut tree behind them, holding hands, squinting into the sun, the horizon at a jaunty angel.

'That's us in Highgate Woods,' she says. 'We used to have a picnic. It was egg sandwiches on that day too. I remember because I was pregnant and they made me feel sick.'

There's not one picture of a baby or child and Wally never mentioned being a Dad.

'I lost her. Miscarriage. We couldn't have no more,' she says her eyes misting over again.
I hold her hand again. Neither of us speaks for a long time.

'Oh no. I never got you your drink. I'm so sorry.'

'Please, don't worry.'

'No, you've come all this way,' she says going to the sideboard and pouring me a glass of sherry.

I sip it.

'Wal thought the world of you, Ella. Thanks for everything you done for him. He was very grateful even if he didn't say.'

'Cathy, Wally was wonderful. He showed me the world through his eyes. And when I look at it from his perspective, I can see it's a great place,' I tell her.

She smiles warmly at me and I can see what a beauty she must have been when Wal fell in love with her.

'I've brought you this,' I say as I hand her the card we all signed, together with a cheque for the British Heart Foundation.

'Oh, thank-you. That's so kind. Please say 'thank-you' to everyone, from me. And Wal,' she says opening the card and glancing at the signatures, overwhelmed.

'Let me know if you need anything, anything at all.'

She nods.

'I'm fine. You look after yourself, Ella. Be happy.'

She walks me to the front door. As she clicks on the light, the bulb blows. She laughs.

'That's Wal, that is. Oh flip, he did all this stuff round the house, ain't got a clue where he kept the spares.'

I help her look and we eventually find a shoe box full of bulbs of all shapes and sizes in the cupboard under the stairs. The first bulb we try, fits. Cathy switches it on.

Even when he's not here, Wally can still light up a room.

Chapter thirty-six

Be honest

Adam and I are walking through Highgate Woods on the outskirts of North London. This is where those in the know come for some much-needed peace and quiet from the chaos of the city. At weekends, it's a favourite haunt with dog walkers. And on sunny summer afternoons, young mums trailing expensively dressed toddlers, head for the shade of one of the Chestnut trees to picnic joylessly on dried fruit and carrot sticks. But it's still early and we are the only ones here, in the clearing in front of the cricket pitch. There's something special about having this place all to ourselves. The cafe is closed so we sit on a bench enjoying acres of green, framed by a brilliant blue sky. As always it takes more than fresh air to sustain Adam. He pulls out a box of ham and brie sandwiches from his carrier bag and hands one to me. Then he opens a can of fizzy drink and sets it down between us on the bench.

'Lovely, isn't it?' he says lifting a layer of bread and examining the filling of his sandwich.

'Yes, it's really delicious,' I reply taking a mouthful.

'I mean sitting here, together,' he says with a smile.

I spin round, suddenly realising where we are.

'We're in Wally and Cathy's spot. The exact place where they ate their picnics all those years ago. This bench must have been put here later.'

I turn to look at the small brass plaque screwed onto the back of the bench.

'In loving memory of Baby Daisy 1958 -1958'

Wally's daughter. My stomach feels hollow.

'Oh, yeah, how was his wife when you saw her. Was she okay?'

'Not yet but she will be. In time.'

'I'd like to meet her. Wally made her sound like a cross between Mae West and Lulu. Next time you go, I'll come with you.'

Adam rips open a packet of chocolate-covered Swiss rolls with such gusto all six tumble onto the grass. He picks them up and hands me one. He tears the foil wrapper off another and eats it in one mouthful, stretching out his legs and leaning back, putting both his arms out along the back of the bench. When I feel his left hand on my shoulder, I jump and he darts forward awkwardly, brushing his lips deliberately against mine.

'Adam?' I ask pulling away.

'Sorry, I thought...'

He looks at my face. I'm not giving him any encouragement. He sits back, downcast before snapping at his sandwich. He chews quickly and swallows.

'Could you fall in love with me? I could fall in love with you,' he says as he stares at me, willing me to give him the answer he wants.

But I reply with the words no-one wants to hear, 'I love you, but...'

'Ella, please don't say that. We love each other; we both know that. Isn't that enough?'

'No, sorry Adam, it never is.'

He jerks away from me, upsetting the drink. It pours through the slats in the wooden bench onto the grass below.

'What an idiot! I can't do anything right, can I?'

'Yes you can. You saved my life, Adam.'

He stares at the ground and scuffs at a rogue dandelion growing brightly and defiantly towards the sky.

'Please, let's just take things slowly and see what happens. You know we can make it work, Ella.'

He is right. Life would be idyllic. We would cherish each other, knowing we had found the one thing everyone is looking for. I adore him. I think I always have.

'It would never work. I would spoil everything. I always do. Even my Dad couldn't bear to stick around me.'

'Ella, no. I can't bear it. From what you've told me, your Dad was the one who was difficult to live with not you. It wasn't your fault.'

I want to believe him but my script has been written for me in indelible ink. How can I change it now? I tried my best. Worked hard, got a good job and looked after Mum but I can't crack relationships.

Now Adam looks broken. He's even stopped eating. I've never seen him so low. I am no good for him. He doesn't need a lush, a failure. He stares bleakly into the distance.

'This isn't something we can solve with cake,' I tell him.

His hands are shaking as he grasps mine.

'Ella, you know we're a marriage made in heaven,' he insists, doing his best to smile.

'Chocolate heaven,' I correct.

I curse myself for being glib. He lets go of my hands and looks away.

'If we lived together we'd be arguing about who ate the last biscuit,' I say to the back of his head.

'If that's all we had to worry about, we'd be laughing,' he tells me without looking round, his voice is tinged with bitterness.

'I don't want to hurt you. You mean too much to me, Adam.'

He turns to face me. He looks confused. Even I'm having trouble working out how we've got here.

'Neither of us has a great track record with relationships,' I say trying to justify my decision.

'That was a bit below the belt.'

'Best we keep everything above the waist, then.'

'Must we?'

I see a flicker of a smile; Jill's right, he is gorgeous.

'Yes, that way we'll always be friends, not many couples can say that.'

'Just friends? You want me to be happy with that?'

Hurt runs through his voice.

'Yes. This way we'll still be together when all our teeth have dropped out from eating too much cake,' I tell him.

His cheeks are wet with tears. I brush them away with my finger and he turns away, embarrassed. I squeeze his hand and he grips mine. Then, I start to cry. I want to run to the school toilet and talk to Mum. But I know what she'd say, 'Be happy, darling.'

Suddenly, the thick grey fog that has haunted me all my life, lifts. Wally taught me to love life. I had better get on with it.

'I can't lose you, Ella,' Adam says, scuffing at the crushed dandelion with his heel.

'You won't, Adam. I promise. 'You make me too happy.'

'Ella, will you …?' he asks.

'Yes, you know I will.'

His face fills with joy.

'D'you love me, Ella?'

'I do.'

He leans forward and kisses me.

'D'you love me, Adam?'

'I do.'

He reaches into the bag with his free hand and takes out a small white box.

Slowly, I lift the lid. He watches closely as I peer inside.

'Oh Adam. It's perfect.'

Very carefully, I take it out of the box.

Encrusted with jewel-like raspberries and elaborate swirls of white chocolate, it is the most beautiful cake I have ever seen.

I better tell Mum, she'll want to buy a hat.

Chapter thirty-seven

End with a bang

I am Ella.

I am Ella Hart.

I am still a pain in the arse.

THE END

If you enjoyed this book a short review on Amazon would be appreciated. Keep in touch, join my mailing list at http://joan-ellis.com and follow me on twitter @joansusanellis

Disclaimer: All persons are fictitious.

By the same author

The Killing of Mummy's Boy

'I slit someone's throat,' the man told the woman on the 4.20 from Waterloo to Portsmouth.
    It was Sandra's first journey back to London since she had moved to the Isle of Wight a few years before. Having a stretch of water between her and the mainland made her feel safe. The Solent could be expensive to cross; some people thought twice before making the journey. She liked that.'

The Things You Missed While You Were Away

'Being paired with a chair at the local National Childbirth Trust anti-natal classes didn't nothing for my ego. Unlike the other mums who were with their husbands, the only arms supporting me through the breathing exercises were wooden ones.'

Coming soon: *Guilt*

'You died on August 8th 1965, a month before your fourth birthday. You were probably dead long before Mum downed her third gin with Porky Rawlings.'